For

Jason Carr

Her White Lie

Her White Lie

Jackie Walsh

hera

First published in the United Kingdom in 2021 by

Hera Books
28b Cricketfield Road
London, E5 8NS
United Kingdom

A CIP catalogue record for this book is available from the British Library.

Print ISBN 978 1 80032 608 8
Ebook ISBN 978 1 912973 64 4

Look for more great books at www.herabooks.com

Printed and bound in Great Britain by Clays Ltd, Elcograf S.p.A.

I

Chapter One

Tara

I can see it clearly. My new life. It's perfect and ready to go. In three weeks' time, I'll be boarding a plane with my brand-new husband and leaving this life behind me. Australia is a long way away but it's going to be wonderful. When I close my eyes I can imagine the sea air filling my senses. The smell of coconut sun lotion on my skin. The sizzle of sausages cooking on a nearby barbecue and beer fizzing from cans.

I'll be meeting Lucas's family and friends for the first time but I feel I know them already from the many virtual calls Lucas has made. At first I was shy, sitting beside him smiling and nodding into the laptop with nothing to say but I soon got the hang of it and joined in.

None of his family are travelling over here for the wedding but that doesn't matter because we'll be having a second celebration when we get there. His parents are throwing us a party, two days after we arrive. I'll laugh and smile and be very polite because I want them to like me. I want his family to be happy that Lucas has found me. To know how much we are in love, how happy I make him, and he makes me.

Of course there's a downside to all this and it's a big one. My dad will still be living here in Dublin, on his own.

Mam died three years ago. Also I'll be saying goodbye to my friends who say they'll come and visit but I know won't. It's Australia, not London.

But we will Skype and Facebook and WhatsApp for the first few months I imagine, maybe even the first year. And then things will move on. I'll fade into the background of their lives. The calls will get less frequent. The WhatsApp groups will slowly dissolve, and I'll be mentioned less and less until it will just be *Tara Moore, do you remember her?*

It makes me sad to think about it but it's the way it is. I have to focus on the good stuff. I have a chance at a brilliant new life in Australia where I'll make new friends. Everything is so exciting; sometimes I feel like I'm the luckiest woman alive.

–

That was ten minutes ago. Now I can barely breathe. My eyes are trying to blank out the image on the television screen. This cannot be happening.

There's a house. Huntley Lodge. It's surrounded by yellow tape. At the side of the building, overgrown shrubbery hides part of a crime scene tent that has been erected because a dead body has been discovered. My heart is crashing against the wall of my chest because I know exactly where that is. I stood in that spot.

A pretty news reporter is speaking into a big fluffy mic saying that initial reports suggest the body has been lying there for some time. I swallow hard, trying to stop myself from throwing up. My head feels like the weight of the world is pushing down on it and I can no longer hear the reporter's voice. It has become muffled, fading into the background, fading like I was supposed to fade.

Rooted to the spot, I feel the chains of my past gripping tightly. I'm no longer able to see Huntley Lodge on the television screen because my vision has blurred... All I can see now is my beautiful new life slipping away from me.

Chapter Two

'Are you okay?' Lucas calls from the sofa.

I should say no but I say yes in the hope he doesn't persist. I can't talk about this now, not to Lucas. I need to get my head around it first. Why now? Three more weeks and I was out of here. The news reporter said the body has been there for some time. It's been three years since I lived at Huntley Lodge. If the police discover that body has been lying there since then, they'll come knocking. They'll ask questions.

A gust of cold air rushes into the room as I pull open the balcony door. With my arms wrapped across my chest I step outside and take a deep breath. The sharpness of the icy air travels deep into my lungs but a shiver of fear travels further, right through my body.

The city lights flicker from both sides of the dark, mirroring waters. Flags hanging from tall posts down the quaysides flap wildly in the gusting winds and I feel something shift inside me.

I think of Faye. Where is she now? Has she seen the report? Faye was my best friend back then. Confident, wild, she made everything exciting and fun. The day I first set eyes on her small skinny body she was standing by the back wall of the school yard, her green skirt and white shirt pristinely ironed and her hair pulled back from her face by a matching green hairband. Faye was scanning the crowd like she was deciding who she would and would not become friends with. A silent confidence oozed from her and it fascinated me how someone who took up so little space could make such a big impact on me. When break was almost over, I leaned against the wall a few feet away from her. Faye lifted her foot up behind her and rested it against the wall. I did the same. She crossed her arms. I crossed mine.

'Are you copying me?' she asked in a quiet voice. I could tell she wasn't annoyed.

'Yes,' I said.

She smiled, revealing her two front teeth were missing. When I smiled, revealing mine were missing too, we both laughed. We were only eight at the time, totally unaware of the years of fun we were about to share.

And now Faye is Dr Faye Connolly. I knew she'd make it. Behind all that confidence was a kindness and willingness to help others that was matched only by her determination to succeed. Faye didn't hesitate the day I asked her for help. I remember it like it was only yesterday but it was more than three years ago when I walked into her bedroom not knowing what her reaction would be. Faye was in the middle of exams at the time and was studying at a makeshift desk Andriu her boyfriend had put together for her. I can still feel the comfort from her gentle smile as she offered to do anything she could to help me. Faye made it seem like it was no big deal. But it was, especially for her.

'Come in out of the cold,' Lucas says now, sticking his head out into the elements and pulling me out of my memories. His soft blue eyes squint in an effort to avoid the ruthless cold wind that hits him in the face. The man was reared on sunshine and surfboards. Embracing this weather seems crazy to him.

'I'll be in in a minute,' I say.

Wrapping my arms tighter around myself, I watch the dark clouds hurry across the sky. The bright moon highlights their journey. I lift my head, close my eyes and let the cold, harsh wind crash into my face. I try to picture Faye. I remember her green eyes sparkling every time she was happy or excited. Faye was smaller and a lot skinnier than me as a kid. Not so much when we grew into our teens. She hated her brown hair, especially when the weather was damp and it would go all frizzy. I wonder if she still has a fringe. Does she still use MAC make-up to cover her snow-white skin? Faye used to say I was lucky to have sallow skin, but she was never jealous of me. Having Faye as a friend was very special and it took a lot of getting used to when she ended it so abruptly. It's something I could never get my head around. Her walking out on me the same week my mother died. My two best friends… gone.

The pain still lives in me. It sleeps most of the time. But now I can feel it stir. Did Faye see the news bulletin? Is she worrying like I am, praying that we did a good enough job covering our tracks?

Chapter Three

Faye

'Holy fuck... is that Huntley Lodge?' I can't believe what I'm looking at. The red-brick kip of a house that I spent a lot of my time living and partying in when I was in college is splattered all over the TV.

My body moves like it's being controlled by someone else in the direction of the screen situated about four feet above my head on the wall in front of me. My eyes fix on the image of the house surrounded by police cars, cops and tape. I strain my ears in an attempt to hear the reporter. The TVs are all set on low volume in this place so as not to disrupt the calm, relaxed ambience we aim to create here at the clinic. But I need to hear this. I need to know what is going on and at the same time I don't need to hear this. I don't want to know what's going on because I never wanted to be brought back there. Things happened at Huntley Lodge. Bad things.

With my face glued to the reporter's lips, I try to match their movements to the mutterings that are barely audible and scrape together the information.

A woman's body has been found at the house. It's been there for a while. The reporter doesn't say how long and I very much doubt they know that yet. How would they?

They've only just discovered it. Taking in a deep breath I try to slow down my racing heart. Is this really happening?

Behind me, I hear footsteps. I glance around to see one of the security guys I'm not too familiar with going off duty.

'Is there any chance I can have the volume upped on this TV?' I say but he tells me the settings are fixed and he's no way of increasing it without climbing up and adjusting it from behind. The maintenance room is all locked up for the day so he can't access the ladder but he suggests I go to the patients' TV room down the hallway. I don't want to do that. I've a load of paperwork to get finished and if I go in there someone will delay me.

'Ok thanks,' I say. My eyes continue to watch the drama unfolding silently on the screen until it disappears into the next story. I take my phone from my pocket and open my newsfeed to see if I can find out anything more.

So far there's just a body. No name, no date, no suggestion of murder. I walk down the corridor and sit at my desk where I open a file, hoping to distract myself. I need to take my mind off the discovery but I'm finding it impossible and now I'm holding my phone again and searching a few more sites. Still nothing. I'm about to stop looking when a news alert flashes on the screen. *Woman Found in Disused Pit*. Shit. I remember that pit. Nobody ever went near it when I was living there. It was covered in weeds and brambles and barely visible. If we hadn't been warned about it when we first moved in, we may never have known it was there.

My eyes devour the information on the screen. Huntley Lodge is currently being renovated and that's how the body was discovered. The builders found it at the bottom of the ten-foot-deep pit while they were digging

8

new foundations for a massive extension being planned to the rear of the old house. The report goes on to say that no one is currently living at Huntley Lodge but it doesn't say when it was last inhabited. Were we the last people living there? I hope not.

I close the phone and picture the building as I remember it. The red brick, the white wooden sash windows all in need of repair. Granite ledges. The old red wooden door with beautiful stained-glass panels. One of the panes of glass broke during a party one night and we replaced it with cheap plain glass. As students it was all we could afford but it looked terrible.

I promised myself I would never let my mind go back there, I would never revisit that night, but I can't help it. Seeing that image of Huntley Lodge has brought everything rushing back. My breath is getting shallower. *Breathe in, Faye...* but nothing helps. It's like the whole cast from that dreadful nightmare has pulled up in a bus inside my head and now they're all stepping off and back into my life.

Tara Moore is the first down the steps. I hate her. The kind of hate you can only muster up for someone you once loved. Tara was my best friend. We grew up together. Did everything together. I loved that girl... I was there when she needed me because I thought she would have done the same for me. But then she did the unthinkable. I didn't know what Tara Moore was capable of.

My mind is rambling, remembering, trying to make sense of the sudden surge of memory bursting through the barrier that I've built to protect it. My head is slumped, tears are welling in my eyes and then I hear the sound of the intercom in the hallway calling my name. My last appointment of the day. Shit. Dabbing my eyes, I take a deep breath and inhale the soft scent of vanilla in the air. I pull a smile onto my face and hope to hide the utter turmoil going on inside me. People need to have faith in their doctors; they need to believe they're strong, that they have everything under control. So this is not the first time I've had to disguise my crumbling interior.

Taking the file from the table, I brush myself down. I lift my head high, shaking off the fear, the truth, the anxiety over what is going to happen now. The knot in my stomach tightens as I walk out the door and, not for the first time, wish I had never set foot in Huntley Lodge.

Chapter Four

Then

'How much?'

'Six hundred euro a month.'

'That's for nothing, why is it so cheap?' Tara's eyes are open wide, staring at me in disbelief and excitement. I'm sitting on her bed watching her try out some makeup her Aunt Rose gave her for her birthday. The room is small compared to my bedroom in my parents' house but it's cosy. We prefer hanging out here. Tara's an only child so unlike at my house, where there are three of us, we don't have to put up with the constant rows over someone touching something belonging to someone else.

'I know, great isn't it? He's a friend of my father's and just wants someone staying in it for a few years until he's ready to renovate it or something like that. Anyway my dad thought of us because it's so close to the college.'

'But that's just three hundred each a month!'

'Two, if we get someone else in.'

Tara turns away and looks at her image in the mirror. Moving closer to the glass, she sweeps lipstick across her lips. Her green eyes are sparkling bright at the thought of us finally getting our own place to live. It's something we always talked about but it's so expensive to rent in Dublin. And with neither of us working we thought the dream would be a long time in the making. But here we are. After just one year in college our wish is coming true.

I know how Tara feels. I was blown away too, unable to believe my luck when my dad asked if we'd be interested in renting the place. The only condition attached is that my name doesn't appear on the lease. The man who owns it is a client of Dad's and it might cause trouble down the line. He suggested we put Tara's name on it.

'This is crazy, Faye,' she says, clasping her hands with excitement. 'Do you know when we can move in?'

'I presume as soon as we want. He's not looking for a deposit and my dad says he'll pay the first month's rent to give us a start.'

'What?'

I nod, then squeal, unable to keep the excitement locked up any longer. I'm so happy to be telling Tara this news, to be the one who found us a place.

'No Faye, he can't pay for me.'

'Why not? He has loads of money.'

Tara's smile disappears. 'That's not the point, I'll ask my own dad.'

'But…' I stop. I don't want this to be one of those moments when our different backgrounds become a thing. Like when my parents invited Tara on holiday with us two years ago but then she couldn't come because the fare to Barbados was out of her parents' reach.

Or the time my mam offered some of my old clothes to Tara. I still can't believe she did that. I was so embarrassed. I couldn't believe the words coming out of Mam's mouth as she stood in the bedroom pointing to a pile of clothes on a chair in the corner of the room. I continued talking as if I hadn't heard her but I could tell Tara couldn't wait to get out of my house.

'Sure, Tara.' I stand and walk to the window and look out into the garden to see if Tara's dad's car is there. 'He's not home, though. What about your mam?'

'Mam will say *yes, go, get out of here.*' Tara chuckles before becoming more serious. 'But she's not in great form lately; she's tired all the time. I don't want to put pressure on her. I'll wait until Dad gets home from his chess club and I'll ask them both together.'

'Fine,' I say, lifting my jacket from Tara's bed.

'Where are you going?' she says.

'Home.'

'God, no, you better be here when I tell them. Dad will freak when he hears I'm leaving. He won't be as bad if you're here.'

My eyes fall on the collage of photographs dressing the frame on the mirror. A history of our friendship since the day we met. On one side, I see a photo of us making our confirmation. I'm in a pink coat, with a cream hat that has a big pink bow at the side and looks ridiculous on me. I'm a good few inches shorter than Tara, who's holding her hand in mine. We're both smiling for the camera.

Further on down the frame and the two of us have become a lot more precious with our smiles. We're standing apart from one another, staring straight ahead like we're in a line-up. Thankfully the 'too cool to care' phase didn't last long because in every other photo, whether at school or getting ready for the local disco, we're wrapped around each other, laughing and smiling. I sometimes find it hard to remember when Tara wasn't in my life.

The light is dimming now, casting a shadow over Tara's face. She switches on the small lamp and we continue to make plans.

'I'll get a part-time job… Oh, I can't believe this is happening, Faye! I can't believe we're leaving home.'

'Can you imagine the parties we'll have?'

Tara stands and moves over to where I'm sitting on her bed. Her eyes open wide in anticipation of what our new journey will entail. Her hand is shaking as she hands me the hairbrush and sits down beside me. 'God I'm sick with excitement,' she says, turning her porcelain-skinned face away so I can brush her long shiny hair that I've always wished was mine. The image in the mirror resembles a perfectly created doll but Tara never seems to notice how beautiful she is.

'I won't be doing this every night when we're living together, ya know.'

'You won't have to, Faye. Next week I'm getting it all cut into a bob. New beginnings, new hairstyle.'

'What?' I'm about to tell Tara she's mad when I hear the front door closing. 'Is that your dad?'

'Probably.' Tara rushes to the window to check if her father's car is in the driveway then turns to me, teeth clenched, blessing herself before saying 'Here goes… let's hope he won his chess game tonight.' Then we both rush out the bedroom door and down the stairs to where Tara's dad has arrived in the kitchen.

Roisin, her mam, is already sitting at the table. I call her Roisin because she told me to. Not something that would go down well in my house. My father expects my friends to call him Dr Connolly and my mam to be addressed as Mrs Connolly. My sister's boyfriend called him James once and Dad spurted the brandy out of his mouth, he was so shocked.

'Hi girls,' she says, when we enter the room. Tara is right. Roisin does look tired and her face is very pale, but

I don't want to mention this in case she says she's sick or something and then Tara decides it's not the right time to tell them she's leaving.

'Mam. Dad. I have some news.'

Tara's father immediately puts down the kettle that he's filling with water and turns around with a look of horror on his face. His mouth is wide open but he's afraid to speak.

'No, Dad. I'm not pregnant,' Tara says, bringing a chuckle from her mother.

'Well what then? What's wrong?'

'Jesus, Niall, give her a chance to talk,' Roisin says, winking at me like she already knows what she's going to hear. That's another thing that would never happen in my house. Mam telling Dad to shut up.

'I'm moving out.'

'Good on ya,' Roisin says.

'What?' Tara's dad is in shock. Her mam is happy.

'We got a house… well, Faye's dad got us one. It's close to the college. Just three hundred euros each a month. Two, if we get someone else to move in.'

Tara turns to me and stares. This is my cue to join in.

'It's called Huntley Lodge.'

Chapter Five

Now

Last night was the worst. I don't think I slept for even an hour. Tossing and turning, worrying about what we did. Then this morning, with only half an hour left before I had to get up, I fell into a deep sleep. Typical. Now I'm like a robot that hasn't been fully charged. Coffee. I need coffee.

The only thing that made any sense during my hours lying awake was my decision to contact Tara Moore. As much as I hate the idea, I have to be sure she doesn't give my name to the cops if they do come calling. My father made sure my name was kept off the lease at the time so it shouldn't be too hard to do. I hope she'll agree. It's been such a long time since I've been in contact with her; almost three years since I walked out of Huntley Lodge that day, never to return. Ignoring all her attempts to communicate with me after that was easy. I didn't want to talk to her. But now I have to. I'll convince her the cops don't need to know I was living there at the time. That it will just confuse things and keep them hanging around asking even more questions. I'll remind her that won't be good for either of us.

The smell of coffee offers hope. I pour a strong dose into my cup and look out the window at the dull morning coming to life. It's only seven, too early to ring Tara so I go to my diary and check the day ahead. Appointment after appointment fills the lines on the page in front of me. Just my luck – it's going to be a busy day. I might be better waiting until this evening to ring her when I have time to talk. I need to find out if she's worried too and if she knows anything more than what is showing up in the newsfeeds. The worst thing that can happen now is the cops will discover the body has been there since we were living at Huntley Lodge. If that happens, they will be all over our asses and, regardless of my cognitive ability, it will be difficult to hide the truth.

I finish my coffee then stand under the heat of the shower for longer than is necessary. If I'm to get through the day with all this in my head, I'm going to have to focus. I put on a pair of blue trousers, comfortable but trendy shoes and close the buttons on my navy silk shirt. I take one last glance in the mirror before heading out the door.

–

Before I know it, it's five o'clock. I got through the day without letting the discovery at Huntley Lodge distract me from the job in hand. And now it's time to deal with it. I leave consultation room number four with a file under my arm and walk down the corridor towards my own room. The smell of something citrusy fills the air when I walk past the reception desk where Anna appears to be finishing up for the day.

'Bye Anna, wrap up warm, it's pretty blustery out there,' I say, my voice showing no sign of the anxiety growing inside me at the prospect of the call I'm about to make.

'See ya tomorrow, Faye,' Anna says, zipping up her jacket. Then she moves out from behind the reception area and I continue with haste down the corridor. I need to ring Tara Moore. I need to talk to her before the cops do. When I reach the privacy of my own space, I quickly sit down at my desk. My finger flicks down the list of contacts in my phone until I reach her name. I'm hoping this is still her number.

With the phone to my ear, I wait until I hear it ring then I cut the call. Why am I so nervous all of a sudden? It's only Tara Moore. Why is my hand shaking, my breath quickening?

I'm anxious. It's like I'm standing at a crossroads on the map of my life and I don't know which way to turn. The thing is, I have learned to live without Tara in my life. I don't want to invite her back in. Especially when I don't trust this woman anymore.

There was a time I trusted Tara Moore with everything. She knew all my secrets, my hates, my wishes, the things I did that I shouldn't have done. The things I should have done that I didn't. But she betrayed me. Stabbed me in the heart with my own knife. I could never trust her again.

Anger simmers below my skin when I think back to that night. My face reddens. I can feel the heat flush through my cheeks. I'm holding the phone so tightly my hand hurts. Releasing my grip, I let the phone drop onto the table… *and breathe in… and out. Take it easy Faye… it's just a phone call… and you have to make it.*

Chapter Six

Tara

I push open the door of the café to the sound of Muriel cursing at somebody over the phone. God love whoever it is on the other end. She does not take kindly to her orders being late.

'So what do you want me to tell my customers?' she shouts, giving me a thumbs-up when she notices me enter.

The smell of coffee is a welcome change to the smell I had to endure on my walk to work. The Liffey is low and stinks today. Every breath was torture to take on the fifteen-minute journey down the quays.

Our riverside apartment is situated in what's commonly known as the financial hub of the city, a thriving space of banks, businesses, theatres and restaurants. It wasn't that long ago when it was amongst the most run-down places in Dublin. An oasis for those who fell through the cracks and couldn't climb out. Now it's up there with the most expensive places to rent in the city centre. I don't actually pay for any of it because it comes with Lucas's job. It was part of the package offered to attract him away from the sun and the sand to the wind and the rain. That, and the promise of a promotion on his return to Australia. All I have to do is enjoy the view, the endless amenities and the one surviving traditional pub that's conveniently situated right beside our block. The glossy green painted exterior of O'Reilly's bar, with its stained glass and warm lighting, looks out of place amongst the cold brick and glass walls that surround it. It's kept busy with clientele from all walks of life. On a Tuesday you could be sipping gin with a poet, Friday a bank manager, Saturday a drug dealer. As long as you don't bring trouble through the door, everyone is welcome. Lucas loves to go there when the rugby is on. He wears his Wallabies gold and green with pride and even though he's the only one not wearing an Irish jersey, he shouts for his team just as loud as the rest of the punters.

'It better not be late,' Muriel says, ending the call before turning her attention to me. She smiles.

'Rotten day, isn't it?' she says. 'Those fools from Cahill's bakery are late with the croissants and doughnuts again.'

Muriel calls 'five minutes' late. The poor van driver is probably stuck in traffic at the far end of the quays, sweating nervously that they have to come in and face the wrath of Muriel. They shouldn't worry, though. Her bark is a hell of a lot worse than her bite.

I yawn when I say good morning and she asks me what has me so tired.

'Were you up all night again making love to that fella?' she says, making me laugh. 'You should keep something for the honeymoon.'

'I didn't sleep very well,' I say, removing my jacket and walking in behind the counter.

'Everything will be wonderful, pet, don't be worrying.'

Muriel thinks I'm stressing out about the wedding. Yesterday she would have been right. I have become more anxious the closer it gets to the day. Hoping everything will go well: that people will enjoy themselves; that my dress will fit; that the best man won't be drunk before the speech. The list of concerns went on and on until last night. That list is now redundant. I have a brand new list and there's only one thing on it. The body found at Huntley Lodge.

As if reading my mind, Muriel comments.

'Did you see they found a body of a woman in the grounds of some old house out by the university? It was all over the news. Apparently it's been there for a while. The house was being renovated and some poor builder chap discovered it.'

I stop walking and listen as Muriel tops up my fear.

'Where did you hear that?' I say.

'It was on the news earlier. Poor fecker, he didn't go in to work expecting to find a dead body... Mind you, if it wasn't for him the poor woman's body may never have been found. Is that Cahill's van outside yet?' she says, walking out from behind the counter to look out the window. Muriel flips the noticeboard on the door to 'open' and I find myself wishing I could turn back time. Get married last month. Be on the beach in Australia yesterday. Far away from this breaking news.

Within two minutes there's a queue and I smile and serve beautiful coffees to the customers. At this hour of the morning most people just want to get their coffee and leave. They're on their way to work and not inclined to wake fully until they absolutely have to. There's very little talk outside what's needed to politely make an order.

It won't be like that later. Come eleven o'clock we'll be providing commentary along with coffee. People are at their best then. The day is up and running. The energy levels are high and they want to communicate.

Today is no different; the main topic of conversation is last night's football match with one or two commenting on the discovery of the body by the builder.

Each time it's mentioned my heart skips a beat. I even flush red once or twice like I'm guilty. No one says anything I don't already know but I am eager to go on my break to check the social media for myself.

Eventually there's a lull and Muriel asks me if I'd like a break. Usually I tell her to go first but today I don't. I make myself a skinny latte, take it to the back room where I sit down and take out my phone. I'm eager to find out if anything new is being reported about the body found at Huntley Lodge. Did they discover the body was lying dead in the pit for three years?

There's nothing new posted on the *The Journal.ie* so I check Twitter and Facebook but still no new revelations. I suppose it's still early; they might not have completed the autopsy yet. I'm just going to have to wait.

My phone beeps. It's a message from my chief brides-maid Amy reminding me she'll pick me up outside the cafe after work as planned. We're going for the final dress fittings tonight. I should be excited but the discovery of the body is ruining everything for me. If the cops call asking questions and discover what we did, I won't be walking down the aisle in my wedding dress or boarding a plane with my new husband. I might not even be allowed out of the country. A rush of sadness slows me as I think of Lucas. Will he still want to marry me?

'Tara,' Muriel calls. The cafe must be getting busy. It's time to get back out front. I stand, shaking my head, shaking the negative thoughts out of my brain. What would Mam tell me to do? She'd say stop worrying about something that may never happen and concentrate on enjoying the wedding.

I walk out to where a queue has formed at the counter and force a smile onto my worried face. 'Next.'

Chapter Seven

I'm standing outside the cafe with an umbrella over my head. Amy is supposed to be here, but she's late. She's been so good helping me prepare for the wedding. Especially with Mam not around. Amy was delighted when I asked her to be my bridesmaid and even though we've only been friends for the past two years, I feel close to her. Not like I did with Faye... but close. The night I bumped into her she was with a group of girls that knew Emily. I immediately gravitated towards her. Amy was funny, she made me laugh. It was what I needed at the time. We arranged to meet again the following week in the same bar and before long we became the best of friends.

I'm hopping from foot to foot trying to keep warm, and my eyes are scanning the cars driving past searching for a little white Mini. Today seemed to go on forever. I couldn't get the thought of that woman's body lying at the bottom of the pit out of my head. Customers kept mentioning it but no one had heard anything new.

I hear a horn beep and see Amy's car arriving. At least now I might be able to take my mind off the discovery at Huntley Lodge and get in the mood for my wedding. I should be enjoying these last few weeks. I'm going to forget all about the news and think only of white dresses and wedding songs.

Amy pulls over and I jump into the car. Immediately I feel better.

'Sorry I'm a bit late, Tar, the traffic is crap on the quays at this hour.' Amy moves back out into the traffic.

'No worries, you're here now.'

'Are you excited? Last fitting.'

'I sure am,' I say, taking a deep breath. This is how I want to feel, excited, alive, looking forward.

'Terrible about that body they found,' Amy says, instantly bursting my happy bubble. I can almost feel the air deflating. Why did she have to mention that?

'Yeah… ah, well, at least it's none of us. Are you looking forward to trying on your bridesmaid dress?'

'I am… You used to live at Huntley Lodge didn't you?' she says.

'A long time ago. Is Emma coming to the hen party?' I try once again to change the subject. Amy wasn't my friend back then. She knows nothing about what happened that night but I did brag about all the parties that went on there. I'm sorry now I ever mentioned Huntley Lodge to her. I don't want to continue this conversation. It's making me anxious. I should be happy. This is my happy time.

'Yeah, she said she should make it.'

'And are we still going ahead with Brogan's first before Coppers?'

'That's the plan.'

Amy turns off the busy quays and out towards Glasnevin where the wedding shop is. It's the same shop where my mother bought her dress all those years ago. Her dress was a lot different than mine. It had a big hoop under the skirt and cut off shoulders. Mam looked beautiful in the photos. Her hair was curled and lifted at the sides, showing off the real pearl earrings that her mother had given her and that I'm going to wear to my wedding. Something old. They're not borrowed, though. I got all Mam's jewellery when she passed away except for one piece, a beautiful silver ring with a green stone that a friend of hers had given her. She wanted her friend to have it back.

'Almost here,' Amy says, taking the roundabout like she's the only car on the road. Someone beeps. Amy presents them with the finger she keeps for these occasions. We both laugh as we eventually arrive and pull into one of the few parking spaces close to the shop. I feel happy again, excited. This is it. The last fitting. I'll be taking the dress away with me tonight and leaving it at my dad's house. I don't want Lucas to see it before the big day. That could bring bad luck and there's enough of that floating around at the moment.

'I see your cousin Emily is already here,' Amy says, noticing her car parked outside.

'Great,' I say.

'I hope you're still saying great when you see who's with her.'

'What do you mean? Who is with her?' I stretch to try and see what Amy saw but all I can see is Emily. She's talking to someone who has already gone through the door of the shop. But who could be with her? A dreadful possibility suddenly enters my head...

'No!'

'I'm afraid yes.' Amy laughs, pushing open the door for me to enter first. I can't believe Emily brought Aunt Rose along.

'Well I guess I had to meet her sometime,' I say, but I'm not at all happy about it. Rose is bound to say something

26

to upset me, something about my dress or the colour of the bridesmaids' dresses. She never could keep her opinion to herself.

When we get inside, Emily rushes over to us. Rose is sitting on a chair by the dressing rooms. She nods sheepishly at me. At least she doesn't expect me to be all over her. I nod back while removing my jacket. The lady who owns the shop, Mrs Beth, is all buzzing and excited for me. She's blabbing on about how beautiful I'm going to look as she brings my dress from the dressing room into the middle of the shop floor. My heart sticks in my throat. I'm going to cry, it's so beautiful.

'You're up first,' she says to me, bringing me into the big dressing room on the right. I look back at Emily and Amy who look as excited as I am. 'Here goes.'

The dress is just what I wanted. I'm standing still, my eyes devouring the picture in the mirror in front of me when I feel a hand landing on my shoulder.

'It's beautiful, Tara. Your mam would have loved it.' With tears in my eyes I think of Mam. She's not here. She should be here. My head blurs with emotion when I try to picture her by my side. Mam would not like me to be harbouring any ill feelings towards Rose. Especially now. If she was here she would tell me to forgive her and move on. So I take my hand and put it on top of the hand resting on my shoulder. 'Thank you, Rose.'

–

When the fittings are complete and Mrs Beth has all the dresses packed for transportation, we leave the shop and try to put the three of them in the boot of Amy's little Mini. Unfortunately, there's no chance they are all going to fit so Emily agrees to drive behind with the bridesmaids' dresses to my father's house which is only about a mile away. Rose is silent when the arrangement is made. She hasn't been at Dad's house since Mam died but I haven't the time or the energy to worry about that sort of thing. There'll be plenty of uncomfortable situations before this wedding is over. I may as well get used to ignoring them.

'Are we ready?' I say, jumping into the car beside Amy. Emily is ahead of us with Rose in the passenger seat.

'Well, that wasn't too bad,' Amy says. 'She was actually quite nice.'

I nod, letting her believe what she wants. But I say nothing. I know Rose. Rose is not nice, shouting at me like she did when Mam was so sick and close to the end. Blaming me for the mess Emily had gotten herself into. Saying it never would have happened if it wasn't for Huntley Lodge.

Chapter Eight

Dad wasn't there when we called so we dropped the dresses into the bedroom at the front of the house which my father has decorated especially for the day of my wedding. It's perfect. Soft white carpet, pale blue walls and three standing mirrors. I don't know how he got it so right; he must have asked somebody. Maybe a new friend. It's probably selfish of me but I wish he was dating someone. It would take the pressure off me when I get to Australia to know he's not on his own. I'm pretty sure Mam would want it too. She'd want him to be happy and to move on with his life. He was always so good to her. So good to me.

I have to admit, I'm very lucky. I've got the nicest dad and the most wonderful fiancé. Meeting Lucas was the best thing that ever happened to me and the timing was perfect. I was still trying to get used to my life without Faye. Learning to make decisions on my own. I missed her backing me up, telling me what to do and pumping up my confidence. It took a while for me to trust my own opinion because I had always run everything by her first, especially when it came to boyfriends. I wonder what she'd say about Lucas. Would she give him the thumbs up?

Amy drops me off right outside my apartment block. She's not supposed to because it's a one-way system but she said certain rules don't apply when you're getting married.

Certain rules don't apply to Amy full stop when it comes to driving. We say our goodbyes. We won't see each other again until the hen party on Saturday night. Walking away from the car, I try to ignore the fear inside me. I can't let it ruin my hen party so I force myself to think about the weekend ahead. The laughter. The drinks. The fun. The dancing. I allow myself to picture what I'm going to wear. The new dress that I bought last month in anticipation of a wonderful crazy night with the girls. I see us all downing shots on the count of three and a wave of excitement surges through me. This is my hen party and it's going to be some craic.

Lucas is standing in the kitchen when I walk into the apartment.

'How did it go?' he says, wiping his hands on a tea towel.

'Great, I love the dress but you won't believe who was there.' I hang my coat on the hooks at the back of the door and kick off my shoes.

'Who?'

'Rose.'

'Rose, the famous auntie that you hate?'

'Don't say hate,' I say; Mam didn't like me using that word.

'Well, dislike a hell of a lot, then,' he says.

I laugh, sitting on the sofa. 'Well, at least it's done with now, I don't have to worry about seeing her for the first time in three years on my wedding day.'

'I tried to call you but there was no answer, I didn't know if you wanted me to keep you some dinner. I did anyway, it's in the microwave.'

'Oh, thanks Lucas. You are so kind to me. Remind me to marry you,' I say, taking my phone from my bag to check the missed calls. 'Sorry, it's on silent.' I always keep my phone on silent when I'm at work and I must have forgotten to switch it back on. There are four missed calls. Three from Lucas and one from a number that I don't recognise.

'Shit,' I say. 'I've missed a call. I hope there is nothing wrong with the wedding.' I start to spiral – maybe it's the band cancelling? Or the hotel is double-booked? Or the flowers aren't available?

'I just need to call back and find out.'

'You have to eat something,' Lucas says taking the phone from my hand. 'You can make your call when you've finished eating.'

'But what if there's a problem?'

'Don't worry, Tara, the problem will still be there after you've eaten.' Lucas knows that if there is something wrong I'll go into a tizzy and won't be able to calm down for hours, never mind eat. I'm lucky to have a man who knows how to calm me down, with reassuring phrases like, *don't fret about it, no one will remember tomorrow*, or, *in the grand scheme of things, I doubt it really matters*, or, *don't worry about it, no one died*. I don't actually like when he uses that last one. Because someone did die. And I do worry about it.

'Well, just a little bit. I'm not hungry.' I'm more interested in finding out who that missed call is from.

'You do know you're going to have to relax when we get to Australia,' he says, handing me a fork.

'There'll be nothing to worry about then,' I say. 'The wedding will be over.' I smile at him, lifting the fork to my mouth, hoping the body at Huntley Lodge doesn't spoil everything. I can't let Lucas see my worry. I have to act like everything is okay. 'It will be all sun, sea and sex from then on,' I say.

Lucas laughs, leaning over the counter to kiss my forehead. 'Well, if you insist.'

—

I'm sitting on the sofa sipping a glass of wine, my feet tucked between Lucas's legs when I suddenly realise I never called that number back. I glance over at the clock on the cooker. 9.45 p.m. It's probably too late now, I think, deciding to ring first thing in the morning.

There was nothing new on tonight's news bulletin about the body found at Huntley Lodge. It wasn't even mentioned and the social media networks have nothing new either. Just lots of condolences under the comments and one or two people asking if it could be the woman who went missing a few years back. Each time I read such a comment my blood pressure shoots through the roof. I have to stop looking.

I look at the clock again. I'm not sure I'll sleep properly if I don't ring now because if someone is cancelling their service I don't have much time to find a replacement. Taking my phone from the coffee table I slip my feet out from under Lucas and go to the bedroom. I flick through to find the number of the missed call. I'm stressing out again, hoping it's nothing to do with the wedding. When I hit the redial button I list every possible thing I think it could be while waiting for an answer. After a few rings the phone goes to message.

> *Dr Faye Connolly is not available at the moment. Please leave a message and your call will be returned as soon as possible.*

My heart stops. That was not on my list. Why is Faye Connolly making contact now after all this time? My hand starts to shake as I lift the phone to my mouth because I know the answer.

'Faye... it's Tara. Sorry I missed your call. Please ring back.' I end the message, gripping the phone tightly in my hand. Faye Connolly is ringing about the body found at Huntley Lodge. She's worried too that the cops will dredge up the past and I don't blame her. If our alibi doesn't hold strong, Faye has a lot to lose.

Chapter Nine

Then

'Smile.'

Faye is holding her phone up to take a selfie of us both standing beside the main stage. I pull my hands out from the pockets of the jeans which are tucked into my pink wellies and force a smile. The light rain jacket that I'm wearing over my checked shirt and a white T-shirt is probably not necessary because the sun is shining in the clear blue sky above my head. But I barely notice because my heart is breaking. I'm giving all that I can to perform in this charade but behind my fake smile my thoughts are crushing me.

I'm also wearing a fake tattoo. A flower on the right hand side of my face, stretching above my eyes. Faye has one of a blackbird with a yellow beak. Faye insisted we stick the tattoos on saying, 'We have to make it look like we're enjoying ourselves.'

I know she's right. Faye is always right.

The stage, a massive steel structure, looks like a giant spider in the middle of the field. Technicians are working, laying wires and connecting supersized amps. Soon it will be bouncing with musicians and singers, setting the night on fire with light and sound and energy. But I won't be here.

Forcing myself to look happy, I form a peace sign with my two fingers and Faye sticks her tongue out.

'A couple more and we should have enough,' she says taking my phone.

Faye captures another few photographs of us at the festival and then we hand the phones to Andriu who is standing beside us with a baseball cap on his head. His eyes are glued to the guys preparing the stage like he's never seen manual work before.

'You know what to do, don't you?' Faye says, nudging him.

'Yes, yes, all under control.' Andriu lifts his hand to salute Faye, his dark eyes gleaming above his smile like it's all some sort of a joke. It isn't a joke. But Faye couldn't tell him the truth about why she needs an alibi. We couldn't risk anyone else knowing. So she said she was faking being here for work. That she could only get off duty to go to her cousin's hen party by telling her boss that she had already bought her ticket to the festival. The photos are in case someone asks.

Andriu fell for it. He believes everything Faye tells him, just like me.

Faye and I have been to every other Electric Picnic festival. Our mothers gift us the tickets for Christmas every year. It's part of a pact we agreed with them when we turned sixteen. If we did well in our exams, we could go to the festival. From that day on, we did well in our exams. So it's the perfect alibi.

'Remember to take a few photos of the stage on both of our phones when Lana Del Ray is playing,' Faye says, leaning in to kiss Andriu before tracing his lips with her finger. It's a quirky thing she does that I don't under-stand. 'And I'll see you tomorrow,' she says, handing him something. I think it's money. Andriu must be broke again and Faye always has money.

'And don't get carried away with the music and forget to take the photos,' she smiles, slapping one last kiss on his lips.

Andriu nods and puts both our phones in his pocket. I feel completely numb walking away from him; my breath is getting shallower as we move against the crowd that's beginning to fill this big green field.

If sometime in the future anyone asks where we were tonight our phones will corroborate our answer.

Pushing through the happy smiles and the abundance of colour floating on all these nameless faces, I drag fresh air into my lungs and try to stop myself from falling to the ground. It's taking all my concentration to see ahead of me, to look normal. This carnival atmosphere with everyone laughing and singing and getting drunk doesn't help. I feel drunk, even though I haven't had a drink. The place is spinning. Moving too quickly, or too slowly, I can't tell. I'm moving at a different pace to everyone else. Trying to pause time.

I need to get out of here.

Faye takes my hand when she notices how stressed I've become. She puts her other hand out in front of her, pushing through the crowd like someone is chasing after us. Faye says nothing, squeezing my hand, letting me know she's beside me.

After what feels like a marathon in chains, we arrive outside where I stop and lean against the side of a food van at the edge of the car park. The smell of food frying adds to my distress and I can feel my stomach lurching. I close my eyes and pray for strength. When I open them again I'm looking up at the blue sky. There are no clouds blocking my view as I hopelessly search for a sign that heaven is up there somewhere. I rest for a few more minutes until Faye suggests we get a move on.

—

The traffic is heavier than we allowed for. There must be quite a few people getting dropped off at the festival instead of using the special bus service. I never thought of that. It's going to take us longer to get to Dublin than we'd planned. But it doesn't matter. Time no longer matters. Not for this. Not for what I'm about to do.

Eventually we arrive outside the house and we get out of the car. My body trembles under Faye's generous hug that cloaks me in support. She knows that what I'm about to do can never be undone.

Chapter Ten

I can't sleep. I lie in bed, listening to the sound of the rain constantly banging against my window. I keep checking my phone in case I miss a call from Faye, which is stupid. Faye is not going to ring in the middle of the night.

Lucas is lying asleep in the bed beside me, unaware of the drama I'm concocting in my head. Does Faye know something about the body? She must have seen Huntley Lodge on the news and I guess in her field it would be easy to find out a bit about it. Maybe she knows how long the body has been there. Or maybe she knows nothing and is ringing to see if I've heard anything. But what does it all mean if she was buried at Huntley Lodge when we lived there? Will the cops think one of us is involved? Will they want to talk to us?

I feel like I'm cheating, not telling Lucas how worried I am. He's always so open about his feelings. Sharing all his inner thoughts. If something is bothering him at work, I know about it. As soon as he knew how he felt about me he couldn't wait to tell me.

'I love you.' He blurted it out over dinner one night in a Chinese restaurant. I was licking sauce from around my lips after finishing off a plate of sticky ribs and doubt I was at my most appealing.

'What?' I said, grabbing my glass of wine and pouring the remaining contents down my throat. I'm sorry now that I didn't say, 'I love you too'. But I hadn't really thought about it and was not prepared to dive into another possible river of heartbreak. As far as I was concerned, Lucas was just another fling. He'd be going home to Australia and I wasn't prepared to suffer the hurt of someone I loved leaving again. But, before long, it became apparent to me that there was something more to our relationship, something I couldn't put my finger on. After a few months, I could feel Lucas slowly breaking down the barrier I had built to protect myself from getting too attached. Could it be love? Eventually, I surrendered to my feelings.

I could see that Lucas did love me. I had to stop paddling in the shallow end or get out of the pool. So I told him. Not over dinner in a busy restaurant but lying on his sofa one night. Just quietly, no big fuss. I leaned in to the warmth of his face and whispered in his ear. 'I love you too'.

After that, things quickly moved into the next phase and within a week I was saying goodbye to Dad and moving in with Lucas.

–

The alarm buzzing at the far side of the bed shocks me back to the present. I didn't drift off to sleep until the early hours and now I would love nothing more than to stay here wrapped up in the duvet for the rest of the day. Still more asleep than awake, Lucas lifts his arm out to quieten the buzzer. He always does that, sometimes two or three times. I check the phone one more time before shuffling out onto the cold wooden floor and heading for the ensuite. I'm knackered, hopefully the shower will wake me up.

Slightly refreshed, I step out of the shower thinking how Lucas and I have already formed so many habits. I'm always first into the shower in the morning. Lucas waits until I'm back in the room before he gets out of bed. Then he goes to the kitchen and switches on the coffee machine. It's almost twenty minutes before either of us verbally acknowledges one another. But today is different. I walk back into the room and Lucas says, 'Are you expecting a delivery or something?'

'Not that I know of. Why?'

'There's someone downstairs. They asked for you on the intercom.'

'Can they not just leave whatever it is in the lobby box?'

'Maybe you have to sign for it.'

'For fuck's sake, at this hour of the morning?' I run a brush through my wet hair and throw on the nearest tracksuit I can find.

'Be a doll and toast me a bagel,' I say, leaving the bedroom. This had better be good, I think. Dragging me down to the front door at this hour!

'I'll toast you a bagel but I won't be a doll.' Lucas laughs out loud as I pull on a pair of slippers and stumble out of the apartment door. I'm halfway down the stairs when I realise I forgot my phone. What if Faye rings back and I miss her call again? Damn it. In the lobby I am walking to the front door when I hear a deep voice call my name.

'Tara Moore.'

I turn to see a man and a woman standing over near the letterboxes. She's about four inches taller than he is and standing with her legs apart and her arms behind her back. She's wearing a blue suit, and a white shirt. If she wasn't also wearing such a poker face, she'd actually be very pretty. The man isn't as stern. He takes a step closer to where I'm glued to the floor. If I move, I'm going to collapse. I know exactly what I'm looking at.

'Detective Evan Mullins and this is Detective Siobhan Lee.' He looks around at the lobby, clearly deciding it is an inappropriate space for an interrogation as he says, 'Is there somewhere we could have a word?'

I nod. I'm nodding like a toy dog in a car window because I can't move any other part of my body. Detective Siobhan Lee notices my state and steps closer. Her voice is a lot softer than her expression when she speaks.

'It's nothing to worry about, Tara, just a few questions. You're not in any trouble.'

I'm not convinced. I know they say that to everyone before locking the cell door. But I have no choice here. I can't have them questioning me in front of everyone on their way out to work. I'll have to bring them up to the apartment.

'Can you give me a minute?' I say. 'My fiancé is still asleep.'

'Sure, go on ahead, we'll follow up in five minutes.'

Slowly, I move towards the stairs and when I know they can't see me anymore I take the steps three at a time. I run to the apartment door and bang on it, shouting, 'Lucas, Lucas!'

Lucas opens the door and I push past him, gasping for air.

'They're here; the cops are here.'

'The cops… where?' he says, sticking his head out the door.

'They're downstairs, they'll be here in a minute. Get dressed.'

'What are the cops doing here, Tara?' Lucas looks a bit confused, probably wondering what the hell he is getting into, marrying me.

'They didn't say yet but I bet it's about Huntley Lodge.'

'Huntley Lodge?' He's standing still, staring at me.

'The house that was on the news, the one where the body was found… can you get dressed, Lucas? They'll be here in—'

'Tara,' Lucas says. 'Tara,' he says again. This time I look up. The two detectives are standing beside him.

'Thank you,' the woman says and moves into the room. The man follows. Detective Lee puts her hand on my shoulder.

'Are you okay, Tara? You seem very nervous.'

I can barely breathe. There are two cops standing in my apartment waiting to ask me questions. Clenching my trembling hands, I turn away from their stare and take a deep breath to calm myself down. I have to act cool. They cannot see how scared I am.

Chapter Eleven

Faye

I'm lying in my bed with the phone in my hand waiting for Tara Moore to ring me back. I left a message earlier when the bitch didn't answer. How busy can she be? It's not like making a cup of coffee takes that much concentration.

That's right. I know what she does. And I know where she does it. That little coffee shop on the quays. It's amazing what you can find out from social media. I also know where she lives. I was able to figure it out by using the location map on Google with one of her 'moving in' bragging photos. Tara was standing outside a modern apartment block holding a big box in her hands pretending to be struggling with it. But that's not what I saw. What I saw was someone saying, *Look at me, moving in to this wonderful expensive apartment! Didn't I do well?*

Pulling the duvet up to my neck I take the phone from under my pillow and check it again. Still no reply. Maybe I should not have come to bed so early because my mind has gone off in a tangent of worry. I should have watched the TV for a while or gone for a walk – anything to relax the tension pulsating through my body. I have to talk to her; she has to know not to mention my name if someone comes asking about our stay in Huntley.

I could ring her back but that would look desperate and I don't want to look desperate. I need her to think this is just a passing request, no big deal. 'Just leave me out of it, Tara,' I'll say. 'I'm too busy to be bothering with such matters.'

I'm hoping she'll just agree not to mention my name without asking me why. Even though she knows why. She knows exactly why. And it's all her bloody fault.

Also, I don't want my father to find out the police want to question me because I know what his reaction will be. He'll freak out and say 'For God's sake, Faye, what have you got yourself involved in now and what am I going to tell Larry?' Larry is the friend of my father's who rented Huntley Lodge to us in the first place. I imagine my father's words echoing in my head. His disappointed voice bouncing off the walls of my skull. I place my hands on my head and urge the torment to leave. Why is this happening now? Will I never be able to say goodbye to the past?

I thought I had. The more time passed, the less I thought about Huntley and Tara Moore's betrayal. It was packed away at the back of my mind in a box marked 'Do not open'.

But now the box is open. The past is creeping out over the edge. Poison seeping into my thoughts. Confusing them, controlling them. I do not need this now but I'm unable to stop the disappointment festering as hate all over again. It's travelling through my body now, that sick feeling swelling in my stomach. My head begins to throb. I can see the empty glasses, the bare skin, the empty packet.

Suddenly I bolt up in the bed, my eyes open wide, staring at the bare wall in front of me like I'm waking from a desperate nightmare. I look around the room, the familiar shadows helping me breathe easier. I must not go there.

After a few minutes I'm relaxed. Well… more relaxed. I'm still a bit edgy so I swallow water from the bottle on my bedside locker and try to take my thoughts somewhere nicer. To my graduation day when I finally put a smile on my father's face. Finally, I had my degree and he could mention me with pride just like he did his other children. *Faye has qualified from medical school.* It's not what she wanted but hell, it's what Daddy wanted. I picture my graduation photo. He's standing beside me with his arm on my shoulder; Mam is on the other side. Mam is her usual grateful self. Her mood seldom changes. She's like an observer standing on the edge of everyone else's life. Unable to comment for fear of being wrong. She just smiles and obeys and makes sure the rest of us have what we need.

I'm happy in this picture. I smile and say 'Cheese' before realising something is missing. I don't know what it is at first. I'm looking around me, scanning the crowd for her face. But she isn't here.

My phone beeps, dragging me back to the present. I sit up in the bed and grab it from under my pillow. But it isn't her. It's just a text from my sister asking me how I am and if everything is okay.

I wish I could tell her it's not. That everything is far from okay but I don't want to bother her.

> All good. Hope to see you at the weekend
> xx

I reply, then flop back onto my pillow.

My eyes don't close. I think they might be afraid to so I look at the slice of sky on view through the slit in the curtains. It's just a peek at space but it settles me to know how big the world is. How unimportant I am. To that bright star twinkling in the far distance, I am not even visible. This brings comfort to me. Reminding me that nothing I do actually matters. Slowly I close my eyes and let peace float through my mind. It warms my body. I feel sleepy; my mind is closing down for the night. Maybe I'll dream of Andriu.

Chapter Twelve

Then

'You get it,' I say, shoving a bunch of towels into the washing machine. Tara's dad was here earlier while we were at college. He fixed the washing machine because it wouldn't empty properly and he also put some light bulbs where they were badly needed around the house. He's really handy like that, which is why he has a key. We can just ring him and the next day the problem is solved. He even cleaned the spare room for us when Robin left last month. Robin was a friend of a friend from college who had moved in two months earlier, a couple of weeks after we did. Then she had done a runner without paying the rent. It took a while for us to realise she had actually gone because it wasn't unusual for her to disappear for a few days. I only became suspicious when I knocked on her door for the third time that week and got no answer. I was pissed off at first but when Tara walked in and saw the room had been cleared out she started to laugh and couldn't stop. Then I started to laugh. We both fell onto the small bed and laughed until we couldn't laugh anymore.

Tara goes to open the front door. Today we met three possible housemates to take Robin's room: a girl out of Tara's history class; a food delivery guy who's over here studying English from Spain and up for consideration because he said he could get us free takeaways; and the third girl, Annemarie, who works in college administration. She's probably the best candidate; she's our age, seems to be a bit of fun and who knows when we might need someone in administration on our side.

'Faye.'

I lift my gaze from the machine settings and look to where Tara is standing in the doorway.

'One more,' she says, her eyes alight with excitement as she pulls a face.

'One more what?' I say, lifting the linen basket to bring it back upstairs. When I see the body walking into the kitchen behind Tara I drop it again and quickly push my hair off my face.

'This is Andriu,' she says, grinning before sticking her tongue out and crossing her eyes. Andriu can't see what she's doing because he's behind her. He's wearing jeans, a white T-shirt and a leather jacket – and if it wasn't 2015 I'd say he was hoping to join the cast of *Grease*. His dark hair hangs loosely to one side of his tanned face. Andriu is a good bit taller than I am and either he works out a lot or he's been blessed by the God of genes.

'Andriu, pleased to meet you,' I say, stepping closer and holding my hand out. He moves forward and takes it, shaking it slowly while his dark eyes hold my stare.

'He's here about the room to rent,' Tara says, standing behind him now.

'He is?' I say, replying to Tara but still staring at Andriu. It's like he has me under a spell. When he eventually releases his grip on my hand I turn away from him.

'Are you studying at the college?' I ask. It's the only place we have advertised the room so I'm guessing he is.

48

'Sort of.'

'Sort of. How can you be "sort of" studying?'

'I'm sort of studying too,' Tara adds in the background, hoping to get a laugh. But it's like we don't hear her.

'My work is top secret,' he says, smiling and showing off a mouthful of gleaming teeth. I take a deep breath. This guy is gorgeous.

'And yourself?' he asks.

'Medicine.'

'Ouch, brainy and sexy.'

He has me now. It's not just his good looks, his broad shoulders or his addictive smile, there's something very mature and sexy about him. Like he has a world of experience behind him and yet remains calm. Whatever it is, he's definitely different to the usual college guys who are always trying too hard. He's cool. That's it. Andriu is cool.

'And will you be looking to move in soon if we decide you're a suitable candidate?' I ask, but before he can answer, I say, 'But let me warn you, we have parties here most weekends so if that doesn't suit...'

'I'm sure I can live with that,' he says, stepping towards the sink and looking out into the back garden.

'Before you ask, she's not ours, she was here when we got here.' Tara giggles.

'Who?' Andriu says.

'Holy Mary, the statue by the wall.'

Andriu chuckles then turns his attention back to me. I want to offer him the room straight away... and join him in it. But I have to discuss it with Tara. We'll need a reference. I don't want to get caught out again like we did with Robin.

'I can give you a month in advance,' he says, as if reading my mind. Andriu takes his wallet from his back pocket.

'Well, we have to discuss it first. There are other candidates.'

'Sure, I understand. Do you want me to wait outside?' He points to the door, casting another smile in my direction. 'Or if it's a problem, don't worry about it. You might rather have a female. I get it.'

'No it's not that,' I say, *not that at all*.

'It's just… I have another offer that I have to reply to today… and…' He leaves his dilemma hanging in the air.

'Okay, myself and Tara will have a chat. Can you wait outside for a few minutes?'

Andriu steps out into the hallway, leaving Tara and me looking at one another like we've just won the lotto.

'What do you think?' Tara says.

'I kinda liked Annemarie from admin,' I say.

'Me too… but she doesn't look anything like him.'

Pausing for a moment, I look at Tara, who's waiting patiently for me to make my mind up.

'He probably has loads of hot friends,' she says, smirking. 'I know who I want.'

I feel like a mammy in a sweet shop holding my decision on whether my child can have something. I've already made my mind up but it's worth teasing it out to build the excitement.

'Okay, sure. We've nothing to lose; he says he'll pay upfront. Let's give him a trial.'

'Andriu.' Tara calls him back in.

The wind blows open the back door when Andriu walks in. Tara rushes over to close it and puts an empty keg up against it to keep it closed.

'If you're happy with the room we'll give it a try for a few months, see if it suits us all,' I say.

'Sounds like a plan, can I move in straight away?'

'Don't you want to see the room?'

I move out to the hallway and Andriu follows. Pushing open the door of the room next to the kitchen, we step inside. An old black leather sofa sits against one wall with a couple of threadbare cushions at each end. A wooden chair with a spindle missing from the backrest sits against another wall. The large black TV looks out of place in the corner of the room. It's the only modern thing in here. My dad bought it for me when I moved in and had Sky come out to rig it up. Andriu nods his approval when I tell him we have all the stations. Then we move back out to the hallway and I take him up the creaky wooden stairs towards the small bedroom at the front of the house. On the landing, the smell of green tea lingers in the air from when I used the shower earlier. Andriu is commenting on how clean the place smells when I open the door and show him his room.

'Perfect,' he says when he walks in. 'Well, perfect for two hundred euros,' he chuckles.

'I know it's small but we don't have any neighbours to bother us and it's close to the college.'

Andriu plonks himself down on the single bed which just about fits along one wall. There's a picture of a single yellow flower hanging on the wall above the wooden headboard. I lean on the bed to straighten it but instead I take it down. 'You'll probably be wanting to put your own stuff in here,' I say, tossing the picture onto the small chest of drawers beside me, before looking back at Andriu. He says nothing, but smiles. I find myself holding his stare a little longer than is necessary and a rush of heat flushes up my face. I get the feeling it won't be the last time I'll be on this bed with this man.

Chapter Thirteen

Tara

I'm sitting with a cup of coffee in my hand that Lucas made for me. The two detectives are sitting on the sofa in front of me. I'm nervous, my legs are shaking, my hands trembling. Thankfully, Lucas is in the room or I think I'd shrivel up and die.

The male detective speaks first, introducing himself for a second time. Then he asks me to confirm that I am indeed Tara Moore. I wish I could say, no; that I'm Mary Moore or Annie Moore or Britney Spears, anything to get them out of here but I'm not. So I nod and take a sip of my coffee.

'Do you know why we're here?' Detective Mullins asks. I shake my head even though I have a bloody good idea.

'Well, it's in connection with your residency at Huntley Lodge. You did live there, didn't you? Do you have the exact dates?'

'I… I… I was there three years ago.' My brain is turning to mush. I can't think straight.

'It's okay. Take your time.'

'I know it was September because we moved in when college started but what year…?' Numbers are dancing in my head, two thousand and… shit, what year did I start college?

'Would that have been 2014?' the detective asks. I nod. 'Until 2016, maybe?'

I nod again, wondering why they asked if they already knew.

'September, we left at the end of September.'

'And Tara, can you tell us who lived there with you?'

'Yes, there were various people there at different times, some just while they were stuck for somewhere to stay but the main people paying the rent were myself, Andriu Fitzpatrick and Faye Connolly.'

'Were they in college too?'

'Andriu was working and Faye was in college. I dropped out the year before we left.'

Detective Mullins is writing down everything I say. It's making me even more nervous. What if I say something wrong? Or get a date wrong? Or— Jesus, I'm no good for this. I wish they'd just get on with it and leave.

'My mam got sick and I couldn't concentrate, so I packed it in for a year. I was going to go back but…' I don't actually have an end to that sentence, so I leave it there.

'Andriu Fitzpatrick. Do you know where we could find him?'

'Is this about the body?'

'What?' Detective Mullins says, lifting his head from the notebook. 'The body?'

'Yes, the body they found at Huntley Lodge?' Shit, I hope I haven't said something wrong but no one was mentioning it and I think I should know.

'Do you know anything about the body?'

54

'Just what I saw on the news. But it's years since we lived there. Why do you want to speak to us? Has the body been there that long?'

'It is about the body, but we haven't got a time estimate yet so we're just talking to anyone who has lived there in the past few years.'

'But you must have some idea.' I can hardly believe the words coming out of my mouth. I put the coffee cup down on the table, keeping my eyes fixed on the detective. 'I mean, it must be pretty decayed if you think it could have happened when we lived there.'

I can feel Lucas's eyes boring a hole in the back of my head. I wonder what he's thinking. Is he feeling sorry for me having to put up with this interrogation? Or is he worrying I might be getting dragged into something that could spoil the wedding? I hope he doesn't think I was involved in any way.

'At the moment, we can't say anything until we get definitive information, but yes, I guess it's already out there that the body is very much decayed. It has been lying there for a while. Exactly how long, we don't know yet. So for now, we just want to talk to anyone who lived at Huntley Lodge.' Mullins glances down at his notebook before looking back at me. 'Can you think of anything suspicious you might have seen, anything that might help us find out what happened?'

I shake my head.

'Andriu Fitzpatrick, do you know where he is living now?'

'Andriu lives in London, but he'll be back here next week sometime. He's coming home for my wedding.'

'Oh, you're getting married.'

I turn my head to look at Lucas. He's right behind me. Lucas winks at me and smiles.

'Yes, to this man, Lucas Jones.'

'Were you ever at Huntley Lodge?' the detective asks, looking up at Lucas. Lucas shakes his head.

'No, we met well after that,' I say, smiling, believing my upcoming nuptials might lift the mood, but no. Detective Lee speaks next.

'And Faye Connolly, where does she live now?'

'I don't know. I haven't seen Faye for years… I know she's a doctor now but we lost contact.'

'Fine.' Detective Mullins closes his notebook and stands. He holds out a card. 'I'm going to give you my direct number. If you think of anything that might be of use to the investigation, ring this number.'

'Is that it, am I done here?' I take the card from his hand.

'For now.'

A wave of relief passes over me. That wasn't so bad. They didn't ask anything too difficult or anything that would have necessitated a lie.

I look at the time and realise I'm going to be late for work. I'll have to ring Muriel to let her know I'm on my way because the cafe can be very busy in the morning. But first I need to get rid of these two.

Lucas is still standing behind me when my phone rings from the speaker stand that's beside Detective Siobhan Lee. It rings a few times before she lifts it.

'Do you want this?' she says. I can see her reading the screen before she hands it to me but now the phone has stopped ringing.

'It's probably work. I'll ring them back.' I take the phone and walk towards the door. Relief washes over me when they walk outside.

'I'll ring if I think of anything,' I say, closing the door behind them, hoping I never have to see their faces again. But something tells me I will. Especially when I look at my phone and see the missed call the detective read on my screen was from Faye Connolly.

Chapter Fourteen

The detective is going to think I'm a liar. I told her I hadn't seen or heard from Faye Connolly in years and the next thing, she sees her name flashing on my phone screen. If I had known before the detective left that it was Faye who called I could have told her the truth. That Faye rang the previous day and I just saved her contact name in my phone in case she rang back. Which she hasn't yet. But then the detective might say, *why is she ringing now, all of a sudden, if you haven't heard from her in years? Are you both trying to get your story straight, Miss Moore?* That would have been worse. My face would have gone red and the detective would have known I was hiding something.

-

We're like ships passing in the night. When I rang Faye back, I got a secretary with a very musical voice telling me that Dr Faye Connolly was with a patient. I told her it was personal and urgent and that I'd missed two calls from Faye already. She said she'd get her to ring as soon as she was free.

I'm nervous. Those cops are not going to go away; they'll keep asking questions, digging and digging, it's what they do. But what if they end up digging in the right place? What will I do then? My thoughts are racing in the wrong direction. I need to calm down a bit but it's hard with so much at stake. I wish I was already on the far side of this planet. I doubt they'd come all the way to Australia to ask if I could remember anything suspicious.

I text Muriel to tell her I've been delayed and will get there as soon as possible. I don't tell her why because the last thing I need is Muriel asking me questions. She texts me back to say it's quiet and there's no need to rush. So I don't.

Lucas waited with me until I'd stopped shaking then he had to run. He made me an omelette first, though. I managed to swallow the whole thing even though every time I thought of the detectives and the body and the fact that this was all happening three weeks before my wedding, I felt like getting sick.

It's a busy time for Lucas, wrapping up things at the company before he goes back to head office. He tells me there are lots of things he needs to sort out and he's training two people to take over his job. Not one. Two. I laughed when I heard that.

I put my plate in the dishwasher. My eyes keep checking the phone which I have sitting on the kitchen island right beside me. I'm anxious to speak to Faye, to let her know that the cops called here. I need to give her the heads-up so she's prepared in case they call to her too. I'm nervous to hear her voice again after all this time because I don't know what to expect. Will Faye be friendly and act like nothing went wrong between us? Or will she bring up the past? Maybe she'll tell me why she just disappeared out of my life without any explanation. I'd love to know why but I've no intention of mentioning it because I've enough to deal with. I'm still wondering what her reaction will be when my phone lights up. My heart quickens. It's her.

'Faye.'

'Tara dear, can you talk?'

The familiar sound of her voice stops my every thought. It echoes around my head, uprooting all the memories I have buried there. Faye's smiles, her hugs, her words of comfort, her words of encouragement. They're all flooding back now, reminding me of what we had, that special friendship, the secrets we have, the unbreakable connection… that broke.

Tears begin to sting my eyes. I can't let Faye know that I'm about to cry so I swallow hard and say, 'Yes.'

'Did you see the news?' she asks, straight up. No beating around the bush for Faye.

'Yes, I was going to ring you but I didn't know if you'd want that so…' I let my comment hang in the air between us hoping it reminds her of all the unanswered calls I made to her when she left Huntley. All the attempts to find out why she ended our friendship had been in vain. Faye never answered. She never even sent a text. Night after night I cried myself to sleep trying to make sense of it all but I never could. I wish I had the courage to ask her the question that haunted me for years. Why did you leave me Faye? Why did you walk out on me when my world was falling apart? My heart was broken. My mam had just died. You were my best friend and you disappeared out of my life. But I won't ask. Not now. That storm has passed. I'm navigating calmer waters now. Well I was until the cops showed up.

'Have you heard anything? Anything about the body? How long it's been there?'

I'm a bit disappointed that Faye has gone straight to the point without asking anything about me. I guess she really doesn't care anymore. I wipe my eyes, feeling foolish for having got upset in the first place. I'm a big girl now. I've a big future ahead of me. Fuck the past.

'Nothing concrete except that the body has been there for a long time.'

'Anything else?' she asks eagerly.

'No… except that it's female.' I don't want to tell her that I think it's the woman who disappeared a few years ago and was never found, because I don't know this for sure yet and she might panic.

'I hope they don't drag us into this, Tara. I can't have cops coming in here asking questions. If they find out what we did, my license will be revoked. I'll never be able to practice again.'

I totally understand where Faye is coming from but I don't know what she expects me to do about it. I'm about to ask when she says, 'If for some reason the cops do contact you, I need you to do something for me, Tara.'

I nod, letting her words filter through my head. This is not a choice for me. Faye knows that. I owe her big-time and now she's calling in the favour.

'Okay.'

'I don't want you to mention my name. Can you do that? Just leave me out of it?'

Other than the sound of my heart bashing against the wall of my chest, I'm rendered silent.

'Your name was on the lease, Tara, mine wasn't, so there's no need to bring me into it—'

I interrupt her before she goes on. 'It's too late. Two detectives called here this morning, Faye.'

Faye doesn't answer. I can hear her breathing, slow, heavy.

'Are you there?'

'Did you give them my name?'

'Yes. Sorry, I wasn't thinking straight. I was in shock and… they'd have found out some other way. The registrar at college or someone else would have given your name. If I left you out and they discovered it elsewhere that wouldn't look good…'

She's saying nothing, so I continue. 'They probably won't come back anyway, Faye. I got that impression.' I didn't get that impression but I don't want to worry her any more than I already have.

'What did they ask?'

'Just who lived in the house and did I remember anything suspicious going down.'

'And you said?'

'I told them lots of people stayed there but only myself, you and Andriu lived there on a permanent basis.' I realise that I forgot to tell the detective about Robin living there for a while.

Faye is silent; I can tell she's thinking.

'Well, good luck to them trying to track Andriu down,' she says.

'Actually, he's coming to Dublin next week.'

The silence that follows is warranted. Faye will not be able to comprehend how I'm in touch with Andriu. Not after what he did to her. She'll probably see this as a betrayal on my behalf. I want to explain to her that he was the one who contacted me but I don't think that'll excuse me.

'Andriu… you've been in touch with him?'

I feel awful now. I probably should not have engaged with him when he made contact but it had been months since I'd heard from anyone. I'd given up trying to contact Faye. She wasn't replying to any of my calls or messages. Then when I saw the message from Andriu,

I was delighted and replied straight away. We stayed in contact after that. Not every day or even every week, but now and then he sends a message.

'Just a few little messages.'

'But you're meeting him next week, are you?'

I can hear someone calling Faye in the background.

'Hang on Tara, I have to go... I'll be there in a minute,' she says to whoever is looking for her.

'Can you call back later?' I say, sounding desperate. I want to explain why I'm seeing Andriu next week.

'I'll call you this evening, but Tara...'

'Yes?' I'm relieved she's agreed to call me later.

'If those detectives return, be careful what you say to them.'

'I will Faye... don't worry.' I know that's easier said than done.

'Okay, got to go. Talk later.'

And then she's gone. Into her world of saving lives and easing suffering. I picture her rushing down a hospital corridor in a white coat to the next emergency room, her petite hand pushing open the door and waving her magic wand.

When I put the phone down, I catch my own image in the mirror and see the tired, worried face of the bride-to-be. This isn't right. I can't be letting this body at Huntley Lodge ruin the most important day of my life. I should be enjoying myself.

I move over to the cabinet with all the wedding paraphernalia and open up the box with the wedding pamphlets inside. The words on the white sparkling cover cheer me up. *The wedding of...* I lift the pamphlet and sniff it. There's nothing beautiful about the smell of this paper except that it smells new, reminding me of the life that awaits me. The sun, the sea, the sex. The barbecues that I never liked going to in Ireland but will probably love in Australia with all my new friends. Lucas has lots of friends. I've met one of them in person when he came over to visit earlier in the year. Others I've met on Skype. They all seem nice, and some of the girls have already friended me on Facebook which is great. I'll feel like I know them already when I get there. It's a pity none of them will be at the hen party.

Closing the lid on the box of pamphlets, I try to swallow the pain that surges inside me. It's an even bigger pity Faye won't be there. How did this happen? Faye was always such a big part of my life; every plan for our future was made together, discussed, dissected and spoken about with such excitement and enthusiasm; we left no stone unturned. Especially when it came to getting married – we had some great laughs dreaming about that. And now she's not even going to be at the hen party. I thought when I met Lucas that I could finally let her go. I didn't think about her as much. I came to accept she was gone for good and I was able to quieten her voice in my head. But hearing her today has brought it all back.

Chapter Fifteen

Even though I didn't get into work until after eleven today the day dragged on. The waiting game has begun. I'm so organised, the wedding arrangements are no longer dominating my time. The only thing outstanding on the list are the weddings suits – which is also the one element that Lucas is responsible for organising. He said there was no need to panic; that the hire shops are full of them, especially at this time of the year. I told him alterations take time and he had better get on it. Lucas eventually made an appointment for this evening. Lucas is the most laid back person I have ever met. So laid back I often have to put my hand out and pull him forward. How he managed to secure the job he has, which has something to do with IT and farm machinery and a greener future, I do not know. But he has and it pays well, and when he returns to the head office in Melbourne he'll be getting a big promotion. This, he says, will give me time to get a job I like. If I want to. He's not bothered one way or the other. Whatever I want.

I asked Lucas not to mention the detectives calling to the apartment when he sees my father tonight. Dad is as bad as me for worrying. Lucas said he'd no intention of mentioning it and I should forget about it too. It will come to nothing. They were just doing their job. I hope he's right. I feel bad that I couldn't do what Faye asked me to do. If I hadn't already spoken to the detective, I wouldn't have mentioned her name. They probably would have found out anyway but at least I would have done what she asked. I would do anything she asked me to. I owe her big-time.

Nothing more was said in the café about the dead body. The story seems to be old news now. The latest shocking event is that of a man who drove himself and his two kids into the sea. Their bodies were recovered early this morning by search and rescue. Both anger and sympathy were expressed by people the tragedy doesn't directly affect. I bet he gets no sympathy from the mother of the two kids.

My step is quick as I walk down the quays. I want to get home before Lucas leaves to go to the hire shop. I need to make sure he's clear about what he has to order.

The black waters of the river Liffey glisten to my right. It's already dark and it's only 5.30 p.m. It won't be like that in Australia.

In front of me, a young man stumbles. He's out of his head on drugs or drink. His clothes look like they belong to someone else. They're hanging off him. When I get closer he stops and falls against the wall of the river, struggling to stay standing. The poor unfortunate guy holds out his hand and slurs something. I probably shouldn't because this is a hotspot for muggings but I reach into my bag and pull out whatever coins I can find. His eyes are focused on my moving hand. I don't know how much it is but I give it to him and watch him wobble as he takes it.

'Thanks very much, Miss,' he mumbles. I smile at him, and whisper to myself the words I say every time. The words my mother taught me when I was very young. 'And there but for the grace of God, go I.' Then I pull my bag closer and walk towards O'Connell Bridge and on to my apartment block.

I'm too late, Lucas has already left. Never mind. I'm sure he'll do okay. After I replace my office clothes with a tracksuit, I switch on the TV and plonk myself down on the sofa with a glass of wine. I have nothing to do tonight so I flick through Netflix in the hope of finding something I can get lost in. Something to kill a few hours when I don't have to think of dresses, or cakes, or flowers or dead bodies. I keep my phone at my side in case Faye rings back because I don't want to miss her call again, even though I'm nervous about what she has to say about me staying in touch with Andriu.

Nothing on Netflix is convincing me to watch it, so I flick off the TV and close my eyes. I'm tired. I would love nothing more than a full night's sleep.

A short time later the ringing of my phone jolts me back to consciousness. It's Faye.

'How is he?' she says, straight away, without leading into it.

'Andriu?'

'Yes Andriu, how is he?'

I shouldn't be surprised that's her first question. She got quite a shock when she heard I was still in touch with him. Faye probably thought she'd never hear or see from Andriu again. She was very much in love with him. I remember that much. They seemed like the perfect couple. Not all hugs and kisses and get-a-room kind of couple, which, as the third wheel on the bicycle, would have probably made my life hell. It was more the way they really seemed to care about one another that impressed me. They planned everything around what the other person liked. I never once heard them fighting until that dreadful night.

I tried to ask him once what had happened but he brushed me off, telling me Faye had changed. I told him Faye was heartbroken over what he'd done but he didn't respond.

'I guess he's alright; I haven't actually met him since he left. I'm not sure he's even been to Dublin since.'

'Well why are you meeting him next week, then?'

'He's coming to my wedding.'

'You're getting married?'

'Yes.'

There's silence for a moment. Faye is trying to digest the information.

'Oh Tara, that's wonderful, I didn't know and here's me waffling on. Who are you marrying? Do I know him?' Faye's voice is lighter, happier, reminding me of how she used to sound when I had some good news to share with her. I'm not sure if she's just being polite or if she really is happy for me because Faye was always able to pretend. Unlike me. Faye used to say I was easier to read than a book and that I should learn how to wear a mask in case someday I needed it. Which I did.

'No you don't, his name is Lucas, he's from Australia but he's been living here the past two years because of work.'

'Well congratulations, Tara, maybe I'll meet him some-time.'

'If you like you could—' I'm about to suggest she could come to the wedding. It would really make my day to be reunited with my best friend on my wedding day. But that's not why she's on the phone and I very much doubt she'd want to be in the same room as Andriu.

'No, no, no.' She stops me before I finish. 'After the wedding sometime, maybe. When this Huntley Lodge

68

business goes away.' When she mentions the name, my shoulders immediately slump. I don't want to think about that now but I know that's the only reason Faye Connolly is on the phone.

'Say hello to him for me,' she says.

'Lucas?'

'No, Andriu. Say hello to Andriu for me.'

'I will.' There's a slightly awkward pause before she speaks.

'Did you hear any more from the police?'

'No. Not yet. Did they contact you, Faye?'

'I think so, was one of them called Siobhan Lee?'

My heart starts to race again and the calm I was feeling earlier vanishes into thin air.

'Yes.'

'Well, she left a message on my phone.'

'Fuck... did she? What did she say? Does she know if the body has been there for three years or more? Which would make us the residents of Huntley at the time.'

'No she didn't say but they must be thinking something like that... So, Tara...'

I'm nodding instead of speaking into the phone. 'Sorry, yes?'

'They'll be asking a lot of questions about what was going on at Huntley around that time.'

I'm taking deep breaths through my nose, trying to relax.

'You know what that means, Tara. You cannot say anything about what we did.'

'I know that, Faye. Christ, do you think I'm stupid?'

'No, I don't think you're stupid, but you're dealing with professionals here. They know how to rattle people, how to get them to say things they never thought they'd say.'

'Well don't worry, I won't be saying anything.'

–

Faye hangs up, leaving me feeling like she has no faith in me. I promised to contact her if the detectives came back and she said she'd let me know how she gets on with the detective if she thinks there's a need to. Then she just told me to enjoy my wedding and said goodbye.

It wasn't quite the reunion I often dreamt about in my head.

Chapter Sixteen

Faye

Each time Tara mentioned his name it felt like something was squeezing my brain. I thought my head was going to burst. Acid burned its way towards my mouth and my teeth pressed down hard, clenching until I thought they might break.

I have cut the inside of my jowl and now I can taste the metallic blood oozing over my tongue. This reminds me I'm alive, I'm human. I don't deserve to be treated like this, to be betrayed like this.

I say hello to jealousy, that green monster who wants to upset me. Someone has what I should have. Someone who doesn't deserve it and it stirs anger in me. Andriu is mine. Why is he in contact with Tara? Why is she inviting him to her wedding?

I lie down and close my eyes. *Count, slowly, one... two... slow your breath down.* It's not good to let my body stay angry like this. They don't deserve to damage me anymore. I must think of the good stuff. How great my life was with Andriu. How he loved me. How I loved him. How I can have all that again.

When I feel I've lowered the temperature under my anger, I sit up straight, stare at the wall in front of me and go back to the source of my distress. I look straight at it.

If Andriu is going to Tara's wedding they must have stayed in touch all these years. Tara did try to contact me for the first few months but I ignored her attempts. I wasn't ready to let her back into my life. She had betrayed me. She had to pay.

I wonder if they spoke about me. They probably laughed at me for being so stupid not to have known what was going on between them.

But then I think. Was I too quick to judge? Was it just a drunken one-night stand that neither of them can fully remember because they were so drunk? It's possible that's why they kept in touch. Maybe they felt guilty and had to talk it through, forgive themselves. But if that's the case, surely Andriu would have contacted me, asked for my forgiveness. I would have given it. I know that now.

But if he could contact Tara, why not me? He had my number. It's all so hard to understand. Maybe I should ask him… or her. I could ask her and make her stand there, mouth open wide, eyes drooping, whimpering a 'sorry' through her pretty little lips when she knows I know. What if I told her fiancé? She wouldn't like that.

There's only one thing to do. I need to infiltrate their little organization and see what is going on. I want Andriu back. Whatever he did that night, it was her fault. She led him astray. Andriu never cheated on me before then. I know now I should not have thrown him out of Huntley but I was so shocked, heartbroken and disappointed I did not know what else to do. I was fuelled with anger and couldn't look him in the face for one more minute.

I should have thrown her out instead.

Swiping my phone open I click onto the Facebook app and see what I can find out. Andriu Fitzpatrick doesn't have a social media presence. I've checked many times in the past and found nothing. Tara, on the other hand, appears to be a member of every self-promoting site that exists as far as I can see.

I type her name into the search engine and watch her brilliant shiny life come up on the screen. Oh wait. Something new. A hen party announcement. I move the phone closer to my face to get a clearer look at the details. Saturday night, November 4th. That's this Saturday. Brogan's pub on Dame Street, then to Coppers nightclub on Harcourt Street. I know that place. I've been there many times.

There are loads of 'likes' and 'see you there' and 'looking forward to it' comments below the post. Tara seems to have fallen into the world of quantity over quality when it comes to friends. She won't find anyone like me, though. We go back a long, long way. We shared so many things, have a real history. Inseparable, like sisters. And now it's gone. Tara and Andriu were all I needed back then. I thought it was the perfect set-up. There was no need for anyone else. As far as I was concerned, our little tribe had it all and I thought it would go on forever; that we were so strong and nothing could break the bond between us. But I was wrong. It only took one night to blow that illusion up, leaving me with nothing.

I flick down through the comments; the only familiar name is 'Emily'. Tara's stupid junkie cousin. I'm surprised to find she's still on the scene. I thought Tara would have given her a wide berth after the accusations made by her auntie Rose. I guess blood is thicker than water.

I'm scrolling on and on down through the comments when I suddenly realise that I'll be in town on Saturday night. I might just pop into Coppers and have a look at all these so-called friends of Tara's. Coppers is so dark it's hard to see someone standing beside you, never mind someone hiding in the corner watching to see what all the friends who've replaced you look like. I don't want Tara to see me. I'm not ready for that yet. I just want to watch her party with all these people. I bet it doesn't compare to the parties we had at Huntley Lodge.

Chapter Seventeen

Then

The sun is so hot it feels like it's only a few miles away. Andriu is massaging suncream into my skin. He gently swirls his hands across my back in circles. His touch makes me feel special, adored, excited. I'm his princess.

Lying face-down on the makeshift sunbed that he made from a plastic pink lilo covered in a towel, I open my eyes to see what progress is being made.

Tara is fussing over some outdoor lights that she wants connected for the party tonight. The last two months were spent with our faces stuck into books, preparing for our exams and now that they are over for this year, we plan to party like mad.

'Why don't you hang them around Holy Mary's neck?' Andriu says, laughing as he puts the lid back on the tube of cream. The statue has been resting against the back wall of the garden since we arrived here. It's a strange sight and no one knows how it got here. It's not like there's a church or monastery anywhere nearby. This house belonged to one of the last operating farms in the city of Dublin according to Larry, my dad's friend who is renting it to us. Most of the land was sold off for new development. The lodge is the only thing remaining. Well that and the unexplained statue of Our Lady.

'I just might,' Tara replies, shouting over the music that John from college is playing from the sound desk. He has it set up outside the kitchen window. He's checking the speakers are working for tonight because anything up to a hundred people could arrive here. It wouldn't be the first time we've had that many. When word gets around that there's a party at Huntley, everyone wants to come.

Tara jumps down from the chair she's using as a ladder and shouts at John behind the desk to plug the lights in.

'Yep, they're working… what do you think?' she says, standing back and staring at the little coloured balls draped along the wall.

'Hmm.' I nod.

'I know it's hard to tell in this light but tonight they'll be lovely. Anyone for a beer?' she says.

I thought she'd never ask. I didn't want to be the first to suggest it because it's still so early and Andriu says I shouldn't drink as much as I do. He thinks I drink too quickly but I slag him and say that's just because he's so old. Andriu is only three years older than me, but honestly, sometimes he sounds so much older. He's often commented on how immature we can get when the shots are brought to the table or the drinking games are suggested. Andriu hates all that stuff now. He's been there, done that, bought the T-shirt.

I can sense his eyes boring through me from behind but I ignore him and tell Tara that I'll have one. Then I hear his voice.

'Are you sure, Faye? Is it not a bit early? You'll be drunk by the time the party starts.'

'The party has already started,' Tara says, handing me a can of cider. She holds one out to Andriu but he says no. Then he stands up from where he was kneeling by my side and heads into the house. Andriu will take this as a loss and he doesn't like losing.

'He can be such a bore,' Tara laughs, pulling the can open and gulping half of it down without taking a break. I don't reply to Tara's comment because I don't agree with her. Andriu isn't a bore, he's just older than us. More mature. He finds Tara's excessive excitement a bit immature. He told me so but I wouldn't tell Tara that because she might get upset. Tara needs people to like her.

—

We've been lying in the sun all afternoon drinking cider and listening to John practising his DJ stunts. The sun has dipped in the sky and my head is a bit woozy from the drink. It's a nice, relaxed, warm feeling.

Already there are about twenty people in the garden and I don't know how many are inside the house but there's a great buzz.

Tara has her eye on one of the guys from third year. She's swooning like a little baby and laughing at every word he says. Her face is burnt red, almost glowing but the guy she's chatting up doesn't seem to mind. He's opening a beer for her. Making his move. I hope he doesn't get too attached because knowing Tara, she'll be into someone else by tomorrow.

I look around at the gathering crowd and realise I haven't seen Andriu in a while. He must be still in his room. He left earlier, probably to put his head down for an hour but that was ages ago.

I roll off the lilo, throwing it to the side of the garden then head into the house. When I get to the stairs Emily is coming down with that dopy glaze covering her eyes. I asked Tara to speak to her and ask her not to do drugs in our bathroom but here she is once more, out of her head. I give her a look, suggesting I know what she's at. But she replies with a look suggesting she doesn't give a fuck what I think. If she wasn't Tara's cousin I'd bar her from the house but Tara says she's a bit of a lost soul and doesn't have any other friends.

'Andriu,' I say, opening the door of the bedroom. The room is dark, the light blocked by the blackout curtains.

'Are you awake?' I say, moving closer to the beautiful shape lying in boxer shorts on top of the bed. How he could possibly be asleep with all the noise I do not know but he yawns, then sits up in the bed. 'Not anymore.'

I sit down beside him and lean in to kiss him. Andriu wraps his bare arms around me and pulls me closer. Then he kisses my head and slides off the bed.

'I better jump into the shower to wake myself up.' He opens the drawer of his bedside cabinet and grabs his shower bag. When he first arrived here, Andriu was in the small box room at the front of the house but since our friendship blossomed into a full-blown love affair, he moved into my room.

There is no ensuite in this house. There's barely a shower. There's just a hose over the bath that has to be pulled at and tugged before the water falls from it. If it wasn't for Tara's dad, it wouldn't work at all.

'Are you okay?' he says. But what he really wants to know is if I'm drunk.

'I'm fine, not a bother.' I smile and watch his long tanned body move towards the bathroom.

–

Sometime later, when the party is in full swing and the back garden resembles a scene from Glastonbury, I stumble over to where Tara is caressing some guy's tonsils with her tongue by the statue. I want to ask her where she has hidden the gin. We have to hide lots of stuff before letting every Tom, Dick and Mary into this place.

I'm about to tap Tara on the back when I glance down the side of the house and notice Emily standing there with someone who doesn't belong here.

Emily is standing in front of them, attempting to hide what's going on. I know I'm drunk but I also know what's going on. She's buying drugs from someone. It wouldn't be the first time and Tara is going to go mad because she warned her. And now the stupid bitch has called her dealer and they're in our garden handing her a packet. I'm all into the 'hear no evil, see no evil' crap but if Larry finds out there are drugs being dealt here, we'll lose the house and my dad will flip.

'Tara, Tara.' I pull at Tara's shoulder, dragging her from the embrace and force her to look down the side of the house.

'You're going to have to do something about that,' I say.

'Shit,' she replies, rushing over to Emily. 'What the fuck are you doing?' she says.

The dealer walks away to the front of the house and out into a waiting car.

'I'm sorry Tara. I… I needed something. I've been so… I promise this is the last time.'

'Fucking sure it is,' Tara says, walking away from Emily, muttering something. I feel sorry for Tara; she only puts up with the girl because she's her cousin and now she's at this crap.

'Don't think for one minute that you're bringing that shit into the house,' I say. Then I follow Tara into the kitchen.

When I get inside, Andriu is listening to some guy who's making everyone laugh by doing impersonations. He smiles over when he sees me and puts his arm out for me to join him. I dance my way over to his side and stumble into his body. Andriu is holding me close, but I pull away when I glance out the window and notice that the dealer friend of Emily's is in the back garden. I thought he had gone off in the car that was parked out front, but no. He's mooching around like he's casing the place. Planning to rob us, maybe? But why is he so interested in the garden? Is he planning his escape route? I'd tell Andriu, only I don't want any more trouble. The last party left us without a pane of glass in the front door when someone tried to gatecrash and Andriu grabbed him to throw him out. It was scary but it also made me feel safe that we have Andriu living here with us. This place is so isolated, anything could happen.

I'm about to go outside and tell the imposter to leave but he turns and walks towards the side entrance. Andriu is calling me over the boisterous laughter that's ringing in my ears but I keep my eyes on the dark shape, making sure he leaves. When I'm happy he's gone, I move away from the window and back into the arms of the man I love. Not wanting to spoil the party for Andriu or Tara, I decide to wait until the morning to let them know what I saw. But I'm worried. What the hell has Emily brought into our lives?

Chapter Eighteen

Tara

I'm actually believing my world has returned to normal when the body found at Huntley Lodge hits the number one spot on the news again. It's all over social media. There are even pictures of the dead woman. Avril Ryan, aged thirty-five, was last seen alive on September 7th 2016. I move closer to inspect the photo. Avril looks happy, smiling. She has a big gap between her two front teeth. Her dark hair settles on the furry collar of her white jacket. Her eyes are hazel-green and she doesn't seem to be wearing any make-up. Her skin is blotchy, probably from the cold. Avril looks like any other normal person. I graze my finger over her image and wonder, did she know she was in trouble when this photo was taken? Was she hiding something behind those big hazel-green eyes?

Sitting with a cup of coffee and looking through whatever I can find about Avril Ryan on my computer is making me anxious because I know this is not just some news story I can close down, then move on to the next. This could ruin my life. The autopsy has confirmed what the evidence found at the scene was suggesting. The body of thirty-five-year-old Avril Ryan who went missing in September 2016 was found in suspicious circumstances. Which I'm pretty sure means murder. It says that the body was found in a disused pit at the bottom of the garden during recent renovations. The pit was ten foot deep with two big heavy steel doors covering it over.

I remember that pit. The owner warned us it was there. Otherwise you'd never notice it. He said it was dangerous; we were advised to keep away from it. Which was easy to do because it was surrounded by brambles and twigs and impossible to get at. Or so I thought. But obviously I was wrong because someone got at it. But who?

I stare at the screen. Huntley Lodge. It all seems so long ago. It's only three years since I lived there and yet so much has changed. Mam is dead. I met Lucas. I'm moving to Australia. I'm no longer glued at the hip to Faye. I never could have imagined any of these things back then. I thought I knew what was coming down the line. Not that I thought about it often because back then I very much lived for the moment – the party at the weekend or the guy I fancied. But when I did think about the future I never considered the loss I would experience or the strength I would find buried deep inside me.

–

Faye hasn't been in touch for a few days so I'm guessing that if the detective did get to talk to her, it mustn't have alarmed her. Maybe they have an idea who killed that poor woman and left her to rot at the bottom of a pit. Her family must be devastated knowing she was lying there, all alone in the cold and the damp. A shiver runs through me when I think about it. Hopefully she was already dead before her body was put into that pit.

The police have to know it's possible she was killed somewhere else and just dumped in there… but not many people knew that pit was there. You would have to be told. But there were other people renting the house before we took it over. They would have known about the disused pit. And even though it was hidden below a lot of brambles, it is possible someone who partied at Huntley knew it was there. In fact, come to think of it, lots of people could know about it. Those detectives will have their work cut out for them.

The pathologist must be finished with the body because the funeral went ahead today. It was sad to see it airing on the news on the salon TV. I was booked into Blush Beauty for a facial as part of the wedding day grooming package that my bridesmaids kindly gave me. It was presented to me at the bridal shower that Amy threw for me, amid a fanfare of cocktails and prosecco. That was a month ago, happier times. Before anyone discovered a body.

With my face covered in cream, I listen to the choir singing in the background as the family follow the coffin out of the church. Hearing the voices reminds me of Mam and I feel painfully sad. Singing was Mam's favourite hobby and the first victim of her illness. I remember her crying when she was told she should no longer sing in the choir. They were the heaviest tears she shed throughout the whole nightmare. I think it was the start of her real-ization that her life was being shut down bit by bit.

The illness teased her. Mam never knew what would be next to go. There was no mercy as it slowly stripped her of her identity. Today you can walk, tomorrow you can't. Today you can feed yourself but this time next month someone else will be holding that spoon and lifting it to your mouth. And as for using the toilet, I'll take that too.

I shake my head. I don't want to go there. I don't want to know how desperate it must have been for her. I like to remember my mother singing, laughing, making Halloween cookies. Dressing the Christmas tree, slagging my father off when he came home drunk on a Friday night. She was good at that, and he took it like any loving husband who was drunk should, by going to bed.

–

When I finish at the beautician's I walk down the road to visit my dad. It's only about a mile and the fresh air revives me. I need to forget about Avril Ryan and focus on what's happening in my life. I'm getting married.

Amy is going to pick me up when I give her a call. She wants to drop off some bottles at my apartment to kick off the hen party tomorrow night. Amy, Emily, Sonya and Emer are meeting at my place first so we can get a head start before meeting the others in Brogan's Pub. Then, hopefully, all hell will break loose.

Lucas is having his stag party tonight in some pub on the south side that I'm not familiar with. It's near his office and they're heading straight from work. He says he expects a good crowd will show up because it's Friday and also because he's using the occasion as his going away party too.

Lucas is going to be in some state tomorrow. I'm not sure he knows what an Irish stag party entails. It's a license for madness – the compulsive drinking, the pub crawls, the no-holds-barred nightclubs and... people have gone missing for days. Christ, I hope he's safe. And that they don't shave his head or his eyebrows or something. Thank God that's not usually a risk with hen parties. They

84

might be just as crazy but there's no disrespect shown for eyebrows.

Pulling my jacket tightly across my chest, I continue my journey towards my dad's house and think about tomorrow night. It's my hen party, for Christ's sake. I can't let this detective business ruin it. Everyone is so looking forward to it… and so am I. It's the perfect opportunity to drag my mind away from Huntley Lodge and concentrate on my wedding.

Chapter Nineteen

The tall oak trees lining both sides of my father's street are now completely bare. The golden leaves that had gathered in bundles by the side of the road last month are all gone. As a kid I used to love playing with those leaves. The council would gather them all up into bundles in the morning so they wouldn't block the drains and as soon as school was over, we'd jump in them, scattering and kicking them in the air.

The cold air is making its way under my coat. Winter is well and truly here. Thank God it's dry. I look up at the blue sky dotted with white fluffy clouds and hope this is the kind of weather we'll have next week. I never thought I'd be hoping it wouldn't snow on my wedding day. A winter wedding had never entered my head when Faye and I imagined our big days. But back then I never thought I'd be marrying a man from Down Under whose job would determine the date. If Lucas didn't have to be back in Australia next month we could have waited until the summer when the days would be longer, there'd be no need for heavy coats and the sun might even be shining.

I continue to walk towards my father's house. As I pass Mrs Sweeney's house she waves at me from her front window. I wave back, drop my head and quicken my step. I don't want her coming out and engaging me in conversation. She's a nice old lady but she'll ask loads of questions about the wedding and I don't really have the time now. I must remember to call in to her before I leave for Australia.

When I get to the gate of my family home, I push it open. I remind myself to make sure that the gate is fully open when I walk through it in my dress next week. I don't want the beautiful lace getting nicked off that rusty handle.

Dad opens the door as I walk up the pathway. His tall, straight, athletic body has buckled slightly over the years. He's grown a beard over the past few months but he promised to shave it off before the wedding. It's not that I don't like it – I hate it.

Dad smiles as I approach him and a rush of happiness flushes over my body. I'm going to be walking down this pathway next week holding a bouquet of flowers with my father by my side.

'Hi Dad,' I say.

'Hi, Pet.' Dad walks down the hallway in front of me and into the kitchen.

'Have you been winning any chess games lately?'

'No, I haven't played much at all this year.' He pushes a box out of my way when I enter the room. 'I'm trying to clear things out to make room for next week,' he says, moving over to lift some envelopes off the table which he hands to me.

'These came in the post. I hope they're full of money,' he chuckles.

'Lovely. Thanks.' I take the cards and put them in my bag. I'll open them later with Lucas. Or in the morning. I doubt Lucas will be in any state to open wedding presents tonight.

'Did you get measured for your suit?' I ask.

'Yes, I did, we'll all look great.' He opens the fridge door and hands me a block of cheese that he says he picked up in Aldi. He must think we don't eat. He's always buying me food. It was the same when I lived at Huntley Lodge. Food would arrive out of nowhere. We regularly came home to fresh bread, cheeses, meats, biscuits, veg, tins of soup or boxes of cereal. There was never any question who had left it there because my dad was the only other person with a key. He didn't use the words very often but I know it was his way of saying, *you're still my baby, I love you and will always take care of you.* And now he won't be able to do that. My heart sinks when I think of how much he will miss me. How will he take care of me from the other side of the world? When he sees something in the shop he thinks I might like, what will he do? Will he pick it up before he realises I'm not here anymore, then put it back on the shelf? I'm gutted with sadness when I think how lonely he will be.

'You should try this, it's lovely,' he says, so I put the cheese in my bag too.

'I'm going to miss all the treats, Dad,' I say, looking into his eyes. For a moment we pause, looking at each other's pain, knowing how much we will miss one another. Tears wet my eyes. I don't want to cry, so I pull away from his stare.

'Have you got your speech ready?' I ask, sitting down on the nearest chair. It was hard to sit here when Mam first died. I could see her everywhere but over time it got easier. Dad owns the space now. He's the one I see.

'Ah, I tried, it's hard... what do I say about your mother?'

'Just say what you want to say, Dad, don't make it hard on yourself. A few words.'

He closes the door of the fridge and sits on the chair opposite me. 'I'll do it later.'

'You know you don't have to mention Mam if it's going to upset you. I can get Lucas to do it.'

My father moves his head back and looks at me like I said something illegal.

'Sure, he never met her.'

'I know but…'

'No. I'll be fine, I just never imagined she wouldn't be with me on this day.' Tears are beginning to twinkle in my father's eyes, so I look away. I'm not good at that sort of stuff.

'She often spoke about it, you know. Your wedding day. She always hoped you'd find someone who loved you dearly and who would let you be yourself.'

'Dad, Mam will be there with us on the day.' I'm trying to comfort him but I can see he's getting more upset. He's not normally like this and I can tell by the redness in his eyes that he must have been crying earlier too.

'I tell her.'

'Tell her what?'

'I tell your Mam that you did find someone who loves you dearly. She should know.'

Oh Christ, I really can't handle this now. If he starts me crying, I won't be able to stop. 'I miss her too, Dad. I wish she was here on my wedding day. But I'm grateful I have you to walk me down the aisle.'

My father stands up and walks over to the fridge again. He opens the door.

'Did you try this yet?' he says, taking out a packet of smoked salmon. 'Take it. Lucas might like it.'

I take the salmon and put it in my bag. I had planned to ask him if he saw the news about the woman whose body was found at Huntley Lodge. But I decide not to. He seems too sad for me to introduce dead bodies into the conversation. And I'm pretty sure he must have seen it, as it was all over the papers. He's probably hoping I didn't see it.

'The suits are going to be lovely,' he says, trying to perk himself up. 'Is there anything you need me to do?'

'Not that I can think of but if there is I'll give you a shout. Other than that, it's the church rehearsal on Thursday evening at six, followed by dinner in the Phoenix Bistro.'

Dad rubs his hands together. 'That all sounds great.' Then he walks out of the kitchen. 'The match is starting in a few minutes,' he says, disappearing into the TV room.

–

Amy is outside the door within a few minutes of me texting her. She must have been waiting down the road. Her face is bursting with enthusiasm when I get into the car.

'Only one more week to go,' she says, squeezing her face with excitement. 'I have the bottles: vodka, gin, Bacardi, red wine, white wine, a bottle of Jägermeister, beers for the lightweights and, wait for it…' She reaches over into the back seat with both her hands and lifts up the biggest bottle I've ever seen. It's about two feet tall and it's full of prosecco.

'What do you think of that?' she declares.

'Where the hell did you get that?'

'A policeman wouldn't ask me that.'

And there it is; the mere mention of the cops and I feel my nerves kick in. Luckily, Amy can't see my face. She's too busy looking at the bottle resting on her lap.

'There's enough there to get an army pissed. I thought it was just the four or five of us coming to my apartment first.'

'Slight change of plan,' she says, returning the bottle to the back seat. 'Apparently they all want to come to your apartment, so I said yes.'

'Thanks.'

'Ah what the hell? Sure, you only get married once.' She looks in her mirror before swerving out into the oncoming traffic. Someone beeps and I jump in the seat.

'I don't know why you bother with mirrors, Amy, you just drive out anyway.'

'You're okay, aren't ya?' she laughs, with a big grin on her face.

The news that there's going to be about fifteen girls instead of four at my apartment is good. Amy's right. I'll only get married once. Well, that's the plan.

'So they're all coming?'

'Yeah, we can get pissed. If it drags on we can skip Brogan's and go straight to Coppers.'

'Whatever, I'm easy.'

'Great, I knew you wouldn't mind.'

We joke and laugh all the way to the apartment. Amy, as usual, pulls up outside the apartment block where she's not supposed to.

'We'll just say we're unloading stuff if anyone asks.'

I hear her but I'm not paying attention because Amy's isn't the only car parked outside the entrance. There's a navy car in front of us. Through the back window I can see the shape of two people and my gut tells me this is not good. The passenger looks like a man and there's no mistaking the fuzzy head of hair in the driver's seat. The detectives are back.

Chapter Twenty

'Drive on,' I say. 'Amy, drive on quickly before they notice me.'

But it's too late. Detective Siobhan Lee has seen me and is stepping out of the car.

Amy is looking at me, then at the detective, then back to me. 'What's wrong, Tara? Who's that?'

I'm taking deep breaths. The detective's eyes have locked on mine.

'It's the cops.'

'The cops. Sweet Jesus, how did they know I was going to pull up here in my car?'

'That's not why they're here, Amy.' Out of the corner of my eye, I can see Amy's head turned towards me. She must be staring in disbelief. My heart is thumping in my chest but I continue to keep eye contact as the detective gets closer.

'What's... going... on?' Amy whispers.

'I'll tell you later; it's about Avril Ryan.'

'Who the hell is Avril Ryan?' We're both talking through closed lips, trying to communicate like we don't want our words read. I don't know why. The detectives would never hear us from here and we're not saying anything bad.

'The woman whose body was found.' I take a quick glance at Amy and see her staring at me. Her mouth is open wide and for the first time since I've known her, I think Amy is lost for words.

I pull on the handle of the door and get out of the car. Acknowledging the detective with a nod, I walk towards her.

'Tara,' she says.

'Yes.' My heart is almost in my mouth now; I'm so nervous. What is she doing here again so soon? They must have discovered something. I try to convince myself that this is all just routine but I'm failing. It seems a bit much calling twice in one week. Maybe they spoke to Faye. Maybe Faye let something slip.

'Can we go inside?' she says.

'Yes, well, okay, but…' I don't want to tell her I'm here to unload half an off-licence full of alcohol for a hen party. Not that she'd care. I'm sure she's been to many herself.

'Okay… Erm… I'll just tell my friend to move on.' I step forward, then backwards and look completely flustered. The detective nods and walks back to her car.

'Amy, you'll have to go, they want to speak to me inside.'

'Is Lucas in there?'

'No, he's going straight to the pub after work.'

'I'm coming with you, so.' Amy rolls up the window and opens the door.

'No, Amy, you better not. I'm not sure that's a good idea.'

'But you're on your own, Tara, and I'm not leaving you on your own. I don't have to listen. I can wait in the bedroom if you want, but I'm not leaving you.'

A part of me is relieved when Amy says this. I'm not sure I would have told her what was going on but she knows now that something is and I could do with some support.

'Okay, but what about the car? You can't leave it here, it might get a ticket.'

'Are they leaving their car here?' she says, nodding at the police car.

'Yes, but they're cops, Amy, they can park where they like.'

'Fuck it.' Amy steps out of the car and slams the door closed. Then she links her arm through mine and walks towards the detectives with me. She must be able to feel my body trembling beneath my coat. She squeezes my arm tighter.

–

My hand shakes as I try to fit the key into the keyhole. After what feels like forever the door eventually opens. Amy and I walk through first, followed by the two detectives. When we step into the living area, Amy asks if I want her to stay. I don't know if I do. I feel stronger with her by my side but what if the detective says something I don't want Amy to hear? No. I'd better not take any chances.

'You can wait inside,' I say. 'I'll be okay.'

'Call me if you need me.' She looks at the female detective before leaving the room.

'I wasn't expecting to see you again,' I say to the detective when she asks me to sit down.

'Well, here we are.' She sits on the chair opposite me. Detective Mullins remains standing with his notebook in his hand.

'Okay, Tara, I'll get straight to the point. You'll have heard by now the body discovered at Huntley Lodge is

Avril Ryan's.' As she sits forward in her chair, I nod my head. 'And you probably know Avril went missing while you and your friends were living at Huntley Lodge.'

Again I nod.

'Did you know Avril Ryan, Tara?'

'Did I know Avril Ryan?' I say in a surprised voice, while pointing at myself. 'No, I never heard of her until last week.'

The detective is staring at me, saying nothing, waiting for me to continue.

'Well I kind of remember hearing about her in the news when she went missing but I don't know her. I never knew her.'

'So why is your number on her phone?' The words echo loudly from the small man standing in the corner of the room. Detective Mullins has jumped in with a ludicrous remark, rendering me speechless. Did he just say my phone number was in her phone? Did I hear right? That can't be. I didn't know that woman. I never met her. What's he talking about? Is this a trick? I look away from Detective Mullins and back to Siobhan Lee.

'What did he say?'

'He said your mobile phone number was found on Avril Ryan's phone.'

'But I never met that woman! I didn't know her from Adam; that can't be. Are you sure it's my number?' My head is going to burst. I feel like a huge boulder is pressing down on it.

'Tell us how you knew Avril Ryan, Tara,' Siobhan says in a soft voice. I recognise that technique from the television. Speaking like they understand: *we know your pain, we know you didn't mean to kill her.* They won't fool me. I remember Faye's warning. *Be careful what you say, they're professional at getting information out of people.*

'I didn't know her, I never met her and I never spoke to her.'

'So why is your number in her phone?'

'I don't have an answer for that. I don't know why. Maybe it's a mistake or maybe someone gave it to her. But I didn't give it to her. I never met that woman. Ever.' I can hear the fear in my voice. It's disguised as anger. My mind is racing. How did they know it was my number? I don't remember giving them my number.

'How do you know it's my number?'

'Simple, we rang it yesterday and you answered,' Detective Mullins says.

'But Avril Ryan went missing three years ago. Maybe someone else had that number back then.' I'm trying to figure out in my head how this could have happened but Mullins's smug expression tells me they have covered all angles before coming here to confront me. He just shakes his head.

'It's your number, Tara. What was Avril Ryan doing with your number?'

'You'll have to ask her,' I say, regretting my smartness as soon as the words leave my mouth. 'Sorry, I didn't mean that but I'm completely in shock here. I do not know how this happened. And it was so long ago.'

I begin to panic. Did I meet her? Did I give her my number? I met a lot of new people at Mam's funeral. I gave my number out to different people when I was helping Dad make the funeral arrangements. But Avril Ryan didn't have anything to do with arranging funerals.

I feel my confidence deflating when Detective Lee speaks.

'Tara, you are the last person Avril Ryan rang before she went missing.'

Chapter Twenty-One

I want to ring Lucas. I want to tell him what happened but if I do he'll rush home and his stag party will be ruined. No. I'll sit here and wait until he comes in.

Amy stayed for as long as she could, making me drink a brandy. Twice.

When the detectives eventually left, she came out of the room. She probably heard everything that went on. I know if it was me I would have had my ear to the door. But she said nothing. She just asked if I wanted to talk about it and I was so drained, I wouldn't have known where to start.

It took Amy seven runs up and down the stairs before she had all the drinks unloaded. I hope I didn't waste her time. The way I'm feeling now there will be no hen party. I'll be lucky to make the wedding.

I asked Detective Siobhan Lee if I needed a solicitor. She said that was up to me, which means I do. I told them I was getting married a week on Saturday and asked them if they were going to be calling here, asking me questions that I didn't know the answer to on the days before my wedding. Detective Lee said they would stay away unless it was necessary. What's necessary to them may not be necessary to me. I'm picturing them standing outside the church when I arrive, white dress, sparkling veil, handcuffs. I feel sick.

And Lucas, what is he going to think? Will he be as eager to take me for his wife if I'm embroiled in a murder case? I can't believe this is happening.

Tears are rolling down my face but they're not from sadness, I don't know how I feel. Numb. That's it. Numb. I should have known something would come along and derail my happiness. It's not right to be that happy. To have all the stars aligned. I don't deserve to be the luckiest woman in the world. Not after what I did. But I just thought for one brief moment I was going to be.

Faye hasn't called yet. If she doesn't contact me by tomorrow afternoon, I'm ringing her. I don't care what she says about it. I want to know what those detectives asked her. Does she know about my number being in Avril Ryan's phone? Can she come up with an explanation for that? And Andriu. He'll be arriving on Tuesday. All happy and where's the pub. He's going to get some shock when he hears the cops want to speak to him. I'd better warn him too. I'll text him to arrange to pick him up at the airport. I'll get Amy to drive and I'll fill him in then.

I'm nervous and completely confused about that number. None of this makes sense. I wish Lucas would come home soon so he can tell me what to do, what to feel. He'll relax me.

Lifting my phone, I check the time, before moving out onto the balcony with the throw from the sofa wrapped around me. It's only half past eleven. Lucas will probably be partying for hours yet. It could be the morning before I see him.

A cold icy breeze brushes my face. The water is still tonight, going nowhere. On the opposite side of the river, I see a crowd of people gathered outside a pub, drinking, smoking, laughing. That should be me tomorrow night. I don't know what to do.

A few minutes later, I go back inside and lock the door. I really should try to get some sleep. I'm placing the throw over the alcohol stockpiled in the corner of the room in case Lucas arrives home and thinks Santa came early, when my phone rings. I rush to grab it, hitting my foot on the corner of the sofa. 'Shit. The pain.' I lift the phone. With my heart beating a hole in my chest I look at the name flashing on the screen and answer.

'Tara.'

Faye is dragging out my name, she's drunk. Which doesn't surprise me. Faye was always fond of getting drunk. 'Merry' didn't satisfy her. 'Just one more', she'd say when I'd tell her I'd had enough. But it was never one more, it was always two or three and sometimes four more. I thought that habit might have stopped when she qualified as a doctor. I don't know why; I'm sure doctors get drunk too.

'Faye, is that you?'

'Tara Moore… soon to be married…'

'Faye, are you drunk?'

'Am I drunk?' she slurs. Then the phone goes quiet.

'Faye, are you there?'

'I'm here.'

'Are you alright?'

'Am I alri…'

God, she must be pissed. I don't want to talk to her when she's like this.

'Faye, maybe you should hang up, I'll talk to you tomorrow.'

'That bitch called,' she says, her voice a little clearer now.

'What bitch?'

'That detective one, she called me, all serious and what did I know… and she said you knew the missing woman.'

'I know, it's all a bit confusing. Maybe we should talk tomorrow, Faye.'

'Why would you tell her you knew that woman? I jusst don't undersssstand.'

'I didn't tell her I knew her. I'll explain to you in the morning, Faye. Look, try to get some sleep.'

'You've ruined me, Tarrra Moore, soon to be marrrried. You've destroyed everything I have worked for.'

'Faye, stop it, what are you saying that for? You're drunk.'

'This is all your fault,' she says.

I think she's beginning to cry. Then she hangs up.

God, will today never end? I wait a few minutes to make sure she doesn't call back then I head into the bedroom to put my thumping head down on the pillow. My eyes are getting heavy. I'm exhausted with worry.

Poor Faye. I feel sorry for her. The detective has her rattled too. Which makes me even more nervous. Faye was never one to crumble easily. She was my strength back in the day, always telling me to relax, that everything would be fine. Faye could take me from a high of ten on the panic chart back to a three with just a few words. A bit like Lucas does now. But Faye is just as worried as I am, this time. She's afraid we're going to get caught.

Chapter Twenty-Two

I don't know what time Lucas arrived home. I must have fallen asleep at some point. The rest of the night was spent tossing and turning and praying the detectives would get a suspect soon so I could get on with my life.

After I had driven myself mad thinking about what the detective said, I thought about the wedding. The fact that I was marrying the love of my life. The man who currently reeks of stale alcohol, lying in the bed beside me. I decided that was the most important thing. I also decided I was going ahead with the hen party. I can't let this Avril Ryan business ruin everything.

Pushing the duvet to the side I step out of the bed and drag myself to the ensuite where I take a shower. I feel like I've been marinated in beer from the smell in the bedroom. Lucas will have some head on him when he wakes up. I'll leave him to sleep another while. I'd leave him there for the day if I didn't have to break the news to him that the cops think he's marrying a fugitive. I need him to reassure me. To tell me everything will be okay.

I'm tempted to ring Faye to see if she's okay but I'll wait and see if she rings me. I picture her holding her head, going to the sink for a glass of water and suddenly remembering she called me. Oh the terror. I've been there. There's nothing worse.

In the corner of the room I see the tower of promise hidden behind the throw. In a few hours' time this place will be buzzing with laughter, music, chocolate willies and bridal sashes. I hope they don't have anything too embarrassing arranged for me.

I step out onto the balcony where the brightness hits me, making my eyes squint. Dublin city is quiet on a Saturday morning. The traffic will come but it will be slower to build. I look at the river rolling like a green army towards the sea. Lifting my mug of coffee to my lips, my hands shake. I sense a sadness roaming through my body. This is not how I should be feeling on the day of my hen party. I should be bursting with enthusiasm. Instead, I'm only half excited. Going through the motions. Finding out Avril Ryan rang my phone has me completely confused and anxious. I'm going to have to wake Lucas up.

'Lucas, Lucas,' I whisper at first. Then I crescendo all the way to a roar. 'Lucas.'

'What the fuck?' Lucas jumps in the bed. His eyes are squinting through an angry expression. 'For fuck's sake, Tara.'

'I'm sorry Lucas, I know you're probably dying but I need to talk to you.'

He slaps his tongue against his dry lips.

'Here,' I say, handing him a glass of water with two Solpadeine fizzing in it. 'Drink that.'

His eyes are only slightly open but I can see the red where the white should be. I cringe; that'll be me tomorrow.

'Lucas, I'm really sorry for waking you, but the detectives called again last night.'

He pulls himself up in the bed and is now resting on one arm and drinking from the glass. When he tastes it, he stops to look at the contents before knocking it all back. Then he hands me the glass. 'Water.'

I rush back out to the kitchen and fill the glass. When I go back into the room, Lucas is sitting up at the side of the bed. His head is a mess, his face green.

'What did they want this time?' he says.

I sit down beside him and hand him the glass. Lucas looks at me, smiles and puts his arm around my shoulder. 'You should have called me. I would have come home, Tara.'

'No, I didn't want to spoil your night. I was alright. Amy was here for a while.'

Lucas stands up and stretches his arms in the air. For a man who doesn't believe in sweating unless he's bathing in the sun, he has a wonderful body. 'The cops, what did they want?' he says, belching as he turns around to look at me.

'They called because they found my phone number in the dead girl's phone, but I don't know how that could be. Could they be lying?'

Lucas walks out to the living area so I follow him. 'Once someone's talking they can be lying, Tara, but that's not the point.' He yawns, moving barefoot towards the sink.

I follow him, watching his every move, listening for his words. His magic. *Tell me everything is going to be okay Lucas. I will believe you.*

'This all happened three years ago, Tara. Your number could be in her phone for any amount of reasons. Don't let it bother you.' He turns to find me standing right behind him. Lucas lifts his hands and holds my head. 'It means nothing. Don't be worrying; they're just doing their job. They'll have moved on to the next person by now.'

'Well, there's more.'

'What more?' Lucas's tone is a little darker now.

'They said I was the last person the dead woman rang before she went missing.'

Lucas takes a deep breath through his nose, once, twice. I can't imagine how he's feeling, trying to hold his body together and his fiancée together at the same time.

'She rang you?'

'Yes.'

'Did you speak to her?'

'No.'

'Did you ever speak to her?'

'No Lucas.' I pull away from his grip. 'I told you, I never, ever met that woman.'

'Okay, okay, sorry, I'm dying here, babe.'

'What will I do?'

'You're getting married, Tara, don't let those guys inside your head. You've done nothing wrong. They can't prove you did. Forget about them.' He turns around and I find myself staring at the back of his head as he turns on the tap.

I wish I could find the courage to tell him the truth.

Chapter Twenty-Three

Faye

I'll just have the one to take the edge off. *What* it's taking the edge off, I don't know. But it makes me feel better, so I'll have one.

I'm sitting waiting for her. She'll arrive in a fanfare of sparkle and laughter, no doubt, surrounded by all those people she calls friends.

I've seen some of them on her Facebook page. All happy and shiny and successful. Living the perfect life, according to Facebook. I used to do it, too. I had a Facebook page and if anyone looked at it they would think my life was perfect. There were no clues. Nothing to reveal that every day I wished I was dead, or that I was someone else, or someplace else. Anything but me, here, alive.

The barman lowers the light and increases the volume on the music. Dizzee Rascal is now dancing in my ears. I don't know how much longer I'm going to be able to sit waiting. I thought they'd be here by now.

Pouring the Coke into the vodka, I pray that I didn't get it wrong. The Event page set up by her friend, Amy, definitely said Coppers night club. Unless there's been a change of plan. I take a large gulp from the glass, letting the gas fizz around my mouth before swallowing. Then I open my phone and check the page again – 'Tara's Last Night of Freedom.'

You would think she was important getting all that attention and her own event page for a stupid hen party.

The place is beginning to fill up now. The music is getting louder, the lights dimmer. I can barely see the entrance anymore so I pull my stool down to the corner of the bar to get a better view. A few feet away, a guy seems to think I'm moving closer to him. He smiles. I smile back but I shouldn't have because now he's walking over.

'Hi,' he says in a nice, soft voice. He's got a handsome face, dark eyes. The guy is so well groomed – his hair, his clothes, his skin. He looks like his mammy spent hours getting him ready. I've never really been a fan of the polished boys. I prefer the ones a bit rough-looking. The ones who don't bother to shave, or gel their hair, or iron their T-shirt.

'Craig,' he says, holding out his hand. He's gripping a bottle of beer in the other one. I don't want to be rude but he's blocking my view. Refusing his hand, I lift my glass and nod. Craig sees this as the *not interested* gesture that it is and steps back to where he came from.

There's a crowd of girls arriving through the door now, waving their arms in the air like they think we're all waiting on them. Some of them are wearing sashes over their shoulders. I can tell it's a hen party but where is she? Where is Tara? My heart starts to race. I take another gulp from my glass and scrutinise the pack.

All lipstick and frills but no Tara. Then I notice one of the girls is wearing a different coloured sash to the others and when she turns, I spot the 'Bride-To-Be' printed on it. My heart relaxes. This is not my party.

It's half past eleven now and they still haven't arrived. I'm thinking I won't be able to wait much longer when I see her. Tara Moore, walking through the door, surrounded by her flock. My heart leaps and my hand shakes as I knock back the rest of the vodka. Tara looks – well, a bit tired but that's probably the drink she would have had earlier. She hasn't changed much. Her hair is still cut in a casual bob. She's still refusing to wear high-heeled shoes, preferring a pair of Dr Martens with her dress. Emily appears to have put on a few pounds. She was so skinny back then, always dressed in black clothes with a white dusting of powder at the end of her nose. I wonder if she still dabbles in it or if she finally quit when Rose found out and caused murder, accusing Tara of leading her darling, little, innocent Emily astray. That made me laugh... It made Tara cry.

For a moment I feel sad I'm not with her. That I'm not the one who set up her hen party Event page. But the feeling doesn't last long.

The pack is moving this way and as Tara gets closer I see a line of worry shadowing her bravado. I could always tell when something was bothering her. The way she only half lifted her smile, the stillness in her eyes. Tara could read me too. She'd know if I was in a bad mood or if I was hiding something. Back then, I didn't mind being read.

Tara won't recognise me. Not with the fake glasses and curled hair that's hiding half of my face. I'm cleverly hidden behind this disguise. When she walks a few feet by me, my heart almost bursts with excitement. I turn to face the bar but I can sense her standing close to me, smiling and laughing, keeping her crowd happy.

I must make sure she doesn't see me. Tara can't know that I'm following her. She'll think I'm mad. I think I'm mad.

When she returned my call the first time I rang her she caught me off guard. I wasn't prepared to talk to her, having just come from an upsetting consultation at the clinic.

I answered the phone and changed my voice, pretending to be my secretary. 'Dr Faye Connolly is doing her rounds at the moment.' I was laughing inside.

When we did get to talk, it was as if nothing had happened, like we just drifted apart even though I was the one who instigated the separation. There were times I wanted to answer her phone calls. Especially over the first couple of weeks. I'd look at her name light up the screen and allow my finger to hover over the accept button. I pictured Tara at the far end of the call and imagined how apologetic she would be if I answered. It made me sad at first, to be cutting her calls. Sometimes I cried but I stayed strong knowing it would get easier over time. I didn't expect her to move on so successfully, though, like none of it mattered. Like I didn't matter. I was quite shocked to hear she was getting married. I was jealous. How fucking dare she?

Abba, now they're playing Abba. My second least favourite band in the world. I know what will happen next. Every female – and some of the males – in the building, will jump onto the dance floor thinking they are in fact, the 'Dancing Queen'. I turn to watch the ructions unfold and true to form, the floor is jammed. It's so easy to predict the masses. It's the ones sitting on their own at the bar you have to watch out for.

My eyes search Tara out. I can see her, dancing in the middle of the group. All hail Tara Moore… bitch.

I look to my right and catch Craig's attention with my eyes. I stare at him and smile. He pushes through the crowd and arrives at my side. He's really broad. I hadn't noticed that the first time he came over. Craig reaches his arm across my back and lifts my glass.

'What's this?' he says, putting his hand in the air to get the barman's attention.

I know I shouldn't, but it will take the edge off things.

'Vodka and Coke,' I say.

I'll just have the one.

Craig orders the drink and I stare at Tara Moore. The first time I met her we were in the schoolyard. I was eight. My name was Faith back then but I changed it when I was fourteen. It was too spiritual a name, too Goody Two-Shoes. I didn't want to be Goody Two-Shoes.

I remember resting against the back wall of the school yard when she came over, all shy and freckly. She clearly had no friends. At the time I didn't want to mix with other kids. They were all so loud and knew everything, or had everything, or were getting everything. Tara smiled and I could see her two front teeth were missing. Tara didn't have everything. We became the best of friends and now look at her. Dancing with all those other girls. I bet they have everything, or they're getting everything.

It hurts, sitting here in the audience when I should be part of the play. This is not the way it should be. Why am I the one getting punished? Why have I no one to dance with? I wish I was someone else. Someone with friends who didn't destroy my life. Someone who had people to go partying with. To plan my wedding with. My head throbs. I need to be that someone, just for a moment, just to ease this boiling anger churning in my stomach. Turning away from the source of my pain, I consider the man standing beside me.

'Do you want to fuck?' I look at Craig who has just put a vodka in front of me. He's about to swallow from his own beer bottle and almost chokes.

'What... what did you say?' Craig thinks he heard me wrong because of the loud music. I lean up towards his ear.

'Do you want to fuck?'

He's nodding and shaking and presumably thinking, *well, that didn't cost much.* 'Erm...'

'We'll have to do it outside. There's a laneway a few blocks down the road with good shelter.'

If he's wondering how I know this, he doesn't ask. He doesn't care that I've been down that laneway before.

Chapter Twenty-Four

If I hadn't shagged Craig, I would have made the last bus home. Now I have to get a taxi. Howth is a good twenty-five euros from Harcourt Street. But he was worth it. For ten whole minutes someone wanted me.

Craig didn't know what to do when we had finished. He pulled his jeans up and politely asked me if I wanted to go back in for a drink. Such a mannerly boy.

I told him it was okay. That he should go back to his mates. I was heading home. Craig didn't offer to put me in a taxi or even wait until one arrived. This one was on me. He jumped up the steps of the club to the entrance door and disappeared in behind the bouncers.

It took almost fifteen minutes before I got a taxi. I had to walk down the road to a crossroads. There were so many people hanging around, jumping in and out of taxis, having fun. As far as I could tell, I was the only person on their own.

When the taxi pulls up outside my parents' house I see the curtain moving in the front bedroom where my father and mother sleep. They can rest peacefully now. Faye is home.

I never thought I'd end up living back here, what with all the money I was going to make and the rich man I was going to marry. But here I am, for now, not forever.

I might do what Tara Moore is doing. Move to Australia. They're always looking for doctors over there. Or I could find myself an eligible bachelor and convince him that I love him. I won't tell him that I'm just looking for a way out of here.

When I think about it, I don't believe I will actually love again. Not the way I loved Andriu. He was perfect. When Tara said she was meeting him next week, I almost threw up on the spot. I thought he was gone, vanished into thin air. But no, she kept in touch. Tara said Andriu contacted her but I'm not so sure. If he was going to contact anyone it would have been me. She must have contacted him. Tara seems to be telling a lot of lies lately. What is she hiding? I don't trust her anymore, not after what she did when she was supposed to be my best friend. I was definitely her best friend. I have the scars.

And why is Andriu going to her wedding? It sounds to me like they're more than just casual Facebook friends. Maybe they continued their dalliance when I left Huntley Lodge. Tara went home to her dad's house for a while but they could have been meeting up. I wonder if she ever went to London to visit him. My stomach hurts when I think about it. How could I have been such a fool?

Sometimes I lay awake at night wondering if I had imagined it all. Did Andriu really exist? Was he really my boyfriend? But he was. I've a punctured heart to prove it.

But why her? Why not me? He could have reached me somehow. Tara said he contacted her through Messenger. Maybe he did try to contact me. I shouldn't have deleted my account. I wonder if he asked her about me. Is it me he's really hoping to meet when he returns to Dublin next week?

The house is eerily quiet when I open the door. I creep up the stairs, hoping not to make any noise. This is my life now. Creeping around, trying not to get noticed.

The cover on my bed is turned down, waiting for me. That will be my mother. She keeps fixing everything around me. Making my stay here as comfortable as possible. My favourite dinners. Favourite bread. She washes my clothes, irons my clothes, makes my bed.

My father is less impressed that I've needed to fall back on them. I'm sure he expected me to be married by now. To be bringing my children to his yacht club to show them off and brag about their IQs. Just like he did with me.

I strip off my clothes and realise I stink. It's probably not healthy for me to go to bed without washing the stranger off me. But I can't switch on the shower now because it's far too noisy. I grab a packet of face wipes from the dressing table. I wipe and wipe until I feel cleaner... on the outside. I don't feel cleaner on the inside. Then I get into bed, pull the duvet up tightly around my neck and I cry.

–

The following morning, I wake with a knot in my stomach. I think it's excitement because I don't feel sad right now. But what have I got to be excited about? Then it hits me. Andriu. But how will I meet him?

Tara will probably be back on the phone wondering if those detectives were questioning me. I don't blame her for being nervous. I'm nervous too. If she does call, I'll ask her where Andriu is staying while he's here. I hope he's staying in a hotel, then I can follow him and accidentally bump into him. Or maybe I should just come straight out and suggest we meet for a coffee. I'll figure it out.

The rain is pelting down outside and this gives me another reason to be cheerful. I won't be expected to go on one of those boring Sunday morning walks along the cliff with my father and mother. It drives me mad, both of them continuously counting their blessings that they live by the sea. Having me as their daughter never seems to shove the number of blessings up.

I'm just about to open my laptop when I hear a knock on my bedroom door. It's a soft knock so that will be my mother. She's very timid. Unlike my father, who's forthright enough for both of them.

'Can I come in?' she whispers. My mother whispers a lot. Either she's afraid to break me or she's telling me secrets all the time. Whatever it is, it can be quite annoying.

'Come in,' I say loudly.

'Your father wants to know if you'd like to go to the yacht club with him this afternoon. There's some event on. You might meet some of your old friends.'

'Mam, I don't want to meet any of my old friends. I'm fine. Don't be worrying about me.'

Her pale face looks to the ground as she pulls back out the door.

'Mam,' I say, waiting for her to stick her head in again. I wish I could make her happier. 'Are you going?'

'If you like.'

'Well, if you're going. I'll go.'

Her face lights up, then she closes the door.

I hate that she worries about me so much. It wasn't exactly the plan, landing back here but I wish they'd stop making such a big deal of it. Constantly trying to fix things. Things they don't even know are broken. Only I can fix things. Only I know what's broken.

I lift the lid of my laptop. My portal into everyone else's world. With my fingers on the keyboard, I continue my quest and type the name of the person who broke me. *Tara Moore.*

Chapter Twenty-Five

Yesterday was boring. I didn't meet any old friends at the yacht club like Mam had hoped, because there never were any old friends. Tara was my only real friend. Mam seems to forget that. I think she's getting me mixed up with my sister, or else she's decided to re-write history. Which wouldn't be the first time.

With my bag packed, I go downstairs and listen to the whispers behind the big white door. Mam will be making a lunch for me, a few snacks, just in case. My father will be sitting at the table, flicking through the pages of *The Irish Times*, telling her she shouldn't bother; that I won't appreciate it. It's crazy to think a thirty-year-old doctor is still being treated like a teenager in school.

I'm about to push open the door when my phone buzzes in my pocket. I'm eager to hear from Tara because I need to know where Andriu will be staying. I need to set in motion a plan to bump into him. Grabbing the phone from my pocket, I'm slightly disappointed to notice a withheld number instead of Tara's but I answer it anyway.

'Dr Faye Connolly?'

'Speaking.'

'This is Detective Siobhan Lee from the Pearse Street station. I was wondering if we could have a word.'

My heart is racing. I knew she would eventually make contact with me but it doesn't soften the anxiety that hearing her actual voice sparks.

'Can I ask what this is about?' I know exactly what it's about but I don't want her to know that.

'It's nothing for you to worry about. We want to ask you some questions about the time you lived at Huntley Lodge.'

'Huntley Lodge. Gosh, that seems like a lifetime ago.' I sound great. Totally in control. It's like I've nothing to hide.

'Would you be able to come to the station or would you rather I called in to you?'

I'm expected at the clinic in an hour so I won't have time to stop off at some station miles from here to chat. And there's no way I'm letting them call here. My father would never be able to let go of that embarrassment. It's going to have to be the clinic.

'Would you mind meeting at the clinic? I won't be able to talk to you until this evening, around five. I'll make sure I'm free then. Is this going to take long?'

'No, it shouldn't take too long,' she says, but I know the answer to that depends on what I have to tell them.

When the detective agrees to call at five, I give her the address of the clinic and close my phone. I'll need to prepare for this because, as I warned Tara, I don't want to slip up. Detectives have a way of getting you to say things you didn't intend to say. I know this because I never meant to tell them I put Valium into my whiskey the night I crashed my father's car into a big oak tree. And yet I did tell them.

I push open the door and walk into the kitchen. Both heads turn to look at me. My father is the first to speak.

'Are you ready?' he says, pulling his heavy weight off the chair with the aid of the table.

I nod. Mam hands me a lunchbox then leans in to kiss my cheek. It's the same routine every time.

'Take care, Faye. Don't forget to ring us.'

'I won't.' I take the box and shove it into my over-flowing bag before leaving the room. Already my brain is calculating what I should tell the cops this evening. I could act as dumb as an old fool or I could use this to my advantage. Drop Tara in it. I'll have to be careful, though. I don't want them finding out what happened or I'll never practice as a doctor again. Not in this country anyway. Maybe Australia.

–

I thank my father for the lift, take my bag from the back seat, then walk up the steps to the front door of the clinic. Another Monday. Another week begins.

'Good morning, Faye.'

Elvis, the security man is on duty today. He's always full of energy and smiles. Elvis is not his real name. He earned it by grooming sideburns the size of two small cats down his face.

'Morning, Elvis,' I say, my head held high. I walk down the corridor, the familiar walls, smells, sounds tapping into my conscience. *Here we go again.*

Anna is sitting at the reception desk. I wave. She waves. Then I carry on to my room, second on the left at the end of the corridor.

Chapter Twenty-Six

Tara

There's a bus broken down on the quays. Which is all anyone needs on a Monday morning. I push through the crowd exiting the bus and continue on towards the café. My head feels so much better today. It took the best part of yesterday before I could open my eyes without feeling pain. Lucas was great; he didn't speak much and brought me lots of water and greasy food when I was finally able to stomach it.

I enjoyed the night, everyone had a great time but I'm also glad it's over. Now I can concentrate on the wedding. The dress, my hair... why did Avril Ryan ring my phone? What could she have possibly wanted? I managed to keep those questions from ruining the hen party but now they're sitting right at the front of my head waiting for some attention. Maybe if I knew more about the woman I could figure out why she was looking to speak to me. But how do I find that out?

With the bright watery sun blinding my vision, I continue on down the quays to the café. I should Google and see if I can find out where Avril Ryan worked before she was killed. It's got to be somewhere on social media and that might give me a clue. Other than that, I'm at a loss. Detective Lee doesn't seem to want to share anything with me – if she knows anything. Faye might be able to get more out of them. They'll be more trusting of her. Dr Faye Connolly. I bet they wouldn't believe she'd lie to them.

The shutters are already up when I arrive outside the café. Muriel must be here already. I turn the key in the door and walk in to find her sitting at one of the tables drinking from a takeaway cup and writing in one of the ledgers.

'Morning Muriel, everything okay?'

'Morning Tara, yes, just getting a bit of work done early. I've to go to a funeral this morning and I wanted to get these orders out before I go.'

The smell of coffee cheers me up so I go straight to the machine and make myself an Americano, with an extra shot.

'Oh sorry to hear that, someone close?'

'Not really but I have to show my face. The delivery from Cahill's will be arriving between ten and eleven so make sure it's correct this time.' Muriel swallows more from her cup of tea, then stands. It always amazes me that someone who owns a coffee shop and brags about the quality of her beans never actually drinks the stuff.

'I've left the checklist there for you.' She points at a sheet of paper which she has placed on top of the counter. Muriel was not happy when Cahill's bakery left her short twelve doughnuts last week. I'm not sure how she knew when she wasn't here but she does a stock check every so often against the till sales and she discovered the error. She's brilliant like that. She knows everything that goes on here. Which is why she's the owner and I'm just an employee. Someday I want to own my own coffee shop.

I've already mentioned this to Lucas and he says we can look into it when we get to Melbourne.

Immediately, I feel excitement taking hold. This time next month I'll be on the far side of the world. I picture myself lying on a beach wearing the big round Gucci glasses I got in a sale last month. My hair will be tied back, I'll have on my red bikini and my skin will be golden brown. In my hand I'll be holding a tall cold drink which I'll hold against my forehead to cool me down. The realisation that this is actually going to happen makes me giddy with excitement as I plug in the till.

But what if I can't go? The fear hits me like a bullet. What if those detectives decide I must stay in Ireland until they've finished their investigation into the death of Avril Ryan? My heart sinks. What will Lucas do? Will he go without me? No. They won't do that. They can't do that. Not without some decent evidence… surely.

With the excitement gone and my head throbbing, I reach for the machine and make a second cup of coffee. This is turning out to be a real nightmare. It could spoil my wedding, force me to make changes, to delay everything. To stay here, making coffee, while my husband takes a flight to the far side of the world. My trembling hand is twisting the portafilter into place when I hear the push of the door.

The first customer has arrived. Hard as it is to do, I put my nightmare on hold and a smile on my face. It's Sean, the solicitor who rents one of the offices above the coffee shop from Muriel. He is always the first through the door every morning. I gulp down some of my coffee and turn to say good morning.

'Let's hope so,' he says, pulling his wallet out of his trouser pocket.

'Why, are you expecting trouble?' I'm trying to sound cheery, trying to ignore the worry coursing through my veins.

Sean laughs too. 'I'm always expecting trouble, Tara. I'm a solicitor, I deal in trouble.'

Sean doesn't have to tell me what he wants because it's the same every time. A double strength latte made with almond milk. I'm reaching down to get the milk from the fridge below the barista machine when the thought suddenly hits me. Sean does deal in trouble. He's the one I should be talking to. I wait until Muriel has moved into the back of the shop, taking longer than is needed to make his coffee.

'Can I ask you something, Sean?'

'Fire away,' he says, checking his phone before putting it back into his pocket.

My heart is racing. Where do I begin?

'I might be in trouble,' I say, placing his coffee on the counter. Sean taps his card and lifts the cup to his mouth. His eyes are focused on me as he takes a sip. I feel foolish, but I have to ask just to be sure.

'Can the police stop me from travelling abroad? From emigrating?'

Sean chuckles. 'There are situations where they can, Tara, yes, but you'd probably need to have murdered somebody. Why are you asking? Did something happen?'

'Well…' I'm nervous to say it out loud. So I check behind me to make sure Muriel is still out of earshot then I lean forward and whisper. 'They might think I murdered somebody or know something about a murder.'

'What?' Sean's chuckle quickly disappears and now he's looking at me in disbelief. 'What are you saying, Tara? Did the police say that to you?'

Oh shit, Sean is definitely going to think I'm a fool.

'No, not directly but they did question me about someone who was murdered. And I'm moving to Australia next month and I'm worried that it might...' My voice sounds really agitated now and I can feel tears welling up in my eyes. Sean puts his hand out and places it on mine.

'First of all, Tara, no, you won't be stopped from going to Australia, so don't be worrying about that.'

I take a deep breath and let the heavy burden float off into the air. Sean is about to continue when the door opens and in walks another regular. Mark from the holiday shop down the road. He shouts hello at the top of his voice and stares at the menu board even though I know he too will order his usual. Sean winks at me.

'What time can you call up to me in the office to have a quick chat? I'll put your mind at ease. You shouldn't be worrying like that.' He says this in a quiet voice so Mark can't fully hear. I'm overwhelmed by Sean's kindness and I feel like crying again.

'Eleven. I'll be on my break at eleven... or one o'clock. I'm finished at one today.'

'One o'clock, Tara, I'll make sure I'm free.'

'Thanks Sean.' I smile with gratitude and move my attention to Mark.

-

The rest of the morning passes with the usual Monday morning customers and comments. I didn't really want to make a big deal about it to Sean but I do feel better now that I've leaned on him. At least now I don't have to be worrying about moving to Australia. Or do I? I wonder if he will be so positive when he hears that Avril Ryan made a call to my phone. It's bound to make a difference. Those detectives will probably never leave me alone now that they have a ball to kick. They'll call and call and poke their noses into every corner of my life. Asking question after question. Shooting from every angle. I will have to stay strong. Defend my goal like a premier keeper. I cannot let my guard down even once because if they discover what I did… the game is over.

Chapter Twenty-Seven

The water is rushing out towards the sea tonight. I'm standing on the balcony drinking hot chocolate. I don't normally drink hot chocolate but the hotel gave us a few samples because we're planning to serve it along with the champagne when the wedding guests arrive in out of the cold. Something different, they suggested. Getting married in the winter would not have been my first choice but Lucas is due back in Australia next month and it seemed the logical thing to do rather than drag him back here next summer.

Faye and I always spoke about the summer sun shining brightly when we dreamed about our weddings. We had it all planned out. I would be her bridesmaid. She would be mine. I can still hear her laughing as she mimics herself walking down the aisle while humming 'The Wedding March'. It was automatically presumed she would be the first to take the plunge. But here we are. And it's me. I don't feel like a winner, though. Instead I feel sad it didn't turn out the way we dreamed it would. With Faye by my side.

With my hands cupping the mug, I look out at my city. I need to frame this picture, to keep it forever in my head – the bridges, the buildings, the lights. Soon it will be a memory. The place I used to live. I will tell my new friends what it was like, what I loved about it and they'll wonder why I left this place. I'll tell them it was love. They'll think I mean Lucas.

Sean seemed quite concerned that the body found in Huntley Lodge dated back to when I lived there. He asked if that was a fact or just a possibility. I said I didn't know. He thought it was very early for the cops to have that information, unless there was other evidence besides the post mortem that led them to believe she'd been lying in that dirty pit for the past three years. I told him that was around the time Avril Ryan went missing. But he said that didn't prove she was killed then, they must have more. He went quiet when I told him that I was the last person she tried to contact.

Sean asked me if I killed Avril Ryan. Not in an accusatory way, it was more of a joke but he still asked. He still got me to say 'No.' I told him the whole thing was a mystery to me and he suggested I forget about it and enjoy my wedding, while at the same time handing me his card in case I needed him.

–

In the background, I hear the unmistakable soundtrack of *I'm a Celebrity… Get Me Out of Here!* coming from our apartment. Lucas loves watching it. Yearning for home, I guess. I'm not a fan of the programme. Some nights I join him to get a feel for where I'm going to be living soon but it's probably not the ideal thing to be watching. I'm not able to look at people eating reindeer's balls and elephant's eyes. Ugh, not to mention the constant attacks from snakes and spiders. Lucas told me that there are plenty of snakes in Australia, sometimes they come into people's back gardens or their outhouses. When he saw my face stretch in disbelief he laughed, telling me not to worry, it didn't happen in the city where we'd be living. I hope he's right.

The chocolate drink has gone cold. I inhale one last view then go back inside to where the light from the TV flickers over Lucas's face. His eyes are peeled to whatever drama is unfolding on screen and I watch as he stares, his innocence, his honesty, his kindness all showing in his beautiful face.

I didn't mention my conversation with Sean the solicitor to Lucas. I don't think it's fair to worry him more than I have to. This is supposed to be the most important time of our lives and I can't let this event from the past interfere with the present any more than it has to.

I might tell Faye what Sean said in case she's worrying like I am. And Andriu. He'll be home tomorrow. I could run it by him. Though knowing Andriu, he probably won't give a damn about the cops. He was never really one to worry too much about anything. One time, two guys called to Huntley Lodge looking for Emily because she owed someone money. Faye and I were in a tizzy. We thought they'd come in and take all our stuff. We were both really afraid but Andriu walked out into the hallway. He told us to wait inside while he closed the front door behind him and dealt with the guys out in the garden. I don't know what he said to them but they disappeared fairly quickly and when he came back inside he wasn't a bit rattled. Faye and I were still shaking half an hour later. I decided then I was going to have to tell Emily that if she didn't stop taking cocaine I'd have to let her mam know. I was not going to stand back and watch her ruin her life.

I reach over to kiss Lucas's lips.

'I'm going to bed. I need an early night.'

He moves his lips closer to me without lifting his gaze from the man on screen. In his fifties, with a dwindling celebrity status, he is jumping around in fear while trying to remove giant spiders crawling up the leg of his shorts.

'Night,' Lucas says, his face cringing at the unfolding torture.

–

Before switching off the light, I check my phone once more to see if Faye has called. She hasn't. Maybe Faye has forgotten about it already or she just hasn't had the time to call me. Her life is so busy, working in a hospital. The media is always reporting on how doctors don't get a minute. Likening them to saints, especially young doctors. Apparently they put in seventy hours a week sometimes, or even more, sleeping in the hospital, eating in the hospital. It seems like a raw deal to me after all those years of studying. I think I'm a warrior if I do an extra shift at the café.

I wonder what Faye is doing now. Is she saving some kid's life? Consoling some upset mother who's distraught that her six-year-old has to have their appendix out?

I put my phone on silent and close my eyes. Faye won't ring tonight. She probably hasn't even had time to meet with the detective yet.

My eyes are closed but my mind isn't. I can't stop thinking about Faye. All that she was to me. I wish she would come to the wedding. It upsets me to think she found it so easy to cut me out of her life, to forget our past, our friendship. I keep going over it in my head. How she stood beside me that night, telling me to be brave. I could not have got through it without her.

My mind is still twisting when the bedroom door opens, casting a ray of light across the dark room.

'Are you asleep, Tara?' Lucas whispers.

'Not yet.'

He walks over and sits down on the bed. He pushes my hair off my forehead and kisses me.

'Are you happy, Tara?'

'Yes, I'm happy, what makes you ask that?'

'You seem a bit down lately. Are you sure everything is okay?'

I look at Lucas and smile. 'I'm okay now.'

'Because you know if you don't want to go ahead with the wedding I can—'

'No, Lucas, no. Don't say that. It's not you. I love you. You're what's keeping me going.'

'Is it the move, then? Are you having second thoughts about living in Australia? Because you know we can stay here, Tara. I could continue working in the Dublin office.'

We've been over and over this. Lucas trying to convince me to move to Australia then telling me I don't have to if I don't want to. He still wants to marry me. He loves me and he doesn't need to be worrying about whether I want to move to Australia or not. The thought of another year here frightens me more than any move.

'Lucas, I can't wait to move to Australia, believe me. It's the most exciting thing I want to do… after marrying you, of course.'

I'm yawning when Lucas leans in to kiss me. He seems happy with my explanation for now but I'm going to have to show a bit more excitement if I'm to convince him it's the truth.

He can't see that someone who's been dead for three years, someone I never even knew, is having this negative impact on my life. But it's going to be hard. I keep asking myself: did I have something to do with Avril Ryan's death? Something I don't know about yet? I get the feeling those detectives think I did.

Chapter Twenty-Eight

I love seeing the moon in the sky even though the sun is already shining bright above my head. It makes me think this day is going to be special.

The traffic is very busy this morning. Car after car after bus after truck all lining up to go a half a mile down the road. I watch the faces of people behind the wheels. Some of them look bored stiff, some anxious and some happy. The happy ones are easy to spot because if they're not actively smiling they're singing along to whatever music is coming from the radio.

Sometimes I can see people arguing and it upsets me. I turn away but the feeling doesn't move as quickly. I've never been comfortable with conflict. I hated it when my parents argued. I would go to my bedroom or put my headphones in my ears until the winner emerged. Usually Mam. Thankfully, they didn't argue often but when they did it made me nervous. I was afraid they would break up. That I'd become one of those children who had to decide who to live with. I worked it out once. I was going to spend the weekdays with Mam because I guessed she'd have the house and that was near my school. And Friday I would go to wherever my dad lived because he always got me food from the chipper on a Friday and I didn't want to miss out on that. Things were so black and white then. When did they become so grey?

There's no arguing today, that I can see. I look up at the moon still refusing to go to bed and I smile. Today is going to be a good day. I'm not going to worry about anything. I'll think only good thoughts. Sauntering towards the café, I'm within sight of the front door when I feel the smile slip from my face.

What the hell are they doing here? Outside the café, I can see the unwelcome sight of the two detectives leaning against their car. Surely they can't call to my place of work? Can they? And how the hell do they know I work here? I don't remember telling them. Maybe I did, that morning in the apartment. Everything has become so confusing and I don't know who I'm hiding what from half the time. But I don't remember mentioning Muriel's café, which means they're checking up on me. Finding out what they can about the girl who Avril Ryan last phoned. The girl who lived in the house where Avril Ryan's body was found.

My stomach heaves. My body starts to freeze up. What now? A thousand thoughts jump to the front of my mind: Who? What? Why? When? Do they know what I did?

My legs briefly buckle from under me but I manage to pull myself together and lift the dead weight of my body forward. When I approach them, Detective Lee steps away from the car and apologises for calling to my workplace but says they have to speak to me urgently.

Her words take pride of place in my head. Every other sound – the traffic, the wind, the screeching of horns, the passing footsteps – has muted. If I cry, will the detectives think I'm guilty? I want to cry. I open my mouth but nothing comes out. For some reason, I think all the people in the traffic jam are looking at me. They probably know the two people standing over me are cops. Cops have a certain look, a stance, they come in twos. They make people nervous. They're unmistakable.

'Is it okay if we come inside?' Detective Lee says.

'I'd rather you didn't. Whatever you've got to say, say it here.' Did I just say that out loud? I'm sounding braver than I feel.

'Well, you could come down to the station if that would be better for you.' Her tone is laced with power. The ball is most definitely in her court. Shit, what do I do now? I certainly don't want to go to the police station. What will Lucas think if he finds out his wife-to-be is being questioned at a police station – and so close to the wedding? A desperate feeling threatens my composure. Will Lucas still want to marry me?

I'm shaking all over and my head is thumping. What am I going to do? I glance to my right. Through the glass window I see Muriel looking out at me. She certainly won't appreciate me walking into work with two cops in tow. I'm about to ask them to wait until I speak to my boss when I hear a voice coming from behind me.

'Is everything okay, Tara?'

I look around and see Sean the solicitor standing behind me. His face is glowing, the watery sun providing him with what looks like a halo. He appears like Jesus rising from the dead. Immediately, I release the trapped tears and Sean puts his arm around me. I'm like a three-year-old crying in the teacher's arms. Looking for a plaster. Where's my plaster?

Sean puts his hand out and gives the detective a card. 'If you wish to speak to my client, call me and make an appointment.'

My client. Why did he say that? When did I become his client?

Detective Lee takes the card, reads it and says, 'Well, if you think you need a solicitor that's fine, but we weren't going to keep you long, Tara, it was just a few quick questions.'

Sean steps in front of me like a bodyguard protecting his celebrity client. I feel safe but I also feel like I've just blown this thing into a whole other dimension. What if they were about to finish with me? Ask one or two more things and then disappear forever.

In the background, Muriel is straining her neck to see what's going on and mouthing at me with concern. I hope she doesn't come outside and join us, so I nod and fake a smile letting her know I'm okay.

'We need to talk to your client as soon as possible,' the detective says to Sean. He turns to me, checks his phone and we discuss a suitable time. Four o'clock tomorrow evening at the station.

The detectives turn away from us and get into their car. I breathe with relief as Sean once again tells me not to worry. But that ship has sailed. I'm worried sick. My body feels like it has been thrown against a wall. The last time I was in a police station, I was getting visa forms signed for my journey to Australia. I was never there as a… what am I now? A person of interest? A suspect?

With my world spinning on an axis of fear, I open the door of the café and walk inside. The person last served is walking out with their takeaway coffee, leaving myself and Muriel to fill the anxious space.

'Are you alright, love? What happened? Was that the police you were talking to?'

She moves out from behind the counter. I really don't want to discuss anything now but I can't ignore her either.

'Yeah, it's nothing; they wanted to ask me about an incident that happened in a house I lived in a few years back. Did the delivery from Musgrave's arrive?' I say, hoping she takes the bait and moves off the subject.

'Yes, it's out back. It's not that house Avril Ryan was found in, is it?'

Shit, she's not letting up.

'Yes, I lived there for a while a few years back. The police are asking anyone who ever lived there if they know anything. But I don't have anything to tell them. I never knew her.'

'According to her brother she was a lovely girl, loved her animals. She worked as a health care worker in an old folks' home or something like that,' she says.

I'm listening to Muriel, aghast. Does she know Avril Ryan's brother?

'They are beyond consoling, God love them all,' Muriel continues, moving towards the sink with a coffee tray. I'm stunned into silence. 'They never gave up hope until they found her body. Terrible… terrible affair.'

Wrapping the belt on my apron tightly around my waist, I pull and knot and take a deep breath. 'Did you know the family?'

'Not me personally. They were distant relations of Eamon's.'

Eamon is what Muriel calls her 'part-time husband'. Sometimes they're on, sometimes they're off. He's a very unassuming quiet guy if you ask me but Muriel finds enough fault in him to send him packing every now and then.

'Which is why I had to go to the funeral,' she says. 'Eamon wanted to show his support even though he hasn't seen them since he was a kid.'

'Was anything said at the funeral about her death? Do they know how it happened?' I say this with my heart thumping in my chest because I can't believe my boss was at the woman's funeral.

'I didn't go to the reception afterwards, but Eamon did. He fell in late and I never got to ask him anything about it. But I'll find out later if you want me to?' Muriel turns her head sideways to look at me. She's trying to gauge my reaction. I don't want to seem overly interested so I continue as if she never said anything. I know Muriel will ask Eamon if he heard anything and she'll be dying to tell me what she finds out, anyway.

'The poor family, they must be devastated,' I say. 'I hope the police find out what happened to her so they can have closure.'

I'm praying someone walks through the door and breaks up this conversation. The longer it goes on, the more chance there is I'll tell Muriel that I was living at Huntley Lodge at the time Avril Ryan was murdered and that I've to go to the station tomorrow to be questioned further.

When the door finally opens, two women from the beautician's a few doors down enter. They're lively, beautiful, and a total tonic from the gloomy atmosphere that I've created. They engage Muriel in conversation while I leave to attend to the delivery out back.

When I'm out of sight, I take my phone from my pocket and check to see if Faye has called but my heart sinks when I see she hasn't. I'm nervous about going to a police station, even with a solicitor by my side. Should I tell Lucas or wait until after I've been there? I don't want him worrying unnecessarily. There's nothing he can do.

The only one who can help me now is Faye. She has to tell the detective that I didn't know Avril Ryan.

I dial her number but there's no answer. Maybe she's avoiding my calls, especially after her drunk episode on Friday night. She must be embarrassed about ringing me like that, struggling to put two words together. That's if she even remembers making the call. She was so drunk it's quite possible she doesn't. Maybe Faye is not avoiding me at all. Just busy making life-saving decisions or delivering bad news to some unfortunate patient. I wish I could have done what she wanted and not mentioned her name to the cops. I know why she doesn't want them contacting her. At least I think I do. But what if I'm wrong? What if Faye is hiding something else from the cops? Something that made her leave Huntley Lodge so hastily. I put my phone back in my pocket and think back to how everything changed overnight.

Chapter Twenty-Nine

Then

The café isn't busy today but still I'm afraid to ask my boss if I can leave. I don't know what excuse I'll give, especially after being out of work for the past week. But I really can't stay here and serve coffee when I'm suffering this pain. I keep making mistakes, handing out the wrong coffee or giving the wrong change and then when someone points it out to me I get all nervous and jittery and have to coax the tears back in behind my eyes.

It's not a physical pain; it's worse than that and nothing will relieve it, not the two Solpadeine I just swallowed or the extra strong coffee I've been drinking all morning in an attempt to stay focused. This pain is dreadful, it's cruel and the only cure for it is time.

The damp cloth feels unusually heavy in my hand. Wiping it over the counter I watch the rings of stain disappear and wonder exactly how much time are we talking about here. A week, a month, a year? Exactly when will my mother's death become a lighter load to carry?

'Tara.' Muriel calls me over to where she's standing by the barista machine. 'I think you should go home, love,' she says.

'But...' I don't know what to say. I'm exhausted.

'Come back when you're ready.' Muriel smiles, puts her hand on my arm and squeezes. 'It will take time, Tara,' she says. 'Take care of yourself and I'll see you in a couple of days.'

Moving to the back of the shop I unwrap the belt on my apron and let that word echo in my head. *Time.* Last week I hadn't got enough of it and this week I have too much. Wouldn't it be great to have a button, to be able to pause, rewind, fast forward? Or a special box to put time away in and take it back out when I need it. But there is no button, no box. Time owns me.

–

The sun is shining bright when I leave the café and it feels like an intrusion into my sadness. Why is everything not dull? I walk to the bus stop and stand with other silent voices and wait for the thirty-nine bus to take me back to Huntley Lodge. Dad was disappointed when I dropped out of college a few months ago. I think he thought I'd go back as soon as Mam died but I don't want to. Not yet anyway, maybe next year.

When I get to Huntley, it's after lunchtime so I don't expect anyone to be at home. Faye will be at college and Andriu at work. My plan is to go to bed, pull the duvet over my head and sleep, something I haven't been able to do properly for weeks now.

I turn the key in the door and step inside. To my surprise, Emily is standing in the hallway. She's just about to leave but then I notice there's an unusual smoky smell. Like something is burning or smouldering. It's coming from the kitchen. Someone must have left a ring on.

'What's that smell?' I ask. 'And what are you doing here?'

Emily sniffs the air. 'I don't know, it's like something is burning.' She takes a cream jacket from a pile of coats hanging at the bottom of the stairs and says, 'I came over to pick this up. I left it here the other day.'

'But how did you get in? Is my dad here again?'

'No, Andriu let me in.'

'Andriu?' I'm confused now because I thought he'd be at work but I haven't been paying much attention to the outside world of late. He might have mentioned something and I didn't hear.

Emily walks over and puts her hand on my arm. 'Are you okay, Tara? You look worn out.'

'I'll be okay. I'm just tired. I'm going to bed for a few hours.'

Emily smiles with pity before asking if I want her to stay. I don't. Emily is the last person I want to see now but I thank her and watch her leave.

A few minutes later, Andriu walks into the kitchen, where I am pouring hot water onto a teabag.

'Sorry about the smell, Tara, I burnt a pot of eggs earlier.'

I attempt a smile and continue to make the tea. 'I didn't know a burnt egg could make such a dreadful smell.'

'Would you rather a hot whiskey?' he says, moving over to my side. He's bare-chested, wearing a baggy pair of joggers. The woody smell from his shower gel blurs the burning smell for a brief moment.

'What?' I say, confused.

'You look so sad, Tara. Let me make you a hot whiskey and then you should go to bed and try to sleep.'

Two hot whiskeys later, my eyes can no longer stay open.

It's after eight when I finally wake. My head still feels like it doesn't belong to me but I get out of the bed and put my dressing gown on over my underwear. I wish Faye was here so I could talk to her. She'd make me feel better like she always does. But she's on student placement and has an overnight at the hospital tonight.

I drag myself downstairs in the hope of killing a few hours watching something on the TV. I'm settled onto the sofa in the living room flicking through the TV channels when Andriu arrives with two glasses and a bottle of wine. He seems to think alcohol is the only remedy for my broken heart which surprises me because he usually never promotes it. Especially when it comes to Faye.

'Wanna talk?' Andriu sits down on the chair opposite the little wooden coffee table that Faye's mam no longer wanted.

'It will get easier, you know,' he says. Hearing his words brings a tsunami of tears to my eyes. I can't help it. If someone says boo, I'm off.

Andriu sits with me. He listens when I tell him how much I miss my mam. We open a second bottle of wine and before I know it, I'm lying on the sofa ready to fall asleep again. My head is spinning from the drink. Faye is so lucky to have a considerate, caring man like Andriu in her life. I close my eyes.

-

'Get out… Get the fuck out!'

I'm woken by screams coming from upstairs. I sit up suddenly. I'm going to be sick.

'You cheating bastard… Get out. Get out!'

I rush out to the hallway and get hit in the face by a flying T-shirt. Faye is tossing all Andriu's clothes over the bannisters onto the floor in front of me. I'm holding my mouth closed, trying to stop the vomit from rising. I rush to the kitchen because I'm not attempting to go upstairs into the unfolding nightmare.

An explosion of puke lands in the sink, once, twice… Christ, I'm going to die here. Sweat drips from my forehead. There is still a massive row unfolding above my head. From the banging and crashing it sounds like she must be breaking everything. Whatever the fuck happened, Faye is not happy. In fact I've never heard her this distraught in my life. Her hysterical voice is crashing into every wall in the house and I can't move to help her. All I can think about is how ill I feel.

I turn the tap on. I'm unable to wish or think or help… I look out through the window to the statue at the bottom of the garden, to the overgrown shrubbery. Something looks different. Cupping my hand below the flowing tap I lift some water to my poisoned lips and drink it. I'm standing still but I can feel everything changing around me.

Chapter Thirty

This morning was endless. Coffee after coffee, cake after cake, sandwich after sandwich. No phone call from Faye. My anxiety danced through my body all day, shooting off the charts one minute, taking a rest for another before bouncing back into action.

Muriel is no fool; she kept looking at me, saying nothing, watching me check my phone every few minutes. Faye never called. The sooner Andriu arrives, the better. I'm looking forward to seeing him at the airport tonight. Amy has agreed to drive me there to pick him up at seven thirty. It's so long since I've seen him.

At least then I'll have an ally. Andriu will be able to confirm to the detectives that Avril Ryan wasn't a friend of ours. She was never even in the house. He'll be able to tell them we never heard of her, that someone else pushed the lid off that slurry pit and put her body inside.

A shiver runs down my spine when I picture Avril Ryan's body lying there. Her cold, wet, distorted corpse left to rot like a rat in a sewer. No one deserves that ending. The final goodbye should be peaceful, surrounded by people who love you. There should be no physical pain, just the angst of loss, lessened by the heightened belief that, yes, we will see one another again someday. A loved one should be holding your hand, tightly, helping you make the transition to the next world with dignity and peace. A smile where possible. Tears at a history well remembered. A life that was worth living.

But Avril Ryan didn't get that. Her life was robbed from her. There was violence, fear, evil. No one smiled through tender tears when Avril took her last breath.

I swallow hard, knowing this could have happened at Huntley Lodge. It's also possible I was in the house at the time, asleep upstairs, unaware of the body being tipped into the pit at the back of the garden. I need to tell the detectives that. They need to know that while I could have been there at the time, any one of hundreds of people could have done this. Someone who once lived at the house or someone who had partied at the house. There were lots of people at those parties. People who knew the unused pit was there. The detectives need to know that.

The lunchtime rush is almost over, just a few stragglers without the chains of clock cards rushing them back to work. I'm usually quite chatty with the customers, laughing, joking, commenting on the latest breaking news. But not today. Today I just smile and put down a plate or lift a cup. My vibe must be easily read because no one is engaging me in conversation. A lot of the regulars are aware I'm leaving Muriel's café in a couple of days. They know I'm getting married and moving to Australia. They are fully aware of my unfolding dream. They don't know that dream is now balancing on a crumbling foundation.

When the last of the tables have been cleared, I go to the barista machine to make myself a cappuccino to take out back. I wash the smell of disinfectant from my hands before lifting the mug. I'm not hungry today. The stress of the detectives wanting to speak to me has my stomach in a knot. Sean says not to worry, that the cops do this;

they have to be certain that I know nothing of use to the investigation before they scratch me off their list. I hope he's right.

I'm just about to pour the frothed milk into the mug when the tinkle of the bell rings above the door behind me. Someone has walked into the café. I look at Muriel counting coins at the till to see if she makes a move to attend to the customer but she remains focused on the money. It's up to me. I force a smile on my face even though one doesn't belong there and turn to see the tall shape of a familiar man.

'Andriu?' I don't believe it. Andriu is standing in front of me. I wipe my hands on my apron before pulling the hairnet from my head. I must look like crap. He looks great.

The three years since I've seen this man have done little damage – some grey hairs sparkling at the edges and a suggestion of age wrinkling the corners of his eyes but other than that, he looks exactly the same. Piercing dark eyes, fine bone structure and a row of perfectly managed teeth. His smile wraps me like a hug. I feel like the cavalry has arrived. But what is he doing here already? I'm supposed to be picking him up at the airport later.

'Andriu.' I rush into his arms and fight the tears that spring forward with relief. Andriu doesn't know what's going on yet. Or so I think. Maybe he does. It's possible the police have contacted him already.

'I can't believe you're here... I thought I was to pick you up later. Did I get the time wrong?'

He looks around at the empty café.

'No, I took an earlier flight. How are you?'

'I'm great, great,' I say, before remembering that I'm not. I don't know whether to get straight into it with him or wait until we've at least said our hellos properly. 'And you... you look great.' I step back to have a better look.

I look at Muriel who is discreetly surmising the situation.

'Is it okay if I have my break now?' I say, knowing she won't mind. Muriel nods, lifts her till tray and walks towards the back room.

'I'm just about to have a coffee, Andriu. Can I get you one?'

'Whatever you're having,' he says.

We're both sitting with our coffees and I'm preparing to tell Andriu all about Lucas and the wedding and Australia when my mouth opens and says: 'Have the police been in touch with you?'

'What?' Andriu leans back slightly. He looks shocked by my opening line. I'm a bit shocked myself so I take a deep breath and hug the mug in my hand.

'Something happened at Huntley Lodge, Andriu. A woman's body was found and now they want to talk to whoever lived there at the time.'

Andriu says nothing, so I continue. 'A woman in her thirties – she's been missing for three years and now her body has been found in the disused pit at the bottom of the garden at Huntley Lodge. Do you remember it, the big steel doors in the ground under all the brambles? Can you believe it? Jesus. And all the parties we had there.'

'What?' He eventually speaks, his eyes lighting up like I've just told him the most incredible news. 'Are you serious?'

'Yes, and the police are on to me because this all happened when we lived there.'

Andriu chuckles. 'That's impossible. Are you having me on, Tara?' He smiles as if waiting on the punchline.

I fill him in on what I know so far. Andriu soon realises there is no punchline but it's difficult to gauge his reaction. I'm in a panic and yet he seems to be laughing it off like it's nothing at all. Cool Andriu. Still nothing fazes him.

Eventually I move on to the subject of Faye and Andriu's mood shifts slightly. He's not chuckling now.

'Have you heard from her?' I ask.

Andriu shakes his head before speaking. 'She did try to contact me once or twice at the start. She sent a few messages but I didn't reply. I thought a clean break was the best thing for us… How is she?'

Hearing him mention her name brings back a lot of memories. Sad memories. Andriu broke her heart. The sound of her crying that night – it was torture listening to her pain travelling through every room in the house. Suddenly I feel like I'm betraying Faye.

'I don't really know. I haven't seen her in a long time. I spoke to her on the phone for the first time a few days ago. I think she's okay.' I remember the sound of her slurred words. 'I hope she's okay.'

'Why? Did something happen?' Andriu says, keeping his eyes on me as he lifts his mug to his lips. I don't want to tell Andriu that Faye was drunk and upset when she rang me; it's none of his business.

'No, nothing. Just the Huntley Lodge thing.'

'Do you think she had something to do with it?' he says, knocking me for six.

'Faye? What are you talking about? Why would Faye have anything to do with it?' My voice sounds a bit defensive.

'No, just when you said you hope she's okay, I thought maybe you…'

'No. God, Andriu. Faye didn't have anything to do with it.'

Andriu places the mug back down on the table, his eyes following his action before he lifts his steady gaze to me again.

'Oh well, that's good,' he says, nonchalantly, but freaking me out at the same time.

'Why do you think she could have had something to do with it?'

'No, I'm not saying that. It's just she had gotten so weird and paranoid before I left.'

He rubs his hand through his hair, saying, 'To tell you the truth, Tara, Faye changed. She'd become possessive or crazy, something I couldn't put my finger on, but she was different to the Faye I had grown to love.'

'But you were the one who cheated on her, Andriu.' I can't believe I'm saying this out loud but I can't let him forget what drove her over the edge that day. She was right to be paranoid.

Andriu pulls back in the chair. 'Wait a minute, is that what she told you? There was more to that than meets the eye... You don't know what she was like, she changed, Tara. Faye had become very nervous, jumpy, like she was waiting on something bad to happen. I had already made my mind up that I was going to take the job in London even before that night.' He leans forward slightly, a half smile appearing on his face. He's locking his stare on me, wanting me to agree with him. But I don't. I know Faye was heartbroken but she wasn't mad.

'I decided to go before things got even more difficult,' he said.

I think back to that time, was there stuff going on that I didn't notice? I was so involved in myself, my own sadness. Had I missed something. Had Faye been in trouble?

Chapter Thirty-One

Faye

Today wasn't too busy. I've had busier days in this clinic. The appointments were at a minimum which I was thankful for. I'm still in consultation room number four but this time there are two detectives sitting in front of me: Detective Siobhan Lee – who seems to be the boss – and her partner, Detective Mullins.

'Thank you for seeing us, Faye. It's important we get to speak with everyone who lived at Huntley Lodge.'

I nod and keep my eyes locked on hers. Detective Lee shifts in her chair and takes out a notebook from her pocket.

'I've already spoken to one of your housemates, Tara Moore,' she says.

Again I nod.

'She told me you were living in the house with her alongside another tenant, Mr Andriu Fitzpatrick.'

'That's right.'

'Have you spoken to either since the body was found?'

I want to say no but Tara probably told her we've been in contact so I decide I'd better not lie so soon into the conversation.

'I spoke briefly to Tara but she didn't know anything either and I haven't seen or heard from Andriu in... gosh, it must be three years or more.' I make it sound like I'm only calculating that figure now. The detective doesn't need to know that it's exactly three years, nine weeks, two days and about nine hours since I last saw him. The day I chucked him out of the house. The day I came home and found the box of condoms on top of his bedside cabinet. The box was open. There was a wrapper on the floor by the bed. It wasn't there when I'd left for work the previous evening because I always make sure the box is inside the cabinet.

The detective doesn't need to know that before I discovered the discarded wrapper on the floor, I found Tara Moore unconscious on the sofa downstairs. Barely dressed. She doesn't need to know I covered her in a blanket and lifted the two empty glasses from the table and the bottles off the floor in case she rolled off the sofa and hurt herself.

The hate is taking over again. I can feel it rising in me, drowning me. It will make me lose control and I might say something that I shouldn't. Casting my eyes to the ground, I stick my finger into the side of my shoe as if clearing something away and I take a deep breath.

'Sorry, something stuck in my shoe,' I say before lifting my head and looking at the detective.

'Do you know where Andriu is now?'

'No, I don't.'

'Okay, not to worry. So, Faye, can you cast your mind back to three years ago when you lived at Huntley Lodge?'

I'm nodding, waiting on further direction.

'Can you remember anything suspicious at all? Anyone unusual coming to the house or anyone acting out of character?'

Mullins coughs into his hand, taking my focus away from Lee.

'Can I get you some water?' I say, standing to walk to the water cooler in the corner of the room.

'Stay where you are, he can get it himself,' Lee says, looking over at Mullins like he's a little kid.

'I'm fine,' he mutters and looks back at me.

'Where were we?' I say. 'Oh yes, anything suspicious, anyone out of place...' Smacking my lips I look to my right, to my left. 'Anyone suspicious?' I repeat. 'I would say at least a hundred different people came through that door in any one month so...' I let that hang in the air for a minute before adding. 'Do you have a name? Or a picture or...'

'Avril Ryan,' Lee says.

I continue to play dumb and yet the anger in me is still very much alive. I try to block out the moment I put two and two together. Tara and Andriu. They had sex. Everything pointed to it: the drink, the condoms, the half-naked bodies. Did they think they were actually going to get away with it? That they could keep their sorry little affair a secret from me... with my IQ? Are they really that thick? I knew someday an opportunity like this would come my way.

'Faye...' Lee interrupts my train of thought.

'Sorry... I'm trying to think. Did you say Avril Ryan?'

'Yes.'

And here it is. Sitting on two chairs in front of me. My opportunity for revenge.

It's a self-harming of sorts. I know that but if I can release some of the anger I have for her, let it flow, maybe then I won't feel as bad. I know it could backfire on me.

But to hell with it. I want my revenge. I will take the blade and make the cut.

'I'm pretty sure Tara Moore knew an Avril Ryan,' I say.

The room falls silent then. I have given the detective exactly what she wants. She can't thank me for it because she can't show her excitement but I know she's holding it in. Detective Lee is looking straight at me and I am looking right back.

I'm fully aware of the trouble this will cause. It's a lie. A great big lie. But I don't give a shit. In fact, I feel better already.

Chapter Thirty-Two

Tara

There's a thick fog floating on the surface of the River Liffey like it's trying to hide something. I make my way down the quays, pushing past the crowds that are walking too slow for my liking. I want to get home to Lucas. I want to see his face and hug his strong body. To be reminded of my future.

Muriel came to my rescue earlier, calling me back on duty before the conversation carried on any further with Andriu. We hugged and he agreed to meet Lucas and me in Reilly's pub on the corner of our apartment block on Friday night. Amy will be there too.

Andriu said he's looking forward to meeting Lucas but I'm not as excited anymore. I'm thinking, maybe I should have left my past where it was and not invited Andriu to the wedding. At the time, I thought it would be nice to have someone from those halcyon days at the reception, but that was before the body was found. Now, having him around only reminds me of the investigation and how close I'm sailing to the wind.

I didn't like what he said about Faye either – that she had gotten weird, implying she had gone a bit mad. It's probably Andriu's way of dealing with the way he treated her, running out on her. Some men get like that when they do something wrong. They become allergic to blame, citing the woman's madness for their lack of judgement. I saw it happen when Mam's brother Derek was caught offside with his young secretary. He decided it was his wife's fault, said she was mad, that she drove him to it. And even though he was her only brother, Mam didn't fall for his nonsense. She was so angry that day, and it wasn't long after her diagnosis so there wasn't a lot of anger left in her, but she summoned whatever there was and read him the riot act.

He lives on his own now. No wife. No secretary. No sister. I sent him a wedding invitation, Derek plus one, but he replied saying he'd be coming on his own.

With my hands tucked inside the pockets of my jacket, I step onto O'Connell Bridge and pray there's still a wedding for Uncle Derek to come to. My step quickens the closer I get to home, and I think of Faye, what she suffered back then and how useless I was for her. I should have noticed if something was wrong. I should have been there for her.

–

Lucas is whistling when I walk through the door. Well, at least someone's happy. He's standing over the cooker pouring cream into something simmering in the pan. It smells delicious, and I tell him so. When he turns to smile at me, it cheers me up and I decide to be happy too.

'What is it?' I say, accepting his kiss before leaning over to look into the pan. Lucas has always been the main cook in this relationship. It's not that I'm a bad cook but I look bad beside him because he cooks everything from scratch. Nothing gets onto his menu that isn't directly delivered by nature. Whereas I often tend to just go for whatever is quickest and easiest.

'Chicken tagliatelle,' he says, stirring the pot. 'With spinach and peppers and...' I kiss him on the lips before he gets to finish. Lucas drops the spatula and holds my face, kissing me harder, deeper, arousing a need in me.

I pull away when I realise I'm crying. Tears are rolling down my face.

'What is it?' Lucas says. 'What's wrong, Tara?' His gaze changes to one of worry.

I don't want this. I didn't want Lucas to be worried about me but I'm unable to hide my fear. 'It's nothing, sorry, Lucas, I'm just a bit tired and nervous and...'

Lucas takes a deep breath. I can tell he's getting a bit fed up with me. I don't blame him. His wife-to-be should be melting in his arms or jumping around with excitement not crying and moaning and freaking out over everything. I have to let him know my worry is genuine.

'Those detectives came to the café today.'

Lucas pushes the pan off the heat and wipes his hands on a tea towel before leaning against the countertop.

'What happened?' he asks.

Wiping the tears from my eyes with the sleeve of my cardigan, I look at him. 'They said they want to ask me more questions and now I've to go to the station tomorrow evening with Sean the solicitor from upstairs, and Andriu thinks Faye might—'

'Slow down, slow down, Tara. One thing at a time. What happened with the detectives?'

While I tell Lucas about the police, he finishes the dish in the pan and plates it up for us both, topping it with some freshly chopped green stuff. Then he opens a bottle of wine and we sit at the small two-person table that

Lucas insisted on buying when we got this place. I thought we'd never use it. I didn't realise how romantic living with Lucas was going to be. He loves making dinner, lighting candles, decanting wine. I'm so spoilt, I'm so lucky, oh God, I'm crying again.

'Lucas, what if this doesn't go away?' I say, sauce dripping onto my chin.

Lucas leans forward and wipes it off with his serviette. 'Tara, this time next month you'll be in Australia. This will be history. Those detectives will be history. You didn't do anything wrong. You need to stop freaking out.'

I felt guilty listening to Lucas saying I didn't do anything wrong. I know now I should have told him but I always hoped I could keep my secret locked away. A lot of effort and time went into pushing it to the back of my mind and the thought of releasing it back into the open again frightens me. Will Lucas still want me? Will I end up in prison? I try to hide my fear behind the glass of wine touching my lips. I'm torn between blurting out the whole truth, possibly destroying everything, and saying nothing. I look at Lucas sitting on the opposite side of the table. His mouth is full of food. His head, full of excitement. I can't ruin it for him.

'I know… I know, but the detectives… I thought they'd have gone away by now.' I say.

'They will.'

'But why did that woman ring me?'

'I don't know, Tara. I'm sure it's a simple explanation. It might even have been a misdialed number. Who knows? You didn't know her. You didn't have anything to do with her murder so let it go, Tara. This will all go away. The detectives will find out what happened. Now eat some dinner.'

The silence that follows is broken only by the sound of the cutlery hitting off the plate. This is not a nice atmosphere and I'm afraid that Lucas will get fed up with my constant panicking. I need to change the subject so I tell him about the surprise visit from Andriu. I don't mention what Andriu said about Faye in the end because I still can't get my head around it. Why did he ask me if I thought Faye was involved? Does *he* think she was involved? Of course she wasn't – unless Andriu knows something about her that I don't. Now that I think about it, it was weird the way she ended our friendship when she left Huntley Lodge. At the time I was confused, so full of grief that I didn't pay any attention to what was happening around me. I thought Faye was leaving to get away from Huntley Lodge and the memories it held of Andriu. I didn't realise she was leaving me too. That she would never answer my calls or try to see me again. If I had known that she was ending our friendship for good, I would have asked her why. But she never gave me the chance. As time passed, I decided Faye wanted me out of her life because of what we had done? That she needed to forget about that night and I was just a constant reminder. But now I'm not so sure. Maybe I didn't know her as well as I thought I did.

I'm telling Lucas he'll get to meet Andriu on Friday when he comes to Reilly's pub and I'm almost licking the plate clean, the dinner is so delicious, when the buzzer goes.

'Who's that?' Lucas says, slightly annoyed that we're being disturbed.

'I don't know.' Then it hits me. 'Shit, I forgot to cancel Amy. She was bringing me to the airport to pick up

Andriu.' I swallow the last of my wine and laugh as I go to the intercom to buzz her up.

'The sooner we get to Australia and I can have you all to myself, the better,' he says. 'No more Amy or detectives or Andriu interfering in our life.'

I laugh at his words but something inside me cries. This is really happening. I'm leaving everyone behind. My dad, my friends, my past.

Well, maybe not the past. I won't be able to leave that behind. What I've done is not going to disappear from my memory just because I get on a plane. Even if it is a twenty-four-hour journey. My past will stay with me. Packed in my head. Baggage that can't be lost at Heathrow.

Chapter Thirty-Three

Amy arrives through the door with four big bags of stuff hanging from her arms. She plonks the bags onto the sofa before commenting on the lovely smell of food.

'Too late Amy, it's all gone.'

I can see her disappointment but she walks into the kitchen area anyway and rubs her finger in the sauce that's stuck to the bottom of the pan.

'Yum,' she says, licking more. 'Are you ready?'

'Sorry, Amy. I should have called you, we don't have to go to the airport; Andriu got an earlier flight.'

'Great,' she says, without moaning. I would have moaned. But Amy is relaxed, and lives in the moment, a bit like Lucas. I'm glad I asked her to be chief bridesmaid because she has practically organised everything for me. She helped me pick a dress, book the hotel, order the cake, the band, everything really.

Amy has moved to the bags she brought in with her and is lifting out what looks like dressing gowns. Three silk dressing gowns with 'Tara's Wedding' embroidered on them.

'Amy, they're gorgeous, where did you get them?'

'Online.' She then pulls out three pairs of fluffy slippers, one with 'Bride' and the other two pairs with 'Bridesmaids' stitched onto the front.

'Amy, you're too good to me, you shouldn't have.'

'I didn't.'

I look at her, waiting for an explanation.

'Your dad rang me and asked me to get something that would make getting ready at his house special.'

'What?' I swallow hard. *Don't feckin cry again, Tara.*

'Yes. He said your mam would have looked after all that for you, so he wanted to make sure it happened exactly as if she were there, the morning of the wedding.'

My heart is swelling. I turn to Lucas. 'Lucas, did you see what Dad did?'

He smiles, nods, then walks to me and kisses my head and I feel blessed, happy, the way I should be feeling the week before my wedding.

'Amy, thank you so much for arranging this for my dad.'

'Are you joking?' she says. 'I thought all my Christmases had come together. Shopping... and I didn't have to pay for it. I loved it. I'm actually thinking of going into business.'

'Well thank you anyway, Amy, you've been brilliant.'

Amy puts her hand out to ward away my inevitable embrace. 'Don't thank me yet, I'm only warming up,' she says, then proceeds to put the gowns and slippers back into their bags.

'Will we take them over now?' she offers.

'What? I'm not really in the humour of going there now.' I can see the disappointment in her face so I look to Lucas for guidance. I don't want to leave him again but soon I won't be able to go to my dad's. Lucas winks at me.

'Okay Amy, we'll go now.'

–

At long last I'm excited. I'm sitting in the car with Amy, talking through the last few bits and pieces that have to be done before the wedding and I can feel energy and enthusiasm bursting inside me. Amy does that for me. She's so excited about the wedding it brushes off on me regardless of my worries. This is going to be a great day. Nothing will get in the way of it.

We discuss the last-minute change that was made to the flowers after seeing the finished bridesmaids' dresses. Amy reckoned our original choice was too contrasting. We tried to guess who would be wearing what on the day. The fact that it was a winter wedding meant there'd probably be lots of fake fur and woolly dresses. Speeches were discussed and dreaded and we decided on a time for the buffet supper to be dished out. The hotel wanted ten o'clock but Amy told me to stand firm with eleven. Ten was too soon. People wouldn't be hungry yet, having had their main meal at five.

When we get to the junction at Glasnevin, Amy switches lanes and once again attracts the howling horn of some unsuspecting driver. I'm going to miss this. Amy, her dreadful driving. Her enthusiasm for life even though she invites death more than most.

'You're going to have to get real driving lessons, Amy.'

'Why? I'm doing grand. You're not dead yet, are ya?'

'I know, but I don't want you ending up in a wheelchair and not being able to visit me when I'm sunbathing on the beach with cocktails and champagne next year.'

'Don't worry, Tara. It would take a lot more than a wheelchair to stop me visiting. I might even stay for a year.'

'Really? Are you messing?'

'No, I thought about it. I might go over for a year. If they'll have me. Don't I have to get a visa or something?'

I'm so excited by what Amy is saying I'm forgetting to breathe. It would be like the icing on the cake if I thought she'd come out for a year. I'm nervous about being on my own. I know I have Lucas but it would be so much easier to settle if I thought Amy was going to be there too.

'Oh my God, Amy, don't say that and not mean it.'

'I do mean it. I might even get an Aussie of my own and stay.'

I take a deep breath, close my eyes and relax. Everything is going to be okay. Australia is going to be wonderful, even better than I imagined.

Another car beeps, disturbs my dreaming. Amy lifts her finger and I laugh.

'Please try and stay alive until you get there, Amy,' I say, thinking to myself: *and I'll try to stay out of prison*.

Chapter Thirty-Four

After a few hours with Amy I am feeling so much better. I return to the apartment positive and eager. I know I'm taking a risk but I've decided to tell Lucas about my secret, get it out into the open before he marries me and hope it doesn't drastically change his opinion of me. I feared it may be a little too heavy for him to carry but now I don't think so.

I'm pretty sure he'll understand. He has a "live and let live" approach to most scenarios so I'm hoping his open-minded attitude can stretch this far. What I'd really love him to say is that he'd have done the same in the circumstances but I can't expect that of him. Not everyone could have done what I did. What Faye helped me to do. But the man deserves to know one way or the other what kind of woman he's about to marry.

When I open the door to our apartment my brave plan is immediately shelved. This is not the right time. Leonard Cohen is moaning from the speakers and the smell of hash hitting me in the face makes me close my eyes, inhale and say, to hell with it. Cohen, hash, and candlelight. There is only one thing going to happen tonight.

I sit down beside Lucas on the floor, take the smouldering bundle from his fingers and watch the city lights stream into our apartment. Lucas has heard enough crap for one day. I'm not going to add to it tonight. This is our time together. Let there be no more interruptions. Lucas puts his arm around me and pulls me closer to him. The warmth of his body against mine melts the anxiety that has been building up inside me. I have been so scared since the body was discovered, I've been neglecting the one sure thing in my life. Lucas gently squeezes me, letting me know he has me. He cares about me. He loves me. Emotion surges through my body. I can feel us reconnecting.

We spend half the night making love, passionate, filthy, love.

–

When I woke this morning I was lying on the floor in the middle of the living room, covered in a throw that Lucas must have draped over my naked body before going to bed.

The sound of the city slowly cranks into action in the background. I sense the smile on my face and feel like the woman I always wanted to feel like. With my arms stretching out I watch the blue sky brightening in the distance and then I remember: I've got to go to the police station later today.

I can almost feel my body getting heavier at the mere thought of it. More questions. For a brief moment yesterday, I was able to forget about the investigation and concentrate on the wedding without feeling all doom and gloom but that's gone now. And probably won't return until those detectives leave me alone. Why are they being so persistent? Do they honestly think I had something to do with it? I wonder if they have spoken to Faye yet and if so, what she told them. Holding the throw around my body I go to where my phone is charging and check to see if there are any calls. I may have missed Faye when I put it on silent last night.

There's a couple of texts and WhatsApps but nothing from Faye. I really hope she makes contact today before I go to the station.

Andriu asked me not to tell the detectives he was staying at Horgan's Hotel. I've to pretend I don't know where he's staying and give them his phone number. He said he doesn't want detectives coming into the lobby and asking for him and I don't blame him. It's very intimidating; you feel like the whole world is looking at you thinking you've done something dreadfully wrong.

In the background, I hear Lucas's alarm buzzing. Still wrapped in the blanket, I hobble to the bedroom to take a shower. Lucas hasn't reacted to the alarm yet so I go over to his side and kiss him. His eyes flicker open. He smiles.

'Time to get up.' I press the alarm off before moving into the ensuite. When I drop the blanket onto the ground, I shiver. 'It's bloody freezing,' I say, stepping into the shower.

'Australia can't come soon enough,' Lucas shouts from the bedroom, cheering me, reminding me of what's in store. Heat, sun, beaches. No detectives.

When I'm ready to leave, I remind Lucas that I have to go to the station after work and because I'm not sure how long I'll be there I'll ring him when I get out. He's forgotten about my having to go to the police station already. I can tell by the way he stalls for a minute before commenting.

'Did you want me to go with you, Tara? I can leave work and… what station is it?'

'No Lucas, I don't want you there. It's bad enough I have to go and Sean the solicitor will be coming with me so you'd just be left waiting.'

'Okay, if you're sure.' Lucas walks over to me. I'm zipping up my jacket when he puts his arms around me and says, 'Don't let them bully you, Tara.' He squeezes me before letting go and I feel stronger all of a sudden. Like he's transmitted some of his confidence to me.

'I won't.'

'And don't let them lock you up before the wedding.' He laughs at his own humour before disappearing into the ensuite.

–

The air is crisp and cold when I leave the building to walk to work. With my scarf pulled up over my mouth, I walk down the quays tossing every possible question the detectives might ask me around in my head. I need to stay focused and not let them distract me from keeping my eye on the ball. There are things I cannot say, things they must not know. I will lie if I have to.

Muriel calls me into the back of the shop as soon as I arrive. She has some news for me; I can tell by the width of her eyes. It's not often I see her this excited so I'm expecting it to be good, or at the very least helpful in some way.

'She had her troubles.'

'What? Who?'

'Avril Ryan.'

I can't move quickly enough for Muriel so she grabs me by the arm and practically drags me closer to her. There's no one in the cafe and yet she's talking rapidly and low like she has some big secret she wants no one else to hear.

'I spoke to Eamon. Allegedly, Avril Ryan had been in trouble a few years before she disappeared. The brother wasn't able to tell him precisely what it was because he didn't know exactly – or at least he wasn't willing to tell Eamon if he did. What he did tell Eamon was that Avril had just gotten her life back to normal when she disappeared. Something to do with a very bad relationship she was in. The man took her for every penny she had. Stole her confidence as well as her future. The poor girl ended up having a nervous breakdown but dropped the charges against him for some reason. Then they think she got mixed up in drugs or something like that.'

Muriel sticks her head out to see if anyone is waiting at the counter before continuing. 'Of course, this was all said with a lot more emotion and sympathy than I'm telling you now. Eamon said the brother was in an awful state. The whole family were.'

I'm listening intently but I'm still at a loss as to how Muriel thinks this will help me.

'Well, don't you think…' She looks at me, waiting for me to be enlightened about something. Then she whispers, 'Do you think you might suggest to the detectives that it was maybe…' She checks once more no one has arrived before whispering, 'Maybe the poor girl took her own life, Tara. She had a history of mental health issues and…' She pauses, then turns away and walks out to the front of the shop saying, 'That's what Eamon found out anyway. I hope it's of use to you.'

I don't want to burst Muriel's bubble by telling her there was a large heavy steel lid that Avril would have had to close after she jumped into the ten foot pit, so I follow her out to the shop and thank her for finding out what she could for me.

Chapter Thirty-Five

Sean pushes on the door of the station and tells me once again not to be nervous, that this is all just procedure. I get some strength from making eye contact with his relaxed expression but not enough to unravel the knot in my stomach. He tells me to wait while he goes to the reception and announces who he is and who he's there to see. Then he nods at me to come with him through a door that someone clicks open for us.

On the way over, I told Sean what Muriel had said but he assured me it was not my responsibility to uncover the events that led to Avril Ryan's death. He said he'd see what he could find out if there was a court case but that rumours and scenarios would be rife in this situation. The best thing I could do was ignore anything I heard that didn't come from a reliable source. I didn't want to tell him I considered her brother a reliable source because that would make me look ungrateful. And I'm not ungrateful. I'm extremely grateful he's helping me.

Sean has been here before. He knows exactly where to go without any instructions. He leads me down a corridor, opens a door and next thing I know I'm sitting in front of a large desk with Sean beside me. Detective Lee and Detective Mullins stare across from the other side of the desk. There's a file open in front of them but I can't read any of it from where I'm sitting.

The room has no windows and is staggeringly bright. My body feels like it's on charge. Every inch of me is trembling. If I could bottle fear, I'd be filling a keg.

Detective Lee is the first to speak and when all the formal introductions are made, rules are explained and buttons are pressed. She asks me if I knew Avril Ryan. I look at Sean who nods the all clear for me to answer and I shake my head. I'm reminded I need to speak the words so I tell her that I don't know and I never knew Avril Ryan.

Detective Lee turns a page in her folder, appears to read something then rests both her arms on the table and says, 'Are you sure you didn't know Avril Ryan?'

I look at Sean again then back to the detective. 'No.'

'No you're not sure, or no you didn't know her?'

'I didn't know her.'

'If my client says she didn't know Avril Ryan she didn't know her,' Sean interrupts. He believes me. He already asked me all this.

'We have testimony that says you did know her.'

'What?'

My body sinks into itself. I want to run and yet I can't move. Who would say that? I feel the bright light dimming. I'm going to collapse. If the detectives believe I've been lying about knowing Avril Ryan, they're going to want to arrest me. At the very least, they're going to destroy my wedding to Lucas. He won't want to marry me if he thinks I've lied to him. I won't be able to move to Australia. I think I'm going to be sick.

Sean is talking in my ear, telling me to take deep breaths and hands me a glass of water.

'This isn't the truth, Sean,' I say. 'They're lying. I didn't know her. I never met her.' The air is barely reaching my lungs so I take deep breath after deep breath. 'Who told you that?' I direct my angry voice at the detective. 'Because they're lying.'

'Faye Connolly,' she says with a smile on her face like she's the cat that got the cream.

'Faye Connolly?' I can barely get the words out of my mouth. Why would Faye say that? What the hell is going on?

'Are you sure?' I say. 'Faye?'

'Yes.'

I turn to Sean, shaking my head, my eyes pleading for an explanation.

'I don't know why she'd say that, I didn't know her. I…' Tears are falling down my face and I hope this doesn't make me look guilty.

Sean turns his attention back to the detectives and asks if they have any evidence other than the word of some distant acquaintance. My body feels numb. What is Faye playing at? I need to speak to her. Behind the buzzing in my brain I hear Sean asking the detectives if they have a definite time of death because as things stand there isn't even any proof that I was living in the house at the time.

The room is getting stuffy. It feels like it's closing in on me. Detective Lee looks at the file in front of her. The last banking transaction made by Avril Ryan took place the day before she disappeared. The last phone call she made was that same day… to me. Lee lifts her eyes and looks at me when saying this. I look away. I've already told her I didn't receive that call. Then Lee says the day I got the call is the presumed date of death, as there was no activity from her after that day. I was living at Huntley at the time; no one is denying that.

Detective Lee's voice is drilling a hole in my brain. She continues to leave no reasonable doubt about the date of death. Sean is telling her that Avril Ryan could have been dumped there any time after she was killed. My head is spinning. The detective agrees and listens as Sean tells her that his client was not involved in the death of Avril Ryan. He suggests the detectives cease any contact with me unless they have some definitive proof that I was involved in Avril Ryan's death.

And that's when the detective drops the bomb.

Chapter Thirty-Six

Faye

It's been a bitch of a day. Barely time for a coffee between appointments. I've missed two calls from Tara so I guess the detective has been to see her. Maybe I shouldn't have done that but maybe she shouldn't have slept with Andriu.

Now I have to convince Tara that the detective misinterpreted what I said, because I need her to tell me where Andriu is staying. The phone rings, once, twice.

'Hello.'

'Tara, it's Faye. Sorry I missed your calls, I've been busy. How are you?'

'Did you tell that detective I knew Avril Ryan?'

She really is pissed off.

'God, Tara, relax there a minute, it wasn't like that.'

'What was it like, then? Either you told her or you didn't.'

I'm almost proud of Tara, she's not holding back. The girl seems to have grown a pair since I last met her. The, *yes Faye, no Faye, whatever you want Faye*, has been replaced with *what the fuck, Faye*.

'The detective asked me if I was sure you didn't know her and all I said was I couldn't answer that for sure. I didn't know if you knew her or not. I said it was quite possible you knew her from work or something and that's what I told the detective. I didn't say you knew her. I said I couldn't say for definite you didn't.'

'Well she seems to think you said I did know her.'

'Tara, I warned you about that. They'll twist things. They'll try to get you to say something you don't mean to say and then they'll rearrange the words. It's all about getting you to admit something. But sure, if you didn't know her you've nothing to worry about.'

There is silence at the end of the phone.

'Tara, are you still there?'

'It's not that simple, Faye.'

'What do you mean?'

'Avril Ryan called me. She made a bloody phone call to my phone. I didn't answer it but according to those detectives I'm the last call she made before disappearing.'

Now, I'm silent. Her words send a shiver through my body. This is not good. I take a deep breath and tell Tara not to worry because I need her to relax. I need her to tell me where Andriu is staying.

'Have they spoken to Andriu yet?' I say.

'Not that I know of. I'm meeting him Friday night so I'll find out then.'

'Where is he staying?' I say.

'Horgan's on the green.'

I finish the call, apologizing for the detective's misinterpretation of what I said and telling Tara not to let this ruin her wedding. I asked her how things were going and her voice seemed a bit lighter when she spoke about the wedding. But she's worried. I'm worried too; Tara was not the only one to be contacted by a stranger.

I think back to the anonymous text that I read on my phone the same day I discovered Andriu was not in love with me. The words in the text message frightened me.

They still frighten me because someone out there knew what I had done.

–

It was three years ago but I can remember it like it was yesterday. I was halfway through my shift at the hospital. A&E wasn't at full capacity but I'd been kept busy all morning. After telling an older lady in cubicle nine that she would have to stay with us for a couple of days to do some further tests, I left the area and went for a break to the coffee shop.

Unlike a lot of my student colleagues, I loved working in A&E. It operated in fifth gear all the time. No one knew what was going to come through the door and there were so many opportunities to learn something new.

The only thing I didn't like was the hours. Sometimes, after doing ten hours on the clock, I would have to stay overnight in the sleeping quarters to remain on call. If my shift fell at the weekend, I might not get to the bed until the early morning when it was almost time to go home. This was one of those shifts.

I went to the public café, Costa, at the entrance to the hospital because I wanted a decent cup of coffee – something the staff canteen found difficult to provide. It was either bitter or cold and the room itself was dull and sparse with hard chairs and metal tables. Unlike Costa, which had a bit of colour and comfort.

With my flat white in my hand, I noticed an empty table in the corner of the café and kept my head down while I walked towards it. I remember not wanting to meet anyone. I was in no mood to chat. It had been a hard few days since Tara's mam died and Andriu was in a strange mood which I couldn't figure out. And on top of all that, earlier that day, I'd watched a young man die from injuries he'd sustained in a traffic accident.

The hospital entrance area was full of people coming and going. All I wanted was a few minutes of peace to enjoy my coffee.

When I sat down at the table, I took my phone from my pocket, hoping to have some news from Andriu.

When I left that morning, he was lying in bed. I kissed him on the lips and he kissed me back. I told him I was on a twenty-four shift and I'd see him tomorrow. I also asked him to check in on Tara because she was so sad but he didn't say anything. He rolled over, turning away from me. I just presumed he was still half asleep. I walked out of the bedroom unaware of how my life would change when I walked back into it.

There was no message from Andriu on my phone. Just a missed call from Mam and a message from a number I didn't recognise. At first I got a bit of a shock when I read it.

I can destroy you.

I clicked on it to see if there was a name attached. Nothing. So I put the phone on the table and lifted the hot coffee to my lips. At first I thought the message must have been sent to the wrong number.

Then it dawned on me like a silent shadow creeping over my body and casting me into darkness. Someone knew what I had done. Someone was threatening me, attempting to blackmail me. I took the phone in my hand again, searching through my history to see if I could connect the number to a person I knew but I couldn't. I thought about dialing the number and was about to when Richard from the x-ray department sat down in front of me. He had a croissant hanging from his mouth and two cups of coffee in his hands. Richard mumbled something before placing the coffee down and taking the croissant from between his lips. A girl I hadn't met before, but whose nametag told me she was Cora, sat down beside him. She said something but I didn't hear her. All I could hear were muffled noises and my heart beating loud in my chest.

Somebody was threatening me. They knew I would be struck off if the truth got out. But who knew? Who would do that? Was it someone here at the hospital? Had someone somehow discovered what had happened?

I glanced around the space in front of me. Patients, visitors, doctors, nurses. It could be any one of them and was most likely none of them. I lifted the coffee to my lips once more and swallowed down half the cup in one go. I didn't know who had sent that text but I was pretty sure I was going to hear from them again very soon.

I didn't hear from them that day, or any other day. I waited, hour after hour, week after week, month after month. Over time, the anxiety of hearing my phone beep disappeared. But there was still a niggling fear at the back of my mind that whoever it was would show up at any time. Someone knew what I had done and they could destroy me.

Chapter Thirty-Seven

I'm sitting by a window, sipping tea from a small white cup dotted with little blue flowers. It arrived at my table on a saucer alongside a small pot and jug. The napkin is as big as a tablecloth, fresh, crisp and white. There's a scone on a plate with a separate little pot of jam and butter and a polished silver knife resting on the side.

Mam would be happy to see this. Her daughter sitting in a Queen Anne chair by the window of a luxurious hotel drinking tea and eating scones like posh people should. Thankfully, my appointment's schedule was very light for the day. I was able to move things around and leave the clinic early.

When I told her I was meeting an old friend in Horgan's Hotel her face lit up with hope for me. Mam loves to hear I'm getting out and meeting people. I know she thinks I should make a better effort to make new friends. She throws a subtle comment my way every now and then to that effect. But Mam doesn't know they're not worth it. Friends can betray you.

I told her it was someone I knew from my college days. According to Mam, Horgan's Hotel is well known for its afternoon tea and she has some lovely memories of meeting her sister there over the years before her sister passed away. Mam has no idea the old friend I'm planning to meet is Andriu. I don't want to tell her yet. I'll wait until we're back together because she might get upset after the way things finished between us.

I hope she'll be happy that I've found love again, because my father won't. He never liked Andriu. He thought he was punching above his weight, and he wasn't shy about sharing his feelings with Andriu. He questioned him so much about his past and his plans for the future and wanted to know so much about his family that Andriu eventually stopped coming to the house with me. He said it was like going for an interview with God.

I lean back in the comfortable chair. From my vantage point in the lobby, I can see who is arriving and leaving the hotel. I can also see the elevators, two large steel doors opening and closing every few minutes. Rich people walking in. Rich people walking out. If Andriu walks out through one of those doors, I plan to rush out and bump into him. If he arrives from the front door, I'll do the same. I'll say I was having tea with friends and was on my way out.

The excitement is buzzing inside me, but to a passer-by I look like a lovely young woman relaxing, enjoying a scone and a pretty little cup of tea, waiting on a friend to arrive.

I've decided not to drink alcohol this weekend. Andriu won't want me if I'm falling around drunk. I need to stay focused if I'm to lure him back into my life.

When the scone is gone and the last of the tea is drained from the pot, a young waiter comes over and asks me if I'm alright and if I need anything else. I tell him I'm fine, just waiting on a friend. I take my phone from my pocket pretending I've received a text and explain that my friend is delayed. I'm not sure he buys it but he tells me there's no problem and I can stay as long as I like. Then he clears the table. If I was anywhere else, I'd order another cup of tea but the last one cost me fourteen euros. Just for tea and a scone. I could get two double vodkas and Coke for that in the pub next door.

A group of four women have gathered at a table beside me, chatting and laughing and clearly enjoying one another's company. The woman who is the centre of attention moves her arms as much as her lips when she speaks and seems to have either just ditched her man or is reliving an old experience for the entertainment of her friends. She's making the whole thing sound like it was a laugh. I bet it wasn't a laugh. I bet she cried her eyes out when she realised her husband was being unfaithful.

It's making me angry listening to her reducing her pain to a funny anecdote to be shared with her friends over tiny sandwiches and tea. I'd love to tell her to shut up. I'm about to tell her to when the door of the lift opens stopping me and sending a rush of excitement soaring through me. Is that him? It looks like him. My breath buckles; am I looking at Andriu?

A tall man with dark hair and a leather jacket is stepping out of the elevator. He is looking downwards watching his step so I can't tell for certain, but it could be him. He's wearing jeans and a white T-shirt under the jacket. My heart is bouncing in my chest when I stand and rush out to the hallway. *Relax Faye, be cool.* An old woman is hobbling in through the entrance on a stick, forcing me to slow down and let her pass. I rush past her but when I get closer to the man in the leather jacket he lifts his head and my heart sinks. It's not Andriu.

—

I've been here for over three hours now and there's no sign of Andriu. The waiter has attended to me twice. He probably thought I'd been stood up as he asked if I wanted anything else to eat or drink but thankfully he seems to have gone on a break or finished his shift. I haven't seen his sympathetic smile in a while.

I consider asking for Andriu's room number at the reception desk but I'm not sure these posh places will give that sort of information out. Unless I pretend I'm a distressed relation with some bad news for him. Or maybe I could pretend to be the detective. There has to be some way of finding out his room number.

Eventually I come up with a reasonable plan that won't make me look like a fool or an imposter so I scan the lobby one last time before heading to the toilet where I take my phone in my hand and ring the hotel.

'I've a delivery for an Andriu Fitzpatrick, could you tell me what room he's staying in?' My heart is in my mouth. They might not believe me but it's worth a try.

'Sorry, can you repeat the name?' the voice at the far end says and suddenly I feel hopeful.

'Andriu Fitzpatrick.'

After a short pause I hear her voice again. 'No, sorry, there's no one staying here by that name.'

'Are you sure?'

'Positive. No Andriu Fitzpatrick. Is there a second guest in the room I could check?'

My mind is spinning. I want to tell her I don't know if there's a second guest. I know nothing about him anymore but I say nothing.

I hang up and look in the mirror where I watch the rage change the shape of my face. My eyes stare angrily, my lips tighten, my forehead shrinks. Tara Moore lied to me. She told me Andriu was staying at this hotel and he isn't. I've been sitting here all afternoon waiting to bump into him, hoping, planning what I'd say when I met him, imagining the look on his face when he saw me. Maybe he'd take me to his room or invite me to dinner later tonight and we'd end up making love and rekindling our relationship. Andriu would realise he was wrong to leave me. He'd realise that he still loves me and we would be together again. But he isn't here. Why did she do that to me?

Taking a deep breath, I gaze at the mirror. 'You won't get away with making a fool out of me again, Tara Moore.' My voice is low, angry, determined. I turn away from my image and walk out the door, through the lobby and out onto the busy street. If I hurry I'll be at her apartment in less than twenty minutes.

Chapter Thirty-Eight

I'm standing across from Tara's apartment building, my feet hurting from the constant pounding of streets in high-heeled boots.

My mother commented on how well I looked when she saw me leaving the house earlier. I was glad to hear the compliment. There are so few around at the minute.

Mam will see this as a sign that things are getting better. *Faye is beginning to look after herself, take pride in her appearance.* Mam doesn't know I'm contriving to meet the love of my life. The man Tara Moore robbed me of.

My hair is tied in a loose ponytail pulled to one side and hanging down over my shoulder. It's all the rage. As is the two-tone colour. The red I dyed my hair earlier in the year has grown out and is now only visible on the bottom half of my hair but it looks deliberate, it looks cool. I think Andriu will like it. He always said I had a funky way with fashion. That was before I could afford to buy new clothes whenever I wanted. I had to make things look their best, adding a bow here or a belt there and it helped that Tara and I wore the same size. We could borrow one another's clothes. Like sisters but without the rows. My own sister never shared her clothes with me. I remember borrowing a denim shirt once from her wardrobe to go to a party and she threw a fit when she found out, resulting in her locking her bedroom door every time she left. Like I was some sort of thief. She need not have worried. There was nothing else in there that interested me.

Having make-up on my face all day feels heavy, like I'm wearing a mask because I don't usually wear make-up at the clinic. The black jacket covering my silver, silk shirt, looks effortless over my tight grey jeans but none of this is stalking gear. I'm freezing, standing here in the dark looking up at a cascade of balconies jutting out from this tall, boring-looking building and wondering which one is hers. Which balcony does Tara Moore drink her coffee on in the morning? Which balcony does she fuck her boyfriend on at night?

The lights are beginning to flicker on in quite a few of these boxes. People are arriving home from their comfortable offices, with their communal toilets and brightly coloured chill-out areas. The apartment block is in the middle of a hub of major financial companies so I imagine the rent is pretty high. Tara's boyfriend is probably paying for it.

I'll have to make my move soon. I'll have to confront her. I wonder what she'd look like dangling from one of those balconies.

Pulling my jacket across my chest does little to keep the cold out. I make my way across the road where I pass the pub on the corner of the building and get motivated by the smell of beer oozing out from the doorway. *Not yet Faye. Not yet.*

There are five entrances that I can see to this apartment block but I remember the one Tara stood outside in the photo when she was bragging about her 'moving in' on Facebook. Block B was written above the entrance door in big red letters. It angered me to think of her lording it up in her penthouse suite with some man while I had been reduced to my single bed in my parents' house in Howth. How did that happen? Why did she get all the luck?

I push on the door of the building as I answer my own question aloud. 'She took it, Faye, she just took it.' Then I stare at the letterbox wall inside the foyer with about a hundred different letterboxes and names and wonder where to begin.

A thought suddenly enters my head. What if her name isn't on any of them? Just the name of her wonderful Australian boyfriend who she thinks she's marrying next week? What the hell was his name?

I scan the names and numbers and I finally come across Tara's name. She's staying in apartment 431. She's on the fourth floor. I hope she's alone.

I look at the first name on the box. Lucas Jones. If he's with her, I'll have to abandon my plan and just play nice. I'll say I was passing and thought I'd pop in to see how she's doing. She might wonder how I know she lives here but I'll tell her I asked at the coffee shop.

The elevator door is about to close when someone pushes on the entrance door and two girls rush in out of the cold. They're a lot more prepared for the weather than I am. Hats, scarves, gloves. A strong smell of perfume fills the small space as one of the girls presses the button that I was just about to. Fourth floor.

The lift moves. My heart begins to thump. I'm nervous and excited all at once. It's about time I confronted her. After all I did for Tara Moore. She's about to find out how ungrateful I am that she spoiled my future by sleeping with my one true love, Andriu.

The elevator opens and the two women step out in front of me. I'm tracing the direction of the apartment numbers when I notice them knocking on a door further down. They're visitors too. Visitors with prosecco.

'Tara, yahoo, only one week to go!' Their hands are waving in the air and they disappear behind the door.

Blood is pulsing in my neck. That was close.

The heat in the building is making me sweat. I am wiping it from the back of my neck when the second elevator door opens and out walks a tall, handsome, blond-haired man in a pair of jeans and a big parka jacket. He's noticed me looking lost.

'You looking for someone?' he says, in a full-blown Australian accent. That must be him. Tara's fiancé. I can't find my voice. So I shake my head, my eyes glued to his gleaming smile as he nods then walks towards their apartment.

Shit. Lucas Jones has seen me. He didn't seem to recognise me, though. Which is good. Tara has probably never shown him any photos of me with her. Her life before Lucas Jones is well buried along with all its secrets. Or so she thinks. I could stop him, call him back and say, 'Do you know what your wife-to-be did?'

Chapter Thirty-Nine

Then

To the rest of the world it's just another Saturday night. To me, it's the night I'm about to witness Tara Moore help her mother leave this world. I'm nervous. I've done as much research as possible but I have no experience in this field. I would much rather be listening to Lana Del Ray on stage at Electric Picnic but I promised Tara I would be by her side to help in any way possible. As well as being completely devastated to be saying goodbye to her mother tonight, Tara is also nervous because even with a potion of relaxants to prevent her mother throwing up the Nembutal, there could be complications that could lead to a lot of pain.

When we first researched the process, Tara didn't want me involved. She thought it was too big an ask. Besides the damage it could do to my career if we were found out, the emotional weight would be a heavy burden to carry. I told her I was going in with my eyes wide open and I could look after myself. That it would be far too dangerous to implement the procedure without medical experience on hand to help if needed. I told her she had to think of her mam. Eventually she agreed it would be safer for her mother to have me here, just in case I was needed to bring her emergency relief. Tara will be the one to inject the morphine if things go badly but under my direct instruction. Tara's afraid if she is found out and it was discovered that I was here, I'll be implicated and my career would come to an end. But I'm already implicated. I know about it and I'm about to let it happen. I'm hoping we don't get caught.

Squeezing Tara's hand, I take a deep breath and lead her into the room where her mother is waiting. I'm immediately struck by how calm Roisin is and how beautiful and relaxed the room feels. I didn't know what to expect. Fear, maybe tears, but Tara's mam smiles at me and immediately I feel at ease. Roisin looks younger than she did last week when we sat by her bed discussing the final plan. I smile back at her, realising it's not that she looks younger; it's that she looks peaceful. Roisin is at peace with her decision.

To my left the silver-grey curtains are open. It was still bright when we arrived home from the festival but now the darkness is closing in, casting an evening shadow across the room onto Roisin's bed.

At the far side of the bed, Tara's dad is sitting, a broken man holding his wife's hand. He looks up at me briefly and nods. I can tell he's glad to see me here. I might not be fully qualified but I'm the closest thing he has to a medical expert and I'm glad to be able to ease his fears. I wish I could ease his pain. It's leaking out through every pore in his body. The man looks about ten years older than he did last month. It's clear this is all too much for him. But he's here, by his wife's side when she needs him most.

Last week, when finalising the plans, we went through every possible scenario. I had researched the dosage needed and the consequences of something going wrong. I played no part in securing the Nembutal. That was all Tara's doing and I was pretty impressed she actually managed to get it.

Roisin wanted a few candles and a Beatles CD playing low in the background. The wall facing the bed is a maze of Roisin's past.

A photo of a very young Tara hangs beside a photo of Roisin and Niall on their wedding day. There are other old black and white photographs – Roisin's own parents and family, I presume. I'm not about to ask.

Among the scattered memorabilia are tickets to gigs, holiday photos, pieces of ornaments, a football jersey, a pair of ballet pumps, a sheet of music and a menu from some restaurant. A whole life pinned to a wall. I cast my eye over the evidence of Roisin's existence and I wonder what my wall will look like. Will I have a wedding photo? Will Andriu be in it?

For the past few days Roisin lay in this bed amongst her past and now she is about to say goodbye to it. I can tell by her relaxed gaze, her stillness, her comforting eyes, that she is not afraid. Roisin is ready. Tara is trembling with fear.

'It will be okay, Tara,' I whisper in her ear, gently squeezing her arm. She needs to know that what she is about to do is right. That I'm with her. Her father is with her. And most of all, her mother needs her to do this.

Tara is shaking. A dose of tablets rattle in the plastic cup as she hands it to her mother. Roisin takes the cup from her and with Tara's help, lifts it to her mouth. She swallows the pills down with some water.

Then Tara prepares the Nembutal. I'm watching over her, making sure she's doing it right. Cloaking her with confidence. Her face is white. I try to imagine what it must be like to give someone you love the one thing you don't want to give them. How strong that love must be. But it's impossible to imagine without a true understanding. Without wearing Tara's shoes.

I am in awe of my friend, her strength, her composure. The fact that she isn't crying or begging her mother to change her mind. This is one single moment in time. No past. No future belongs here.

When the dosage is ready I move away from the bed to a chair against the wall. I am just an observer. This is not my mother. This is not my pain and yet I can feel it seeping into me, tugging at my heart, teasing my strength. Don't cry, I say to myself. Don't spoil it for Roisin.

When Tara hands her mother the cup, the final dose, 'Sergeant Pepper's Lonely Hearts Club Band' starts playing from the speakers, hoping we enjoy the show. I'm thinking 'Let It Be' or 'Hey Jude Don't Be Afraid' might be more appropriate but no one else is blinking an eye at it. Maybe they can't even hear it. Or maybe it's exactly what Roisin wants.

–

Then we wait. Tara's dad clutching one hand, Tara stroking the other. Nothing is said. Nothing needs to be said. The love, the loss, the sadness and the gratitude is so intense I can almost touch it.

It takes less than an hour before the last breath heaves its way out of Roisin's lungs and with it, relief. Everything has gone to plan. There was no vomiting, no pain. No excruciating release. Roisin smiled, then closed her eyes.

Tara kisses her mother's forehead, tears rolling gently from her eyes. I'm almost paralysed with sadness for her but this was the plan. It's what Roisin had insisted on.

Nobody is to be in the room when the nurse arrives the next morning to find her. Roisin wants it to appear like she has done it all herself. That no one else was involved.

I walk over to Tara's side and wrap my arms around her, coaxing her away. Tara lets go of her mother's hand for the last time.

Chapter Forty

I'm leaning against the cold steel, the number 431 pressed against my face. I'm listening to the fun unfold behind this large wooden door when my phone vibrates in my pocket. It's Mam, I know it is. No one else ever calls anymore. Not even my brother, because apparently he's fed up listening to my sarcastic bullshit. When I'm ready to talk like a normal person, he says, he'll speak to me. Huh, normal. What's normal?

Ignoring the phone, I walk away from the door and back to the elevator. I'm pressing the button for the ground floor when it occurs to me that Andriu might arrive at the apartment for drinks. Tara said she was meeting him in a pub later but I know now she says a lot of things that aren't true. Like when she told me Andriu was staying in Horgan's Hotel. Now I don't know whether to believe her. Still, my mind indulges in the possibility that I could bump into him at any minute.

The excitement lifts my mood. I check my reflection in the silver panel of the elevator door and remember my mother's words. *You look lovely, Faye*. Which reminds me: I'd better ring her back. She'll be worried. I told her I'd be home for dinner. Chicken arrabbiata no doubt. It's the same every Friday. I happened to mention that I liked it when we were in a restaurant once, long before all this crap started, and my mother remembered.

Mam had never cooked Italian before then, except for maybe spaghetti bolognese or heating a pizza. But when I had to move back in to the house, she found a recipe in some Jamie Oliver book and now she cooks chicken arrabbiata for me every week. I think she's trying to tell me she loves me without using words.

I step out of the elevator, my feet no longer sore. I'm looking all around the hallway but Andriu isn't here. With my flimsy jacket pulled once more across my chest, I leave the building and walk to the far side of the street. The only thing I can do now is wait. Then I will follow them to whatever pub they go to. I will definitely bump into Andriu if I do that.

I wonder what he looks like now. Has he still got that silly hairstyle where the top is twice as long as the rest of his hair and drops down over his face like a black mantilla? His sideways grin always made me blush when it was accompanied by a subtle wink. That meant he was thinking about the love we had made the night before. Or the love he planned to be making that same night once we had left whoever's company we were stuck with.

Andriu was always in T-shirts and jeans. Even when going to work, which surprised me because he was management. But he said suits and ties were for old people and his company didn't insist on them. They were up and coming, more like Google.

I remember buying him a shirt and tie once, hoping he'd wear them to my Christmas party at the hospital but he didn't.

The only time I saw him in a suit and tie was when his father died and he looked really handsome in it. I remember him standing at the doorway explaining once again that he didn't want me to go to the funeral with him because I had exams coming up. I wanted to go. I wanted to meet his family. I had only ever heard stories about them – his sisters, his mom, his older brother who lived in the States. I wanted to be there to comfort Andriu when he succumbed to the loss. He hadn't cried since hearing about his father's sudden death, trying to stay strong for everyone else, but I knew when it came to the church and the graveyard he would be devastated. He would need me to hold him… but no. He insisted he'd be okay and refused to take me away from my studies.

My exams were still a few weeks away but Andriu was thoughtful like that. He wanted me to do my best. Taking a deep breath, I let the icy air travel deep into my lungs and blow out a white cloud of smoke. I wonder if Andriu will wink at me tonight?

The phone beeps, dragging me out of the trance I've fallen into. It's Mam again. This time I answer. I tell her that I'm doing great. I'm having a lovely time with my friend. I hold my hand over the phone briefly and pretend to be laughing with someone before telling her I have to go and that I'll be home later. She stutters, which means she's nervous. Mam doesn't know whether to believe me or not. I try to reassure her that everything is fine and ask her to leave my dinner in the microwave in case I'm still hungry when I get home. I know she won't relax now until the key turns in the lock. Mam treats me just like she did before I left home to go to college. She forgets I'm a woman of the world now. That I can look after myself. There's nothing I can do to ease her anxiety. I have to live my life. I have to wait for Andriu.

Over an hour has passed and I'm still standing here. With the river Liffey flowing behind me, I lean against the wall. It would be so easy to lean back and fall in if I wanted to. I don't want to though. I want to meet Andriu.

It's difficult to hear the water moving because of the noisy traffic but when there's a lull and I concentrate I can hear it. It's rhythm. The sound of the earth breathing.

Another hour passes. The cold air doesn't seem to bother me so much anymore but the lights flashing on the premises opposite do. Reilly's Bar. I really could do with a drink… but what if I miss him? What if Andriu arrives when I'm in there? I take one last glance over at the entrance to the apartment block where I see no new activity, then I step away from the Liffey wall.

I'll have one. Just the one.

Chapter Forty-One

Tara

'Will you miss us?'

Emily is half drunk and we're not even in the pub yet. She and Amy have polished off a bottle of prosecco and now they're opening a second bottle.

It was Amy's idea to meet here at my apartment before we went to the pub. She said it might be our last opportunity to say goodbye to the place where we spent so much time laughing, crying, solving the problems of the world, while sitting on the balcony drinking gin. I wanted to say no, but I couldn't because I knew she was right. We did spend a lot of time on that balcony watching people passing by and making some very inappropriate comments about them. It's just that I've lost a lot of the romance for this place in the last few weeks with all that's going on. It's hard to convince yourself you're going to miss a place you can't wait to leave.

When Lucas found out the girls were meeting at the apartment, he decided to invite his best man, Ronan, and two other mates from work who are coming to the wedding. It's like a mini wedding rehearsal. Only I'm not at all in the humour for any of it. I'm scared after what that detective said at the station when she dropped a bomb on my world. I couldn't believe she mentioned the site. I had to be clever and act dumb. My bag of secrets was in her hand and she was pulling on the zip. I can only hope she doesn't get it open.

I'll have to try and put my worries to the back of my mind for now and make an effort to enjoy myself because it's almost time to go to the pub and I don't want to leave Andriu sitting in Reilly's on his own. I could have asked him to join us here at the apartment for the pre drinks, but then the rest of the gang might never leave and I don't want that. I'm afraid I might get too drunk and blurt something out about what happened at the police station.

I have to stay focused until I speak to Andriu. Thankfully nobody has noticed I'm only sipping my drink or they'd be asking questions. I need to talk to Andriu about what the detective mentioned with a clear head. I'm hoping he can remember something of use and my best chance of getting to speak to him on his own, without everyone else listening to the conversation, is in the pub.

'Of course I'll miss you,' I say putting my arm around Emily. 'I'll miss you every day and I'll particularly miss you when I see prosecco.'

Emily laughs. 'And I'll miss you,' she says. 'And I'll particularly miss you when I run out of prosecco.' She lifts her glass in the air. I lift mine and we clink glasses.

'To Mr and Mrs Jones,' she says.

Lucas is taking three more cans of beer out of the fridge and he sees me looking at him. 'We'll go after this,' he says, handing the cans to Ronan and the two mates whose names I can't remember.

Amy is busy chatting to the taller guy. The one with the charming smile and designer clothes. She's giving him the attention she doles out only when she's very interested in a man. Her eyes are all dopey and fixed on his. She's nodding in agreement with his every word. I wish she'd say something and mention his name; I don't want to have to ask Lucas what it is again. He'll think I'm losing it and I wouldn't blame him. I've been so jumpy and nervous these past few days.

Lucas thinks it's because the wedding is a week away that I'm so anxious but it's not that. In fact, I wish the wedding was today and I was jetting off tomorrow. Leaving this place before the detectives discover anything else.

If we had gone with the original date, October, this wouldn't be happening now. I'd be dodging kangaroos instead of the police. But the band that Lucas wanted wasn't available, and as he had no other requests, letting me pick everything I wanted from the hotel to the meal to the service, I couldn't really disappoint him. So we changed it to November. One month later. I thought it wouldn't make any difference. How wrong was I?

The body hadn't been discovered in October. I'd never have heard of Avril Ryan on the far side of the world. And if the police did try to contact me through the Australian police, they probably would have just called me up to ask me if I knew anything. I would have said no, I'd never heard of the woman and that would have been the end of it. But here I am. One month and I'm in a completely different situation.

I'm feeling very nervous since Detective Lee asked me about the 'Cabhrui' website. I played dumb. I had to. My heart was in my mouth and I think I lost at least a year off my life with the shock I got. I hope I disguised it well.

My mind has been tortured ever since she mentioned it. I wanted to ask her what the site had to do with Avril Ryan but I was afraid that would make me look interested and she might pick up on that and think I was hiding something. Sean did ask, though, and the detective said they came across some information on Avril Ryan's hard drive that suggested she might be involved with the site.

I think Sean noticed a chip in my façade because when we left the station he reminded me it was important I hid nothing from him. He needed all the facts if he was going to help me. I told him he had all the facts. I had never met Avril Ryan. Which I believed to be true.

But now I'm not so sure. The more I think about it, Avril Ryan must have had something to do with that website or the detective wouldn't have mentioned it in the interview.

I didn't tell Sean the 'Cabhrui' website the detective mentioned was where I illegally sourced the Nembutal for my mam's death three years ago.

Chapter Forty-Two

It took another half hour before we packed into the elevator and left for the pub. The smell of alcohol in the confines of the small space did not go unnoticed by the couple who were waiting to get into the elevator after us. One of the women was just short of holding her nose. Her face shrivelled up when the door opened and the waft of beer hit her.

'Sorry,' Lucas said with a grin on his face as he stepped out. He put his arm around my shoulders and we walked out the door.

Lucas has been really busy this week wrapping up at his office. He had to stay late most nights which didn't bother me. I was busy with the last minute stuff for the wedding and I had to rearrange some of the seating arrangements when we got a final attendance number. I was glad I had something to keep me busy because when the middle of the night came and I lay in the darkness of the bedroom, the heat from Lucas's body radiating into mine, my mind took off in search of its own adventure. Exaggerating every possible scenario including, would you believe, what I would study if I did end up in prison.

This could go on for hours well into the morning trying to piece together the jigsaw from the few pieces of information the detectives had given me. Why did Avril Ryan ring me? What had she to do with 'Cabhrui'?

The only thing I can come up with is that she actually ran the site. Avril Ryan may have been the person who sold me the cocktail of drugs for my mother.

I didn't see enough of the woman to identify her. It was all very brief, a clandestine mission that Andriu drove me to.

I first made contact with the website on my mam's laptop because she wanted nothing to connect back to me. I didn't know what I was looking for so Faye helped me. Both of us sat at Mam's kitchen table staring at the screen like we were shopping for clothes. The consequence of what we were searching for didn't dawn on us in that moment. We even laughed when we thought we might be making progress and would end up on some obscure site of no relevance. Dad wasn't in the house at the time, which was just as well because he wouldn't have been any benefit to us. He crumbled at the mere mention of anything to do with my mam's request. I wouldn't even ask for a lift to pick up the package. Thankfully, Andriu was insured on Faye's car. Faye was able to tell me what drugs to google and possible online communities that might support our mission. It took a lot of hours searching before we came across the 'Cabhrui' website. It was very vague and didn't directly say it supplied Nembutal. But it mentioned it, so we made a simple enquiry. Immediately the connection was erased and further communication took place over a burner phone that the seller said would be destroyed as soon as the transaction was completed. To my eyes, the seller was just words on a screen; there was no name, sex or nationality mentioned. The seller, however, needed my mother's information to ensure the case was legit and that she was terminally ill. I don't know how they checked that out. Maybe they worked for one of the terminally ill support groups or in the health board offices. I didn't ask. I didn't need to know.

It took over a month after the initial contact before I found myself standing outside the library on the far side of the city, taking a small bag from a female wearing dark glasses. She wore a coat with a big furry collar that hid most of her face, even though it was really warm out. The transaction was brief. I thanked her and she thanked me, saying that what I was doing for my mother was a great thing.

When I got into the car, I could see her doing a double take. Even through the dark glasses I could tell she was staring at the car. The woman was not at all happy that I had somebody with me. I didn't recall being instructed to come alone – maybe I was supposed to have copped on to that part by myself but I didn't drive, there was no direct bus and it was much too far to walk. I turned my head away from her stare and asked Andriu to drive on.

Could it have been Avril Ryan? The question sits uneasily with me. If so, why did she ring me on the day she disappeared? Did she want an update on how things had gone for my mam? I can't suggest that to the detectives or they'll know I broke the law. I'll be charged. I won't get to live in Australia with Lucas and the sunshine and barbecued everything.

'I hope it's a bit warmer next week,' Amy says, pushing on the door of Reilly's pub. 'If not, we're going to freeze.'

'We'll be on the dance floor by this time,' Emily says, hurrying in after her.

The pub is busy when we get inside, the lights dim, the music not too loud. We get a spot big enough to accommodate us all in the corner. I glance around to see if Andriu has arrived yet but I don't see him.

Lucas takes everyone's order and waves down a young waitress who's walking past us. He's telling her what we want when I feel a hand landing on my shoulder. I turn and look up to find Andriu standing there.

'Jesus, that's creepy,' I say, jumping up to hug him. 'Were you hiding?' Then I turn and introduce him to everyone. Andriu is wearing the same clothes he was wearing the other day. Jeans, T-shirt and a leather jacket.

Immediately I notice Amy's eyes locking onto his good looks. She pulls a stool out from under the table and asks him if he wants to sit there.

'No,' I say, louder than I mean to. 'He's sitting here, beside me, we have a lot of catching up to do.' Then I pull up a stool beside me and Andriu sits down. When Lucas has finished giving the young waitress the order he stands up and puts his hand out, forcing Andriu to do the same. 'So, you're the famous Andriu,' he says.

'And you're the famous Lucas. Congrats on landing such a dinger.' He shakes Lucas's hand.

'Thanks, I think so.'

I can't put my finger on it but I don't think Lucas likes Andriu. He's not fully smiling. Lucas is holding back, staring at him a bit longer than is necessary. Maybe Lucas thinks we were an item once upon a time. That Andriu bedded his woman. Men can be like that, threatened and territorial. Lucas should know he has nothing to worry about.

By this stage Amy has reverted to plan A and is now practically sitting on Lucas's friend's knee, who I discover is named Ryan. Emily is deep in conversation with Barry and Lucas has turned away and is recounting some bad joke for Ronan, the best man. I hope it's not a speech rehearsal.

With everyone in deep conversation, I turn my stool slightly away from them to get a more direct one-on-one with Andriu.

'Nice guy,' he says, meaning Lucas.

'Yeah he'll do grand, for a few years anyway.' I laugh at my own joke, lifting my glass to swallow some gin.

'Has he money?'

'Andriu, don't be so rude.'

'Well has he or hasn't he? I'd hate to think of you arriving in Australia and discovering you had to skin crocodiles for a living.' Andriu lifts his pint of Guinness, breaking the seal on the white collar as he swallows. Then he licks the frothy moustache from his lips. An image of Faye brushing her finger over his mouth jumps into my mind and suddenly I feel sad. What really happened between them? They were so good for one another. I want to ask Andriu but if I go down that road I may never get to the subject I really want to ask him about.

'Did you hear from the detectives yet?' I say, staring at him from above the rim of my glass as I take another sip of my drink.

'Yes, actually, they called me on the phone. Thanks, by the way, for not mentioning where I was staying.'

'And?'

'They asked me if I knew the woman. I said no. Then they asked if you knew her. I said I didn't know but I'd never heard you mention her name, or Faye for that matter.'

'Did they want to meet you?'

'They said they may need to contact me again, but…'

'But what…?'

Andriu puts his pint down and rests his hands on his knees. He looks up at the ceiling briefly before saying, 'Tara. Do you think Faye could have something to do with it?'

'What?' Why the hell is he bringing that up again?

'It's just… ah, nothing.' Andriu lifts his pint and swallows a large gulp of Guinness.

'No. Not nothing. Why did you say that, Andriu?' I don't like where this is going. Is Andriu suggesting Faye killed that woman? Because if he is… Faye was wonderful, Faye was kind, Faye would never hurt anyone. Could she really have changed that much? My heart is beating fast and I'm praying he gets to explain himself before someone interrupts us.

'I shouldn't say it, I know, but it seemed to me like she was going a bit crazy, Tara. And it seemed to get worse after that night, the night when you left the festival to be somewhere more important.' Andriu leans in closer to me. 'Did something happen that I don't know about?'

My heart is racing. Why is he bringing up that night? Does he know something? Did the detective mention the 'Cabhrui' website to him too? I don't know what he's suggesting but I need to find out.

Lucas stands up. 'Same again?'

Ryan interrupts him. 'No, this is my shout, Lucas, you got the last one.' Ryan moves away, leaving Amy with no one to chat to. She turns her attention to me and Andriu but I give her such a look she knows to back off.

'No, nothing that I can think of.' I look away from Andriu and stare at the ice melting in the glass in front of me. Was I wrong to expect my friend to assist me? To sit there and watch me administer a lethal dose to my mother while she waited with a vial of morphine in case something went wrong? Oh God, what did I do? I lift the glass and down the rest of my drink in an attempt to slow down the panic rising in me. And then I think, but she's a doctor, she knew what she was doing, she offered to help.

'Andriu, why do you think Faye could have something to do with the murder? Do you think she killed the woman? Faye could never do that. For God's sake, Andriu.'

He notices the disbelief and anger creeping into my voice and decides to back off. 'Forget I said anything, Tara. I'm sorry. I shouldn't have said that about Faye.'

'No you shouldn't.'

'Look, there's no point opening old wounds. You don't know what was going on between us back then. How crazy she'd become. She accused me of sleeping with you, for God's sake.'

'What? Why would she think I slept with you?'

Baffled by Andriu's comment, I remember the night she tossed Andriu out of Huntley Lodge, her words flying angrily throughout the house. Andriu had been unfaithful. That much I could make out. My heart was bleeding for her and when I heard her shout that she could trust no one anymore, I wanted to run up the stairs and hug her, tell her she had me. That she would always be able to trust me. But I was puking into the sink at the time and I didn't think it right to interfere. I thought the next day would be better when she'd calmed down. I would talk to her then, remind her she could trust me. That we would always have each other. But when the following day arrived, Faye never mentioned the row. Or Andriu. Or anything that happened the previous night. She just left.

Christ, after all she did for me, I really hope she doesn't think I slept with Andriu. But I'm confused as to why she would think that? What would even put that idea into her head?

Chapter Forty-Three

My conversation with Andriu ends abruptly when Emily pulls her stool over beside him. They both seem very familiar with one another. I want to join in and laugh and pretend I'm enjoying myself, but what Andriu said about Faye is worrying the hell out of me. I really hope I get a chance to tell her I did not sleep with her boyfriend. I would never do anything to hurt her. I pull my seat back to make room, because Emily is almost sitting on Andriu's knee. If Faye thought I had betrayed her, it would explain why she left so abruptly and never returned any of my calls. But why didn't she confront me? I know she never bought into forgiveness. Faye was a 'one strike and you're out' kind of girl but this was me. Tara. Her best friend. Why was she so quick to believe it without even giving me my chance in the dock?

Pushing her blonde hair off her face, Emily leans forward, smiling, and tells Andriu it's lovely to meet him again. She asks him all the right questions, about his job, how long he is in Dublin for, whether his hotel is nice... All the questions I should have asked him but the truth is, I wasn't interested in the answers to those questions.

The only thing I'm interested in finding out from Andriu is what he knows about the Avril Ryan investigation. What did the police say to him and has he any idea what Avril Ryan was doing in Huntley Lodge? Everything else he has to say seems surplus to my curiosity. He made light of what the detectives asked him which leads me to believe he isn't worried about them. Not like me. I'm worried sick. I think I'm the one they're focusing on.

We've been here for hours now and everyone is at their loudest, vying to be heard over the laughter and music. Lucas is looking at me from the far end of the table. His eyes are glossed over from too much beer. He mimes a kiss in my direction and I send him one back. He's the only thing keeping me sane at the moment.

Amy is currently tapping her fingers on Ryan's leg for some reason. He seems to be as interested in her as she is in him. Maybe they'll become an item and Amy won't want to move to Australia next year. I was delighted when she suggested she might come over but now I'm not as fearful of being on my own over there. I might even prefer it.

Ronan is up at the bar trying to get a last order out of the barman before we're all turfed out. I'm pretty sure it was Andriu's turn to buy a round but he didn't offer. He's chatting away to Emily now and Emily is doubled over in laughter at something he has said.

I feel like I'm unable to fully enjoy myself. Andriu has added to my worries instead of easing them. What he said about Faye is freaking me out. But what if he's right and Faye was unstable at the time? Could she really have thought I slept with Andriu? Was I so engrossed in my own grief that I didn't notice Faye was crumbling too?

I can't think about that now. Not here. Not in the company of all these wonderful, cheery people who are just out to enjoy themselves. I need to relax and emotionally join the company. Laugh a bit. The show must go on.

These are my friends. The people who'll be celebrating my wedding with me next week. I hope.

In a couple of months, I'll be longing to be in a crowded noisy pub with these people. Thinking back to all those carefree days that we spent together. All the fun I had with Amy and Emily and… I wish Faye was here.

Three gin and tonics are lined up in front of me on the table. I'm way behind everyone else so I lift a bottle of tonic and pour it in on top of a gin, then I swallow the whole drink in one go. The noise seems to fade to the background as I take the next drink over and sit beside Lucas. Lucas puts his arm around me.

'This time next week, Tara, this time next week.' His words bring a smile to my face. This time next week I'll be Mrs Jones. Dancing amongst my friends and family in a beautiful white dress. My dad will be dancing beside me, his awkward moves making me laugh. He'll smile even though he's sad. But he'll also be happy, because I'll be happy.

'Would you take my grave as quick?' Ronan says, placing the last round of drinks down on the table.

'I would if it was as comfortable,' I say.

Lucas pulls me onto his lap but Ronan insists I have his stool and goes searching for another one. I'm sitting down when my eyes are drawn to Andriu at the far end of the group. Emily is still talking away to him but he's looking towards the front of the pub. I look over to see what's so interesting. A woman in a black jacket and grey jeans is walking out the door. I didn't get to see her face. Maybe he thinks he knows her. She's gone now.

I bring my attention back to Ronan and ask him if he's all ready to make his speech next week. I hint at him that I'm hoping the speeches are short, they can be so long-winded.

An hour later and we're standing outside the door of the pub waiting on a taxi for Emily and Amy. Everyone has had enough and I'm thankful that no one suggested returning to the apartment.

The lads decide to walk home because it's only two roads behind the pub. When they've parted, Emily and Amy get into a taxi, screeching with excitement in anticipation of next week's wedding.

Andriu says goodbye and walks off in the opposite direction. He's excited to be going to the wedding and feels less of an outsider now that he has met some of the guests. I get the feeling he's looking forward to meeting Emily again. They got on a lot better than Emily's boyfriend would approve of. Andriu told me to get in touch if the cops get in contact again but that I shouldn't worry too much.

Tiredness is swimming through my body, shutting down each section as it passes through. I can't wait to fall into bed.

Lucas is dying to pee, hopping from foot to foot when we get into the elevator. When the door opens, he rushes down the corridor and fumbles with the key before he darts into the apartment.

I follow, entering the familiar space with a heavy heart. I'm marrying this wonderful man next week. I need to tell him why I'm so worried about the investigation. What I'm afraid will come to light before the detectives are finished with me.

'That was a great night,' Lucas says when he comes out of the toilet. He takes his jacket off and flings it onto the sofa. There is still some pizza left in one of the boxes from earlier on. Lucas takes a slice and shoves it in his mouth cold. 'Your friend seems to be a bit of a scrooge,' he mumbles through a mouthful of food. 'I noticed he didn't offer to buy a drink all night.'

I knew he didn't like Andriu. Lucas never has a bad word to say about anyone even when they deserve it. He's always, 'Ah, give the man a break.' Or 'Sure, you don't know what they're going through.' Sometimes I think he should be writing quotes for Instagram.

I yawn, my mouth opening wide, dragging in as much energy as it can fit. Then I cry. Unplanned tears stream down my face. I no longer have the power to keep them locked away.

'What's wrong?' Lucas says, his voice filled with worry. 'Did something happen, Tara? Are you okay?'

He hurries over to where I'm standing at the patio door. The city is twinkling through the glass. I'm looking up at the dark sky, at the lonely moon looking back at me.

'Tara.' Lucas puts his hand on my cheek and turns my face to his. 'Tell me, what's wrong?'

I sniffle, then wipe my nose with my hand. I'm about to rub my eyes when Lucas wipes them for me.

'This can't go on Tara… you're going to have to talk to me.'

I look into his eyes, his deep blue eyes, and nod. My mouth is bone dry. The tears have dried me up, or was it the gin? I gather spit with my tongue, swish it round my mouth and speak.

'There's something I have to tell you, Lucas.'

I walk away towards the kitchen area. I'm going to need a strong coffee to get through this.

Chapter Forty-Four

Then

My father hasn't spoken in over an hour. He just sits by the side of the bed, ashen-faced, listening to Mam. He runs his hand through his hair every now and then as if massaging his brain, trying to understand what she is saying.

When Mam has stopped talking, she puts her hand out for him to hold. He leans forward and with both hands, he grips her hand tightly.

'Are you sure this is what you want?' he says. But he knows it is. I know it is. Mam has spent many a night and day lying here, just lying here in this same bed unable to move, thinking about it.

It's as clear as the water that flows down Daylight mountain. Mam has absolutely no doubt in her mind. She wants to die. She wants us to help her leave peacefully before the disease gets a chance to drag her from this world screaming and crying.

I listen to her words like I'm sitting watching a performance. Her thin lips move with more precision than they have in some time. Her eyes seem void of emotion. It's as if she has rehearsed this speech so often in her head, its contents no longer affect her.

She speaks about the facts, the menu of pain that lies in front of her and the awkward disrobing of her dignity.

She leaves no reasonable doubt as to why she should revisit her decision. Since day one she has educated herself on everything she could expect from her diagnosis and while it has been hard up to now, the hardest bit lies ahead. She has searched and found no reason to allow it to occur. The disease has taken enough from her and she does not want it to take her last wish. Her decision is final, and she hopes we can allow her that. Mam also hopes we will help her.

Afraid to move my eyes from her face, look at my father or see Mam's frail body lying there, I sit paralysed in the chair. Then her hand, resting on top of the covers, opens and reaches out to me. I look at it. The thin bony hand. It makes me nervous but I put my hand in hers and she squeezes it with the little strength she has left.

I lean in closer to my mam, turning her hand over until I am squeezing it. I take a deep breath and in that moment I move from being my mother's daughter to being my mother's saviour.

'Of course I'll help you, Mam.'

I don't question her decision. It is her decision. I know this has to go as smoothly as possible for my mother's sake. For all our sakes.

I tell her I know a few people in the medical world. Faye immediately springs to mind. I can trust Faye. She would want me to trust her, but I will tell her not to get involved, just to point me in the right direction because what I am about to do is illegal.

Exactly how this is going to play out isn't decided by the time I leave the room, but I promise my mother I will do what I can for her. I will make it happen.

I'm doing my best to stay calm but on the inside everything is shaking. My legs are barely able to hold me up. I step out of what has now become Mam's downstairs bedroom because she can no longer walk upstairs. Then I fall to the ground.

I'm lying here, unable to move, howling silently. My mouth is open, my body is screaming but I cannot let her hear me. I have to absorb as much of her pain as possible. Tears burn every inch of my face as I plead with God to stop time from passing.

My father eventually comes out of the room and nods at me to join him in the kitchen. His red face appears to have swelled up from all the crying and it's hard to focus on his eyes because the pain is so heavy behind them.

'We have to do it,' he says.

'I know.'

The words screech out of my mouth. I fall forward into my dad's arms. We sit there, hugging, crying. I want to ask him what he thinks. But his opinion doesn't matter, my opinion doesn't matter – not even God's opinion matters now.

When the last sigh of weakness leaves my body I replace it with a plea for strength. The strength I am going to need to see this through.

Chapter Forty-Five

Lucas is watching me from the far side of the small table. I'm sitting cross-legged on the ground. There is silence between us. The mug of coffee sits untouched on the table in front of me. I'm not sure if Lucas realizes I've finished talking, or if he just can't find the words to express how he feels. His face is partly shadowed by the single light-bulb glowing in the corner of the room. I want to get up to fetch some water but I need him to say something. I want to know if he still loves me. Does he still want to marry me?

'I'm sorry Lucas. I should have told you before now.' My voice is low, weighed down by sadness. I lift my hand and reach for the mug but the coffee is cold now. I've been talking a long time.

'Do you want a fresh one?' Lucas says, stretching his arms out when he stands up from the sofa. It's late now. Lucas is tired. I'm tired. The clock in the kitchen is out of sight but I'm guessing it must be after three in the morning.

'No, I could do with a glass of water.'

What feels like a cold breeze passes over my body. My teeth chatter. I wrap my arms around myself and turn around to check the patio door is closed. It is. It must be my nerves. It's been a few minutes since I finished telling Lucas my secret and he still hasn't commented. Is he finding it hard to digest? Maybe I shouldn't have told him at all but I couldn't go through with the wedding knowing I was keeping something this big from him. At first I thought I could. That I could keep it locked away but I understand now that it will never leave me. No matter how hard I try to forget about it something will bring it back to life. I have to learn to live with it. It's part of me. Part of who I am and Lucas needs to know that. If I'm going to be spending the rest of my life with this man I need to be able to talk about this whenever I need to. Lucas probably thinks it's a bit much landing this on him now. Right before the wedding. Gosh I wish he'd say something. Anything. *Just speak Lucas.*

He walks over to my side with the glass of water and puts it down in front of me. Then Lucas returns to the sofa. He leans forward and stares at me. My heart is thumping in my chest and my hand trembles when I lift the glass. The cold water sends another shiver through my body but I swallow it all in one go. The thirst returns as soon as I'm done.

'I think you were very brave,' Lucas says. I shuffle forward on the floor, closer to the table, closer to Lucas. I'm nodding, I want him to say more. He looks up, rubs his hand down his face before smiling at me.

'You should have told me before now. I can't believe you've been carrying that around with you all this time. Christ Tara, we're about to get married. You have to know you can lean on me.'

'I know Lucas, I'm sorry, I was going to tell you but every time something would get in the way and...' Looking away from Lucas's stare, I start to cry.

'Don't cry Tara.' He says, moving off the sofa to my side. Lucas puts his arms around me and I sob. The relief is overwhelming. I have told Lucas what I have done and he has responded by putting his arms around me. My eyes slowly close. I'm clinging to his embrace when I hear the words.

'Would you do it for me?' Lucas whispers. I lift my head and look him in the eye. 'I'd do anything for you Lucas.'

'Well that's good to know.'

A few more minutes pass with Lucas holding me tight before he suggests we go to bed. It's been a long day. My body is tired. I'll fall asleep right here in his arms if I don't move now. Just to get from the living room floor to the bedroom takes a lot of effort. I eventually stop yawning when my head hits the pillow. Lucas wraps his body around me and I'm about to drift off when my eyes open wide. Clutching his arms close to me I say.

'Would you do it for me?'

Lucas hugs me. His words melt my heart as he whispers in my car.

'I'd do anything for you Tara.'

Chapter Forty-Six

Faye

My feet have gone numb. My body is shivering from the cold but I have to wait here. I have to meet Andriu. This could be my only chance before he goes back to London. He needs to know that I have forgiven him, that I still love him.

The four vodkas – at least I think it was four – have worn off now. But I had to drink them. I found it hard to watch the two of them, sitting together, talking, Tara turning her chair so she could have Andriu all to herself. I wonder what they spoke about. Was I even mentioned? Were they planning another rendezvous? A last fling before the wedding?

I'm lucky the pub was full, or I would not have been able to stay there and spy on them. At one point, I thought Andriu might have recognised me. His glance hovered on me for a minute. Our eyes met but I quickly turned away and stood up and left. I couldn't risk bumping into him in front of her. I want to talk to him alone.

The phone buzzes in my pocket. My mam is doing my head in. I can't answer it because Andriu is in my sights now. He's walking towards the next bridge. I quicken my step, my freezing hands holding my jacket closed over my chest as I shuffle in these cursed high heels. I cross over the road and follow him along the Liffey wall.

'Andriu,' I call out but he doesn't hear me. So I move quicker. I'm almost running. I am running. 'Andriu!' Why can't he hear me? Is he wearing headphones?

'Andriu!' I'm just a few feet away when he turns and stares at me in silence. 'It *is* you… It's me, Faye.'

'What are you doing here?' he says.

My smile fades. My heart slows. Andriu does not look happy to see me. If anything, he looks the opposite.

'I saw you from across the street and I couldn't believe it was you. I thought you were in London. What are you doing here?' I say, doing my best to sound cool while every part of me is ticking like a time bomb.

'Faye, I don't really want to talk to you,' he says, shaking his head like I was the one who broke his heart.

'But Andriu, can't we just talk? I need to talk to you.'

Andriu turns around saying, 'Leave it be, Faye.' Then he walks away.

What will I do? I can't just leave it be. Why won't he talk to me? I follow him.

'But Andriu, listen to me, please, just for a minute.'

He stops and my heart kicks back into overdrive; he's going to talk to me. Andriu turns around.

'Okay, one minute.'

One minute, what will I say? I should have rehearsed this but in my head I imagined Andriu would be delighted to see me. That he'd want to talk all night long. We would discuss everything and make plans for getting back together. I did not expect this response. What will I say?

'Andriu, I just want you to know that I forgive you.'

'Okay,' he says and turns back around. He's walking away. What is wrong with him? Tara must have poisoned his mind. I rush forward and grab his arm.

'Andriu, I still love you, I never stopped loving you…'

He puts his hand on mine, his touch a bolt of lightning shooting up my arm. But then he pulls my hand away.

'Go home, Faye.'

'But Andriu please, I—'

'Go home, Faye. You need help,' he says.

'But Andriu, hear me out, please.'

Andriu stops. He turns and walks towards me.

'I'm sorry, Andriu, I shouldn't have flown off the handle that night. I shouldn't have asked you to leave. I miss you, Andriu. If I could go back, I'd do things differently.'

'Sorry Faye, but that was a long time ago. I've moved on and you should too. I pity you, you know.'

I don't normally accept sympathy easily, in fact I hate it. It makes me feel like a loser, a failure. It's another way of saying, *I'm glad I'm not you*, but from Andriu, I'll accept any form of attention. Even if it's tainted with a hint of malice.

'I tried, Andriu. I tried to move on but I couldn't get you out of my thoughts.'

I lower my head shyly and lift my eyes to look at him. He steps forward and moves his face closer to me. For a moment I can feel excitement rushing to my head. Is he going to kiss me?

'Were you following me?' he says. His boozy breath lands on my face.

'No, I just saw you across the street and…' Shit. Andriu must realise it was me he recognised sitting up at the bar. He'll think I'm crazy.

'You need to go home, love, or wherever you should be. You should not be here.'

He said *love*, Andriu said *love*. My heart is swelling; it's going to burst. A flurry of heat shoots through my body. I'd better do what he says.

'But can we meet before you go back to London?' I say, hopeful now as he knows I still love him and that I'm still available.

'Sure,' he nods. His eyes stare through me. It's like he's trying to figure me out. I wish he'd ask me to come back to his hotel with him. Maybe I'll suggest it.

'I'm freezing here, Andriu,' I say, my teeth chattering. 'Is your hotel nearby?'

'I think it's best if you go home, Faye. It's not safe around here. Are you still on the same number?' So he remembers my number – or at the very least didn't delete it.

'Yes.'

'Okay, go home, I'll catch up with you before I go back.'

I let him go. Leaving me feeling a lot happier. I would have loved to go back to his hotel. To make love all through the night. But I should have known Andriu wouldn't take advantage of me. He's not like that. He cares about me. All I need is time to rekindle his love for me. To remind him how great a couple we were. Then we'll get back together.

Taking the phone from my pocket, I notice I've missed about five calls from Mam. I open the phone and text her that I'm on my way. Then I look back and watch Andriu's handsome shape fade into the dark night.

Chapter Forty-Seven

The following morning I'm feeling excited and motivated and I even chance a tune in the shower. I haven't heard my own singing voice in a long time. I put on a pair of jeans and a bright yellow T-shirt then I plaster cream on my face. My skin has dried up a lot lately. I need to take better care of it. When I get to the kitchen, Mam and Dad are sitting at the table. Mam jumps up and asks me if I would like sausages but her voice sounds nervous. She's wearing a navy skirt and white shirt with a navy trim. Her hair is perfectly set.

Mam always likes to look her best even first thing in the morning when she's frying sausages. I say yes to the sausages but a sense of dread is growing inside me. I sit down at the table and wait for the bad news. I know it's coming because my father hasn't said anything yet and that's how he usually starts delivering his bad news, by saying nothing.

'What's wrong?' I say.

My mother turns her attention to the frying pan and I look at my father. I hadn't noticed how much he's aged until now. His silver-grey hair is now snow white. His eyelids droop a little heavier over his eyes. He looks away from his paper and sighs.

Mam is silently buttering bread at the countertop. The poor woman gets into as much trouble as I do. I bet my father gave out to her last night, telling her not to cover for me.

'Were you drinking last night?'

'I just had one drink, Dad.'

My father turns his attention back to the paper. It's his way of saying *you're not fooling me. I've heard your bullshit before*. He will never forgive me for losing my driving license.

Mam turns to look at me and mimes, *do you want some tea?* I smile at her and nod. For the next while, no one will say anything. Eggshells will not be broken. My father will decide when normality can return but, until then, Mam and I will sit and eat and be grateful. I wish I didn't have to stay here. It's ridiculous being treated like a kid again. I can't wait until I get my own place.

–

I'm sitting in my bedroom with nothing to do but daydream. I wonder when Andriu will ring. I wonder when I can go to London to be with him. I wonder what our kids will look like. I have a strange energy boiling inside me, a sense of needing to do something. I can't just stay here in my room while Andriu is floating around the city, probably with nothing to do. He might welcome some company.

I dial the number I have for him in my phone but it's no longer in use. I could ring Tara. She must have his number. But I don't want to talk to Tara; she might ask more questions about the dead woman and I can't go there. Not now, not when I'm feeling so positive. I'll text her instead.

Within ten minutes she sends me Andriu's number and without planning what to say I dial it. My heart leaps when he answers.

'Andriu, it's Faye.'

'Faye, what are you doing ringing me?'

'I thought you might like some company. Do you want to meet for a coffee?' I'm holding my breath, praying that he'll say yes.

'You shouldn't be calling me.'

'But?'

'Faye, I don't want to meet you. I don't want you calling me, either.'

'But Andriu, I thought…' I can feel the pain like a knife ripping a hole in my heart.

Why is he being so mean? I thought he understood. I thought…

'Is it Tara?' I say.

'Tara? What are you talking about?'

'Do you love her?'

'Sweet Jesus, Faye, where does your madness end? Of course I don't love Tara. Tara is getting married.'

'But you stayed in touch with her, you slept with her.'

'What are you talking about? When did I sleep with her?'

'That night, when I was at work, when you were both drinking.' Why is he acting so clueless? 'When we had the big row… I asked you to leave and…'

'I never slept with Tara Moore. When I said I was sorry I slept with her I didn't mean Tara, I meant Emily. It was Emily I slept with the night before I left. But no. You wouldn't listen to me. You just kept shouting and screaming and throwing things and when you said Tara's name you went completely mad. I couldn't quieten you down to explain you had it wrong so I just ran out of the place while I still could. Is that why you hung her out to dry, Faye?'

'What?' My hand is shaking so badly I can barely keep the phone up to my ear to hear him continue.

'You told the detective that Tara knew Avril Ryan. Did you kill Avril Ryan, Faye? Is that why you told the detective that? Is that why you've gone mad? You can't live with yourself.'

There are no words to describe how I feel. I have been wrong all along. How could I have believed that about Tara? But Andriu must have known I would think he was talking about Tara. She was lying on the sofa when I came home that day, conked out, half-dressed. They had both been drinking. I saw the empty glasses. The box of condoms on his bedside cabinet. No one mentioned Emily. What has this man done to me?

And now he thinks I killed Avril Ryan. He thinks I'm mad. Andriu doesn't love me. Did he ever love me?

'No,' I whisper before ending the call.

I drop my head onto the pillow. What the hell is going on? Why did Andriu ask me if I killed Avril Ryan? Is it because I lied to the detective about Tara knowing Avril Ryan? Does he think I'm trying to shift the blame to her?

Fear washes over me, bigger than the fear that has been washing over me for years. It's heavier. To lift it, I'm going to have to be stronger.

I sit up on the bed and let reality sink in. Andriu Fitzpatrick does not love me. He might even hate me. He will tell people I killed Avril Ryan. He will tell the cops.

I can't let that happen.

Chapter Forty-Eight

Tara

I'm watching the commuters get off the bus at the 22a stop for the last time. They'll do it again tomorrow, but I won't be here to see them. My journey is changing course. This is my final day working for Muriel in the café and while I'm sad to be leaving because I'll miss Muriel – she has always been very good to me – I'm also happy. Happy to be moving on to new exciting things.

Telling Lucas about my mam's passing has helped me see more clearly. We spent most of the day yesterday just lying around, talking, spending time on our own. Lucas assured me I had done the right thing, and though I didn't need his reassurance and never doubted my decision, it was nice to hear.

I don't know why I delayed telling him and maybe if it hadn't been for the discovery of Avril Ryan's body at Huntley Lodge bringing it all up again, I wouldn't have. But I'm glad I did. It's over now. Lucas has seen the darkest side of me and he still loves me.

The worry of Avril Ryan being associated with the 'Cabhrui' website hangs heavy in my mind. Lucas and I talked about it. We searched Google for the website to see if there were any clues but we couldn't find anything. It was gone. We googled Avril Ryan but there was nothing new that I didn't already know. Lucas advised me to push it out of my head and enjoy the week ahead. I told him I'd try, and I will try, but it's hard, especially when Andriu suggested Faye might have been involved. Was he serious or just thinking out loud? Trying to get his own head around the events of that week when Faye threw him out of Huntley Lodge.

I refuse to believe that Faye would hurt anyone. It would be so out of character for the Faye I knew and loved for all those years. But I am surprised she told the detectives I may have known Avril Ryan. Is she trying to shift attention away from herself?

Here I go again, trying to figure it out. I need to let go, if only for a couple of days to concentrate on the wedding. Then I'll be leaving and this nightmare will soon be a distant memory. At least I hope so because this could really mess things up.

-

I've a to-do list as long as my arm to get through and the first thing on that list is my dad. So today I'm calling in to see him after work to make sure he has everything he needs to walk me up the aisle and that the house is ready to receive the bridal party. I'll give the place a once-over, make sure the bedroom that we're getting prepared in is clean and ready and that he's removed all those empty suitcases and boxes from the landing that I asked him to.

I look down the quays and see big black clouds approaching in the distance. The river is full of energy this morning, flowing at a great pace. The air is damp and I'm adding to my list of things to do, in my head, when I see her image. Avril Ryan. Her face is on the front page of the newspaper being read by a man who's leaning against a barber's shop door. My heart sinks. Something has happened. Some new information must have come to light if her picture is on the front of the newspaper again. I want to go over to the man, grab the paper and see what's going on but I can't do that.

The nearest newsagent is one street down to my right. I take the first turn I come to and rush down the laneway to the store. Inside, I walk over to the newspaper stand and lift the paper with Avril Ryan's face on the front of it. Her hazel-green eyes are staring at me from the page. I never realized how beautiful she was before. I'd been so obsessed with not getting dragged into the whole mess that I never paid much attention to the woman who was killed. What she must have gone through. And why did she end up at the bottom of that pit? How does her family survive knowing their sister, their daughter, their niece has been killed? God knows how many people's lives were turned upside down when Avril went missing, and now they must go through this fresh, ruthless pain. This grief that removes all the hope from their hearts of ever seeing Avril alive again.

I take the newspaper in my hand and a feeling of guilt washes over me. I don't know why but it's as though I believe deep down that somehow I have something to do with this woman's death. Have I? For a brief moment I imagine everyone in the shop is looking at me, thinking I am responsible for her murder, which is stupid because no one is looking at me. No one is looking at anyone.

I pay the cashier and leave the shop. If Lucas could see me now he'd say I wasn't doing a very good job of pushing the investigation to one side and concentrating on the wedding. But I have to find out what's new. Have they arrested somebody? Have they discovered some new information? Can I stop worrying about this now?

The answer is no. I can't. The police haven't arrested a suspect. They are making a fresh appeal for information. Asking the public to come forward if they can remember anything, no matter how small. My eyes are glued to the words on the page as I also try to navigate my way down the road without walking under a car. After a few lines, the paper directs me to page ten. Which is what I intend doing but when I turn the page I bump into a buggy coming from the opposite direction. The pain shoots down my leg.

'Sorry, sorry,' I say to the girl pushing the buggy and bend down to rub my knee.

'Watch where you're going, for fuck's sake,' she says, pulling the buggy away from me before walking on past. For a split second I want to cry. I feel so vulnerable. Why was she so mean to me? It was clearly an accident. But then I think, *feck her* and walk on towards the café. Reading while walking is proving dangerous so I shove the paper into my bag. I'll finish the article when I get to work.

Sorry You're Leaving Us. The banner is the width of the café, hanging above the service area in silver and blue. My mouth is open with surprise and delight. I can't believe this. Muriel is playing 'The Wedding March' music on her phone and Helen, the new girl who's taking my place, sings along with it. Dah dah da-dah. They're both standing behind the counter with great big smiles on their faces. Imelda and Anna from the beauticians on the corner are standing to my right clapping. Noel from the travel agent's is also here and Sean. Sean is clapping too. I can't believe this. All this for me.

'Oh my God. Thank you so much, I don't believe this,' I say and suddenly I feel tears rolling from my eyes. But they're not tears of sadness, these are tears of joy, happiness, appreciation. These people love me, they care about me. What the hell am I doing moving to Australia?

Muriel walks out from behind the counter and hands me a small package wrapped in wedding paper with a card attached.

'A few of the regulars made a collection, Tara. They wanted you to have this to thank you for all your smiles over the years. You've been a wonderful part of the café and we're all going to miss you.' Muriel is choking up. Her eyes glisten with tears.

'You shouldn't have… but thank you so much,' I say, grateful. I know I'm experiencing one of those moments when you realise how lucky you are. I am lucky to have known these people, to have served them coffee. I'm experiencing a moment that will soon become a scene from my past. One I will always recall with a smile.

'Well, open it,' Muriel says.

I rip the paper off to reveal a mug in a box. *Dublin's Best Waitress: Tara* is painted on the front of it. I laugh. I love it.

'Look inside it,' Imelda says.

When I pull the mug from the box I see a wad of notes tucked inside and I'm rendered speechless. I was not expecting anything like this. There must be a few hundred euros there.

'It's your tip,' Sean says, and everyone laughs.

'A well-deserved tip,' Muriel says.

–

I hug everyone before they leave the café and thank them at least a hundred times. There are loads of 'best of luck' wishes and 'stay in touch' comments. I'm giddy with happiness and heartbroken with sadness at the same time. Mostly, I'm blown away by their kindness. I was not expecting that. I can't wait to ring Lucas and tell him what they did for me. I'm moving up a gear now. I can't wait for the wedding.

I'm still thanking Muriel when she hands me a coffee and tells me to take my time. I go out to the back of the shop and hang up my coat for the last time. I'm taking my bag from the floor when the newspaper falls out. It opens on page ten.

Avril Ryan was thirty-four years of age when she mysteriously disappeared. Her body was found at the bottom of a disused slurry pit at Huntley Lodge. It mentions the 'Cabhrui' website for the first time and says the police are only interested in information about Avril Ryan and are not interested in pursuing any other avenues with regard to services provided by the site.

My breath buckles, my eyes open wide and I read it again. Does that mean they're not going to arrest anyone who used the services of the website? That's what it sounds like to me. If that's the case, I have nothing to worry about. I'm free. This is great.

I continue down the paragraph and read about her life. I already know a lot of the information on the page from social media. She was single. She had a love for dogs and took care of her elderly neighbour.

What I didn't know was that Avril Ryan was a keen chess player. It took a minute for this to sink in. I had to read through the section a second time to make sure I read it correctly. Avril Ryan is a chess player. My dad is a chess player. Could he have known her? It's not like every second person you meet plays chess, especially at club level, so it is possible. They might even be from the same club. In the background I hear some laughter and a lot of voices. The café is getting busy and Muriel will expect me to finish my break. I roll up the newspaper and shove it into the pocket of my jacket. I catch my image in the small wicker framed mirror that hangs on the back of the door. My face is pale. I rub my hands on my cheeks and take a deep breath to slow down my racing heart. It's like I can't get a break. What do I do about Dad? I'll have to ask him if he knew Avril Ryan but what will that mean if he does? The detectives will want to talk to him if they find out the man who did all the maintenance at Huntley Lodge knew Avril Ryan. So I sure as hell won't be mentioning it to them but I do want to know if he knew her.

'Tara,' Muriel calls out to me, breaking my train of thought. I move away from the mirror. I close my eyes briefly and beg God that Dad never heard of Avril Ryan. I don't think I could handle what that would do to my paranoid head.

Chapter Forty-Nine

Sean is sitting behind his desk when I walk into his office. The cuffs on his crisp white shirt stick out below the sleeves of his light blue suit as he signs the paper in front of him. He has skin like satin that any woman would be jealous of. Sean, as always, looks like he's stepped out of a magazine. His partner Flynn is just as handsome but hails from a different tribe altogether. He's a bricklayer who works for a company that builds bespoke mansions. He's been to the coffee shop a couple of times with Sean, his work clothes covered in the dust of someone else's dream as he tucks into a double helping of the house special cheese and bacon toastie.

'Tara, you wanted to see me. Come in,' he says, moving out from behind his desk and pulling a chair out for me to sit on. Sean sits beside me on a dark wooden chair that screams designer. I messaged him earlier to see if he had a few spare minutes to talk to me. I don't know what to do about what I found out in the paper, about the cops not pursuing users of the 'Cabhrui' website.

'Have you seen this?' I say, handing the paper to Sean and pointing at the relevant section. Sean reads it while I inhale the mild woody scent of his aftershave.

When he finishes, he leans back in his chair and scrunches up his face briefly before saying, 'So, you do know something about this website.'

My face is reddening. I can't see it but I can feel the heat flushing over me. I'm so embarrassed I didn't tell him when he asked me after we left the station the other night.

'Sean, I'm sorry. I got such a shock when the detective mentioned the website that I couldn't think straight but the thing is…'

Sean leans forward, his elbows resting on his thighs. He's looking intensely at me, waiting for me to continue, to explain myself.

'Sean what would you say if I told you I did use the services of the "Cabhrui" website?'

'I would say don't mention it to the detectives. It's up to them to find that information out. Don't go handing it to them.'

'But it says they're not going to pursue any charges if—'

Sean interrupts me. 'Tara, this is a trap.'

I nod, hoping he'll elaborate.

'If Avril Ryan was a facilitator for this website, they may be going on the assumption that she was blackmailing somebody who used it or someone was blackmailing her. It might be fine for other people to come forward and say they used the site, but Tara, I would not advise you to.'

I'm getting nervous, feeling weak; this is all very frightening. Why not me? I grip my hands together to stop them shaking.

'You were, remember, one of the people living in Huntley Lodge at the time of her disappearance. You were the last person Avril Ryan tried to contact. Your number was on her phone. Don't put fuel on the fire. Don't mention the website. If they discover it some other way, we will deal with that then but for now say nothing.'

I'm taken aback by this advice. So I ask him. 'But what if they find out the truth and discover I lied?'

'That won't make any difference to the facts, Tara. This is about managing the truth. Not lying.'

I don't know what to think. I have to do what Sean is saying because he's the one who knows how it all works but it seems so wrong. I thought that if I told them, they might leave me alone. Avril's unanswered phone call to me could be explained. But Sean is right. If blackmail was involved it wouldn't look good for me.

I'm trying to think if I have anything else to ask him when a sudden bolt of dread flashes through me. Faye. Could Avril Ryan have been blackmailing Faye?

'Are you alright, Tara, what's going through your head?'

'Nothing... It's just...' I don't know whether to mention this to Sean but if I keep holding back on him he's not going to be impressed.

'Well, my friend Faye, she helped me, she's a doctor. Maybe...'

'Maybe what, Tara? Avril Ryan was blackmailing Faye?'

I nod to let him know that's what I was thinking. Sean stands up.

'Tara, that is your friend's problem and I don't mean to sound callous here but I represent you. My job is to give you the best advice that I can and for now I'm telling you not to give that information to the detectives. You'll be out of here in a few weeks, Tara, don't give them a reason to delay your leaving.'

My teeth chatter. I rub my hands up and down my arms trying to warm them as an icy wave shivers through my body. My mind is a mess, full of too many thoughts. Thankfully, Sean is able to direct me. If it wasn't for him,

I would surely have fallen into the trap and added to their list of reasons for suspecting me.

'Did you find out any more about what Muriel said, about Avril Ryan being harassed, the trouble she had in her past? Do you think the detective knows about that?' I say, lifting my bag from the floor and making to leave. I know how busy this man is. People come and go from this office all day long. I serve coffee to half of them.

'Again, not your problem, Tara, but I'm pretty sure the detective knows all about that. The family would have told them. Now, rumour has it you have a wedding to get ready for.' Sean smiles and sits down behind his desk.

I thank Sean before walking out of his office even more confused than I was when I walked in. The old wooden stairs creak as I make my way downstairs and out through the door onto the busy street. I'm trying to push my fears out of my head but now I can't help thinking about what Andriu said about Faye. How she had become weird. Asking if I thought she could be involved in the murder. Andriu must know something about Faye that I don't. Something that made him leave. I need to talk to him to try to make sense of this.

It's okay for Sean to say that Faye is not my problem. He doesn't know that she is. I was the one who dragged Faye into all this. I gave her name as the support medical person that would assist me. The suppliers of the Nembutal insisted I had medical expertise with me in case something went wrong. I shouldn't have been so abrupt with Faye on the phone when she called me last week but I was annoyed she had told the detective I knew Avril Ryan.

I push open the door of the café for what I sincerely hope will be the last time ever.

The moment of happiness that embraced me this morning seems so far away now. My mind is bending with endless scenarios and Faye is not the only one I'm worried about. I've yet to ask my dad if he knew Avril Ryan.

Chapter Fifty

Dad is standing with his back to me on the porch polishing the letterbox. He has headphones in his ears so he doesn't hear me calling him while I walk up the pathway. He jumps when I tap him on the shoulder.

'Jesus,' he says, 'you frightened the life out of me.' He leans in and kisses me on the cheek, taking the polish and cloth with him as he pushes the door fully open.

When I step inside the house, his hard work becomes apparent. There's a beautiful fresh smell of vanilla and everything is gleaming.

'Gosh, Dad, you've been hard at it. The place looks great.'

The hallstand, usually covered in letters and crap, is completely cleared and there's a candle burning in a glass ornament in the centre of it. I can tell the doors have been washed down because the usual scuff marks around the handles are nowhere to be seen. The kitchen is also spotless when I step inside. The smell of disinfectant saturates the air making me cough briefly. I hate that smell.

When I see a vase of flowers at the centre of the table, I begin to question what's going on. My father never bought flowers in his life. Even for Valentine's Day. He always bought my mam perfume or chocolates, saying flowers were a waste of money.

So what is this? Is there someone else involved, a woman maybe? I'm about to jokingly ask but before I get a chance to say anything he walks over to the vase in the middle of the kitchen table and tells me that Mrs Higgins from two doors down sent the bouquet to brighten the place up for the wedding. I'm biding my time before asking him if he knew Avril Ryan because I want to sound casual rather than jumping straight in like I'm working for the prosecution.

'She mustn't have had any faith in me,' he says.

'Well you've certainly done a good job, Dad, thanks.'

'More cards have arrived.' Dad takes a bundle from the table and hands them to me. I put them in my bag to open with Lucas later. Then I make my way upstairs to admire the great job he has done cleaning the bedroom that the bridesmaids and I will be getting ready in on Saturday morning. Amy and Emily will be arriving here at seven for breakfast and bubbles before the hairdresser arrives. The make-up girl is booked in for eleven. I hope she has time to do the three of us before the car arrives at one.

The dresses are hanging from the wall, where I left them. Taking a deep breath, I unzip the bag covering my dress and hold it open to look inside. My heart lifts with joy. It really is beautiful. My hand glides over the white lace and I feel a twinge of pain in my heart. I miss Mam. I wish she was here now. She'd love the dress. I know she would.

'Do you need me to do anything else?' Dad says.

'No, everything looks perfect.'

Before going back downstairs, I check the second bathroom to make sure he waved his magic wand over that and I am not disappointed.

'And your suit?' I say.

'Hanging up, ready to go. The only thing left for me to do is prepare my speech which I'll have a go at later. You won't be wanting anything too long?' he says, following me down the stairs.

'God no, just a few words Dad, and as I said before, only if you want to.'

Back in the kitchen, I'm checking the list on my iPhone, making sure I'm leaving nothing out when out of the blue my father asks, 'Will Faye be at the wedding?' He's opening a cupboard and putting the polish inside. I'm completely shocked because my father has never mentioned Faye since the day my mother passed away.

'Er, no, actually, I don't really see Faye anymore.'

'Ah that's a pity,' he says, but my curiosity doesn't want to leave it at that.

'Why are you asking about Faye?'

'I was just wondering would she be there. I haven't seen her in years and she was such a good friend of yours...' Then he pauses before saying, 'A *great* friend, I would say... I thought she'd be there. I never got to thank her.'

I'm speechless. I don't know what to say except, why now? Why is he asking about Faye now when he hasn't mentioned her once in the last three years? Does he know something?

'Is Lucas excited?' he asks, changing the subject.

'Yes, he's really looking forward to it. Imagine, it's his first Irish wedding and he's the groom. Hah!'

'He's a lucky man.'

I laugh out loud but I'm not laughing inside because I want to bring up the subject of Avril Ryan without sounding like I've an agenda.

'Have you been playing any chess lately?' I ask, taking a glass from the cupboard above the countertop. Even the glass is spotless.

'No, I haven't played much this year. There are a lot of new kids on the block,' he says, rubbing his elbows. 'Real whizz kids, too smart for the likes of me.'

My heart is beating fast now. I want to ask but I have to make sure I don't upset him.

'You know the woman who was killed at Huntley Lodge, the body they found there two weeks ago? She used to play chess. Maybe you knew her?'

'What was her name?'

'Avril Ryan.'

'Avril Ryan... Do you know what club she was with?'

'No.'

My father is sitting at the table, his face hidden behind the flowers so I can't read his expression.

'Is everyone coming to the wedding?' he asks, moving swiftly off the subject of Avril Ryan.

'Yes, so far we haven't had one person who can't make it.'

'I guess that would be the time of year. A lot of people would be on holidays during the summer months.'

'Probably.'

Dad doesn't seem to want to talk about Avril Ryan. Which surprises me, because she played chess just like he did. I thought he'd be more interested for that reason. I can't imagine it's a huge community, so it's possible their paths did cross. After a few more comments about the wedding and next week's weather forecast, I want to bring the subject of Avril Ryan back into the conversation, but he cut me off so short the first time, I decide not to.

Chapter Fifty-One

Lucas laughs when I tell him about the possible chess connection between my dad and Avril Ryan. Pouring wine into a glass he tells me I'm losing it. The steak Diane which he has cooked smells delicious and for once I'm feeling hungry. Besides drinking about ten cups of coffee today, I don't remember eating anything.

'Well, he didn't really answer me when I asked if he knew her. He just asked me if I knew what club she was with and when I didn't have the answer he changed the subject. But he never actually said he didn't know her.'

I'm starting to hear the madness myself and I laugh along with Lucas. 'I am mad, I know. Are you sure you still want to marry me?'

'Well I bought the flights,' he says, causing me to spit out the wine when I burst out laughing.

'You know, this will probably be our last meal here together. We've the rehearsal Thursday, I'm staying at Dad's on Friday, and tomorrow night Amy is driving me to Dad's with all the stuff we need for the morning of the wedding.'

'And Wednesday, I'm having a couple of pints with the blokes from work,' Lucas says.

'Is that your last day?'

'Yes, I'm all yours after that. A whole month before I have to go into the office. It will be strange going to work without a jacket.'

'So, cheers.'

Lucas clinks glasses with me then turns to glance out at the city. 'I'm gonna miss this place.'

'Me too... and I'm really going to miss my dad.'

Lucas smiles and clinks the glass again. 'He'll come and visit... we're going to have a great life, Tara. Australia will be as good to us as Ireland was. I know you're going to love it there.'

I smile at Lucas, at his innocence, his faith, his excitement, all oozing from those big blue eyes that I've become so familiar with.

'Do you think we'll ever come back?' I say.

'Whatever you want, Tara. I told you, if things don't work out I'd be willing to return here with you.'

If I hadn't got a head full of worry, I'd believe I was the luckiest woman in the world. But I have and I'm scared.

'I'm going to do my best to make it work, Lucas.'

'I know you will.'

When the meal is finished I put the plates in the dishwasher and wipe down the hob. Lucas is sitting on the sofa looking at the TV.

Now is my chance to pack a few things to bring to my dad's, so I go to the bedroom and take a case from the top of the wardrobe. A photograph falls down from under the case. I take it in my hand and turn it over to see who it is. Faye stares back at me.

The photo was taken on the wall outside my house when we were little. Even then, she had her arm around me. We were so innocent, making funny faces at the camera. I rub my finger over her face and whisper, 'What happened to us, Faye?' I put the photo on my bedside cabinet wondering how it ended up on top of the wardrobe.

I convince myself that it must have been in the suitcase when I moved here from my dad's house. It seems strange that I'm only finding it now. Maybe it's a sign, telling me to ring Faye. To ask her if she's okay.

Without thinking twice, I dial her number. With the phone to my ear, I wait for it to ring but I'm asked to leave a message as the contact is unavailable. Faye must be in some part of the hospital with no coverage. She could be in an operating theatre for all I know, saving someone's life. That's Faye. I hate to think she's worrying and has no one she can talk to about this. She needs to know she can talk to me.

'Faye, it's me, Tara, ring me when you get this message. We need to talk.' I put the phone down on top of the photo and hope she might ring back.

Andriu is right about one thing; Faye did go off the rails a bit. Especially that night when she had the big row with him. She barely spoke to me after that.

The night she told me she was leaving Huntley Lodge came as a massive shock. I had just lost my mother and was about to lose my best friend. I couldn't get my head around it and I was so absorbed in my own pain, I failed to notice Faye's.

Was Faye being blackmailed? That would drive anyone mad. Especially as she was studying medicine. The white coat and stethoscope were only a few years away. If it got out that she helped me assist my mother's passing, her career would be over.

But would she not have told me if she was being blackmailed? Especially when it was my fault?

Not if she killed the blackmailer.

Stop, Tara Moore, don't be so ridiculous. You know that didn't happen. But something did happen and the only way to find out is to ask Faye.

The sound from the TV travels into the bedroom, cheering, shouting, music. Suddenly there's a different sound, a ringing. I turn away from the wardrobe and see my phone flashing on the bedside cabinet. I rush to grab the phone and look at the screen. My excitement is short-lived.

Why the hell is he ringing at this hour of the night?

Chapter Fifty-Two

Faye

My father said nothing when he pulled up outside the clinic this morning. He just sat silently waiting for me to get out of the car. Usually he utters a few words before I go through the big blue door.

He's fed up with me, I can tell. Fed up with the endless lies, the manipulative stories. He was so disappointed when he found out I was drinking at the weekend.

The stress was written all over his face – his skin greyer, the lines on his forehead thicker. His eyes did their best not to meet mine as he looked from the side mirror to the rearview mirror, feigning concern he might be blocking someone behind us.

It was hard to watch him like this. Like he had given up all hope and was now just going through the motions until it all ended, wherever it was going to end. Good or bad, it was clear he was losing the will to care.

I wanted to tell him I felt different now. Something had happened, a breakthrough he might call it. A correction of sorts. I had been mistaken about the world I was living in. I had been lied to, given false information that pushed me down a slippery slope, where I glided through muck, clung to roots, slipping time and time again.

My father glanced briefly at me before turning his head away again. Dad looked like he was about to cry and just wanted me out of the car. I felt awful. It was my fault. Me and my selfish 'poor fucking me' ways. I had to fix this.

'Dad,' I said, disturbing the awkward silence. The word reverberated around the car like we were in a big hollow space. My father turned to look at me. I stared at his sad eyes for a moment, then leaned in to kiss his cheek.

'It's going to be okay, Dad,' I said, then jumped out of the car before he had time to reply.

I walk through the doors of the clinic. Waving good morning to Anna behind the reception desk I continue on down to my room at the end of the corridor. Aoife is in her bed when I get there. The poor girl has only been here for two weeks so she's still in shock. Before that, Joanne was my roommate. She did really well and was released after only two months of therapy. I haven't heard from her since she left, which is a bit disappointing because we really did hit it off.

Aoife is asking me about my weekend when the door opens and Nurse Catherine walks in. She's wearing a black woollen dress and flat grey ankle boots. Catherine always ties her hair back off her bony, shiny face. There are no uniforms here. There's no need for them. It doesn't take a genius to figure out who the patients are. Pain is carved all over our faces, in our gait, our tortured smiles. We're the ones walking with sagging shoulders, darting eyes. Nervous, looking for signs, waiting for the world to collapse.

Catherine hands me a little plastic cup with the yellow lid like she does every Monday morning. If it turns out that she discovers alcohol in my pee, my weekend pass will be revoked and I certainly don't want that to happen. She pushes open the door to the bathroom that I share with Aoife.

'When you're ready,' she says, but she doesn't mean this. It's not when I'm ready. It's now, or I fail.

I take the cup and walk into the room, closing the door behind me. I can hear her chatting away to Aoife while searching my bag. So many things are forbidden that it's hard to remember at times. Face wipes. I can't imagine being so desperate for alcohol that I'd suck on a face wipe. But I guess they're covering all corners. Or so they think.

I stand up onto the toilet seat and reach into the small air vent at the top of the wall, pulling out a plastic Ziploc bag full of urine. I hid it there last thing before leaving here on Friday. Then I place the bag and the plastic cup on the radiator before pulling my knickers down.

Catherine knocks on the door.

'Give me a minute, it's not that fucking easy to piss on demand,' I shout out to her. I've developed quite a vulgar tone since coming here. It's either a last line of defence or a show of resilience. Whichever, it gives me a sense of control.

I press my hand down on the bag. That should be warm enough now. I take the lid off the cup and open the corner of the bag, carefully pouring the contents into the cup while peeing into the toilet bowl. Then I tighten the lid of the cup, pull up my knickers, wash the plastic bag out and wash my hands. I stick the empty bag back into the air vent before opening the door and handing the cup to Catherine. This is the third week in a row I've managed to complete the trick flawlessly. I could be a circus act.

'Thank you,' Catherine says before asking me if I had a nice weekend. It's important I remain positive if I'm going to appear like I'm making progress so I say, 'Yes, lovely, nothing too exciting.'

'Did you watch *I'm a Celebrity*?' she says, causing a glitch to appear in my confidence but thankfully Aoife butts in, commenting on the latest goings-on and surreptitiously updating me in the process. My week in here is spent watching *I'm a Celeb* on the TV at night. If I didn't have an up-to-date comment ready, alarm bells might ring. Catherine might say, *so what were you doing if you didn't watch it? Were you out? You know you're not supposed to be out after ten o'clock when you're on weekend release.* Then I'd have to make up some story about a visit from my sister or a headache that sent me to bed early and I'd be nervous because I'd know she was on to me. They're very smart in here. Just not as smart as me.

Catherine eventually walks out of the room with the cup in her hand and I'm left to unpack the fresh clothes my mother ironed with the precision of a brain surgeon. I know she's nervous. Mam finds it hard to deal with someone like me. Someone not quite right. My brother and sister gave them no trouble – a fact my father regularly imparts to me.

'Faye Connolly.' The door opens and Fionn, one of the counsellors, calls my name.

'Here.'

'Consultation room four in ten minutes.'

The file where I keep all my notes and questions and progress, if any, is in the drawer of the desk that stands at the end of my bed. When I have my clothes put away, I take the file and walk to the door. Aoife is writing in her notebook. She lifts her head and smiles at me as I leave the room. Walking down the corridor my body grows heavier. When I reach the door of consultation room number four, I take a deep breath and push it open. And so it begins. The quest for answers. Why is Faye Connolly an alcoholic?

Chapter Fifty-Three

Sometimes I think I'm never going to get out of this place. That my life will be spent explaining myself. What I did, what I didn't do. Why I did it. Why I didn't do it. It's all just an attempt to unravel the mystery of my twisted mind. My misdemeanours. Why do I not care about myself anymore? Why do I hurt the people who love me? Intelligence doesn't help. That just means there are more wires to unravel. More things to go wrong.

Apparently I'm a 'complex character'. That's how Fionn described me to my father when he demanded answers for my acute demise, after just a few days of therapy. My dad thought the more money he threw at the problem, the quicker he'd get results. This place costs 10,000 euros a month. Dad must have expected me to be skipping through the meadows by Christmas. He doesn't understand about all the wires.

I don't actually agree with Fionn but I don't tell him that my problem is not complex. It's quite simple, really, I just can't share it with him. Instead I make like I'm buying all his crap. I like to give him something to work on so I speak about Andriu sometimes. How I'd built my world around him and then he walked out on me. I was so dramatic when I first mentioned him, making it sound like a breakthrough, a revelation, a demon released. I even cried. I imagine Fionn had a celebratory bottle of wine that night. At last he was getting somewhere with the complex character. If only he knew.

That's the thing I don't like about this place. Fionn believes I can tell him anything. That what I have to say to him won't destroy me even further if I let it out of my head and into the world. He's a true believer that people can be fixed. And maybe some people can but not me. I'm broken beyond repair. I just need to find a way to operate with the cracks so I can get out of here and back to some sort of normality. Which is why I'm playing their game.

'Today's session went well, don't you think?' Fionn says, walking out the door behind me. Fionn is only a few inches taller than me and full of hope. He has more faith in me than I have in myself. He never fails to remind me of my achievements and even though he makes me confront the darker side of my personality, to him, my life is not all about failure.

There are times I genuinely cry in a session and don't have to fake it. Today was one of those times. I let myself replay the night my mother walked into the hospital. I was lying on a bed in A&E, my face covered in blood. The irony wasn't lost on me when a young student doctor arrived beside the bed just like I had done the previous month. He tried to explain to my distraught mother what had happened. But how could he? I didn't even know what had happened. Why I had driven at full speed into a tree. It's not like I planned it. One minute I was going for a drive to clear my head, the next minute I was wrapped around a tree. I waited for Mam to ask if I was trying to kill myself. Or if it was an accident. But she never did.

I can still picture Mam standing by my bedside, the disbelief, the confusion, the pain carving a whole new expression on her face. She was wearing a navy coat with a soft pink scarf hanging around her neck. Mam never left the house without carefully brushing her hair and putting on some lipstick… but that day she did. I hate that I hurt her like that. I can be such a selfish cow at times.

I nod at Fionn and mutter a yes, while wiping my eyes. Today's session did go well. Then I head back to my room and find Aoife lying on her bed, crying. Everyone is crying. What sort of place is this?

'Are you okay, Aoife?' I say, putting my hand on her head. But it's a stupid question because if she was okay she wouldn't be crying. She wouldn't be in here.

Aoife lifts her head off the pillow. Her eyes are swollen; her face is red and wet. For a brief moment I want to laugh. It erupts inside me, the madness of it all, but I manage to hold it in and watch as she rubs her eyes with her fingers. I never ask her why she's here. It's early days for Aoife.

'What time is it?' she asks, sitting up on the bed.

I take my phone from the drawer in the bedside cabinet and see that it's almost five, time for tea. Egg sandwiches and Jaffa Cakes no doubt.

I notice Tara has called again. I'll call her back tonight when I can get a bit of privacy. Aoife usually goes to the TV room after supper.

Exactly when you can make a phone call isn't the only thing governed in here. They control the WiFi also. You get one hour a day, but that's only after you've proven yourself. I've proven myself. I can troll whoever I want for sixty minutes every day. Which is great. It's where I get my energy to stay angry.

When the egg sandwiches are swallowed and those who haven't proven themselves yet head to the communal area, I go back to my room and lift my phone. Holding down the button and waiting for the WiFi signal to flash on has become so satisfying it's like having a drink.

I quickly scan through the headlines in *The Journal.ie*. Money missing from the football association claims the number one spot. Then, an earthquake on some island leaving hundreds of inhabitants without homes. I find it strange the earthquake doesn't make it to the top spot ahead of the missing money.

After reading a short update about Avril Ryan's investigation and finding nothing new or of consequence in the report, I decide it's time. I'd better ring Tara back in case she decides to come here. I don't want her to find out I'm a patient in this clinic, not a doctor.

Chapter Fifty-Four

It's six in the morning. There's a fog sitting on the grass outside the window. The bottom of the trees that line the walled garden aren't visible at the moment and the trees look like they're floating across the back wall. The wall doesn't have any barbed wire, even though this clinic feels like a prison. The barbed wire is in our heads.

Only people who want to get better will be admitted here. Or so they think. *This won't be easy. Are you prepared to put in the hard work?* I remember their words, chiming in my head like church bells when I'm trying to sleep. I nodded and nodded.

Three months ago it seemed like the better option. The only option. Things could not go on the way they were.

The hospital management where I worked were as good as they were legally allowed to be. It was impossible to keep me employed once they had it figured out. At first, nobody suspected anything was wrong. I was so clever. Feigning illness, migraines, I even faked a miscarriage once. But my shaking hands and tardy timekeeping soon revealed the problem. My job demanded responsibility, accuracy, concentration; there was no room for error. No room for me to be anything less than perfect.

'Contact us as soon as you're feeling better,' the staff officer said. I remember his concerned look. I could tell he was embarrassed for me. Why? I don't know. He worked in a hospital. People get sick all the time. I was sick.

After that, things went from bad to worse. It was my sister Deirdre who alerted my parents to the fact that I'd lost my job. I showed up at her house one night looking for money. I probably shouldn't have knocked on the door drunk because her eight-year-old son Elijah answered and I fell in the door on top of him. I didn't scare him. I know that much for sure because I can still picture him laughing while she was shouting at him to go back inside. I laughed too.

I don't think I've laughed since. My sister Deirdre, my brother Morgan and both my parents all moved up a gear in their quest to fix Faye. Phone calls were made. People in the know were contacted. The local GP was summoned to the house to give me the once-over and a box of pills that would help get me through the next few days. Everyone agreed, Faye needed help.

Except me. I was still happy to fall under a bus if that's what was in store. And I almost did, but instead of a bus it was my father's brand new Mercedes that got the job. I drove it out from the driveway in the middle of the night and ran it into a beautiful Sessile oak tree that stood tall at the bottom of my parents' road. An image of me climbing that tree as an eight-year-old flashed in front of me just before I hit it. I was wearing denim dungarees and a pink T-shirt. My hair, tied in a ponytail, was swinging from side to side and I was about to turn around and look when – a loud crash shattered the quiet. My body lifted into the air with a force I didn't understand. I didn't know why I was floating in mid air. The crashing sound was followed by a hissing sound and then my head hit the windscreen. It was like I'd been whacked with a baseball bat. I could smell something burning. It got stronger... and then nothing. The next thing I remember was the screaming, the screechy, noisy, aching screaming. Someone was shouting at me, trying to open the door. I wanted to see who it was but something sticky and dark had formed a blanket over my eyes. I'm not sure how much time passed until I was pulled out by two medics and strapped onto a stretcher. My head was secured in a brace and I was put into the back of an ambulance. A stranger's voice told me I was going to be okay. I was alive and I wasn't sure how I felt about that.

Thankfully, the tree survived. As did I. The Mercedes, however, had to be replaced. I often think my dad would rather it had been the other way around.

–

Aoife's whimpering breaks the silence. She stirs in the bed, lifting her face off the pillow. I remember how terrible it was when I first arrived here, especially the first weekend before I was given weekend release. It wasn't the fact that I was alone in the room. I liked that bit because it was the only time I felt I wasn't being watched. That every little thing I did wasn't being noticed, recorded and analyzed. But the realisation that I was only at the start of this barbaric journey was frightening. The months ahead were going to be painful and there was a lot of doubt in my mind as to whether I'd be strong enough for it.

'Don't worry, Aoife, you'll be getting weekend release soon. You'll get to see whoever it is you are missing.'

I want to ignore the fact that I can hear her crying into her pillow. It's impossible to comfort everyone in here every time they cry. I do my best. I have put my arm around her a few times and told her things would get better, like Joanne did for me. It never really cures anything or helps anything but in that moment, when you feel the heat of another broken soul embrace you, you're happy to bathe in hopeless comfort.

Oh damn it. I can't leave her like that.

I move away from the window and over to Aoife's bedside where I lie down beside her and rest my head on her pillow.

'You know what we should do, Aoife? This time next year we should meet up. Somewhere beautiful. Somewhere with trees and birds and blue skies and hot coffee and people walking their dogs. We should meet and talk and be proud of ourselves. We'll know we've made it, but we won't mention it, Aoife. We won't talk about what it took for us to get to that beautiful place. We'll just be happy to be there, to be meeting up.'

Aoife sniffles, lifts her head and looks at me. 'You promise?'

'I promise, Aoife. This time next year.'

Chapter Fifty-Five

When I get back to the room later that evening, Aoife isn't lying on her bed as per usual and that immediately raises a red flag but I guess maybe she's gone to an early group session or is still in the dining room. I throw my notebook onto the bed and turn around to find Nurse Catherine standing there.

Her eyes are fixed on me and she doesn't look her usual happy self. Something is wrong. Has something happened to Aoife? Is that why she's not here?

'Where's Aoife?' I say. 'Is she okay?'

'Aoife's fine.'

'Is something wrong?'

'I need you to give me a sample, Faye,' she says, handing me the container with the yellow lid.

She holds her grip on the container a second longer than she needs to, making me pull it from her. My heart is sending panic waves throughout my body.

She knows. Did she find the bag or did she send the sample to the lab? They do that sometimes. They don't believe their own little strip of telltale paper so they send it out to have it analysed. Shit, one way or the other I am in trouble.

I'm about to close the door when she puts her foot out to stop me like a prison warden. It's hard to believe this treatment costs ten thousand euros a month.

'Leave the door open,' she says.

'But—'

'Open.' She almost growls the word.

My hands are trembling now. If I give her a sample, she'll know I was drinking at the weekend. Which means I'll be thrown out. Or at the very least, with a bit of begging, I might get off with just losing my weekend privileges. One way or the other, my father will find out. Everything I thought was within my reach earlier today is being pulled further away from me. Discovering the truth about Andriu and Tara had released me from the chains of my past. Erased the nightmare I was living with and brought me hope that I might be able to commit to this treatment. But now...

'Is there a problem?' she says, noticing my delay.

'No, I just don't need to pee yet.' I look up at the vent. I should not have done that because then she looks up at the vent. I have confirmed her suspicions.

'It's not there,' she says.

'What... what's not there?' My throat is so dry my voice cracks.

'This.'

Catherine holds up the Ziploc bag that I had hidden in the vent. Out of nowhere a strange feeling cascades through me. Like someone has pulled a plug and drained all the fear out of me. I don't care that I've been caught. It's almost a relief.

I look down, scuffing my foot backwards and forwards across the cold tiled floor before lifting my head.

'Yes. It's mine. I did that.'

The next breath to enter my body is slow and deep and brings with it a sense of peace.

The following two hours are touch and go. There's a meeting between Fionn and Catherine and Margaret, the head coordinator of the facility. I was called in to make my appeal to be allowed to remain at the clinic. I said very little. I was sorry. I wouldn't do it again. I was ready to commit to the programme. I didn't think I held much power over their decision so I didn't say anything else.

Fionn requests a one-on-one session with me and they agree. We talk. I tell him what has happened with Andriu. Which made me hate Tara and my life. I even tell him about the threatening text I received the week after Tara's mam died. We talk for over an hour.

It feels good. For the first time I am communicating for real. Not interpreting my life but seeing it for what it is and accepting what has happened. I don't want to soak in my past any longer. I want to stop drinking, to be a doctor again. I tell Fionn I am ready to commit if they'll still have me. That is the easy bit.

The hard bit goes on behind the door while I wait outside. It doesn't take too long though. Fionn must have recognized my epiphany wasn't fake because after about twenty minutes I am called back into the room. The decision is made. I will be given one more chance. And one more chance is all I need to get my life back.

Chapter Fifty-Six

A few hours later I'm summoned to the same room but this time Detective Lee is sitting on a chair at the far side of the room when I step inside. She points to the sofa opposite for me to sit down. Today she's wearing her hair differently. It's rolled up at the back of her head but her face is still framed in red wispy stray bits. She's wearing dark trousers, a big woolly jumper with what looks like a snowflake pattern across the front of it and a rain jacket which she removes when I enter the room.

Scratching my arms through my long sleeved T-shirt, I sit down, thinking that the heat in this room is going to roast her. Detective Mullins, her partner, is sitting on a low stool beside her. He shifts awkwardly because his legs are far too long for the stool and his knees are almost reaching his face. He looks like her elf.

After a few more unsuccessful moves to make the stool work he must realise how stupid he looks because he stands up. Then walks to the wall where he takes out his notebook. Mullins rests his foot up against the wall behind him.

When I see him do that, it reminds me of the day I met Tara. How she copied me when I had my foot up resting against the wall. I swallow. My heart sinks when I consider the damage I've done. How could I have thought that badly of Tara, believing that she would sleep with my boyfriend? Why didn't I have faith in our friendship? I should have at least asked her if it was true but I was so upset and with Andriu gone I decided to hate her instead.

What must she have thought? I left her when she needed me most. Walked out on her the same week she buried her mam. Andriu was gone. I was in pain, confused and I wanted her to be too.

'Faye, thank you for agreeing to meet with us again. I know it's not ideal…'

The detective glances around the meeting room, which is the one I usually have my sessions with Fionn in. She speaks softly, acknowledging my situation, believing me to be weaker than her usual subjects because I'm in here. The detective is wrong. I'm stronger.

I starc directly at her, letting her know she can stop the crap talk and get on with it.

'Something has come to light, Faye and we thought maybe you'd be able to help us.'

'I'll try.'

'As you know, we are investigating the murder of Avril Ryan at Huntley Lodge sometime after the eighth of September 2016, when you were a resident there.'

'Yes,' I nod.

'Have you remembered anything you want to tell us?'

'No.'

'The "Cabhrui" website, maybe?' She holds my stare.

'Sorry?'

'"Cabhrui", a website that helps people who want to end their own life.'

'What about it?' My heart is hammering on the wall of my chest but I'm so good at lying now, I can easily disguise my shock. 'Never heard of it,' I say, following my comment, as all good liars do, with a bit of embellishment:

'Is there really a website that does that? I thought that was illegal in this country.'

'It is, Faye, but that's not what we're interested in. We're here because the site was run by Avril Ryan. It's possible someone knew she was running it and was blackmailing her.'

'Or she was blackmailing someone who used it,' Mullins adds.

Inside, I'm wilting. Is this true? Could Tara have got into trouble with the woman? Was Avril Ryan trying to blackmail her? My eyes are still focused on Detective Lee. Shaking my head from side to side, I put a calm expression on my face and tell her I know nothing about the website. Then she mentions Tara and it takes all my strength not to punch her in the face to shut her up.

'You don't see Tara Moore anymore,' she tells me.'

'No, we went our separate ways... boyfriend trouble.' It's the first thing I can think of.

'Oh? She never mentioned that.'

'She doesn't know. I did something I wasn't proud of and I found it hard to hang with her after that.'

Detective Lee frowns.

'Oh. It's nothing illegal,' I chuckle. 'I was young... stupid.'

Detective Lee isn't impressed by the lack of interest I'm showing. She's staring me down. Trying to make me think she can see through my lies. But she's wasting her time.

'Okay,' she finally says.

'Is that it?' I say, about to stand.

'No, there is one last thing.'

Mullins moves his foot off the wall and stands forward. He pushes his steel-framed glasses up on his nose. I get the feeling Lee is about to reveal the real reason she called here today.

'You received a text, Faye, around the time Avril went missing. Avril Ryan sent it to you. Can you tell me about that?' She shifts forward in her chair.

Breathe, Faye. Keep your eye on her and slow down your breathing. Don't let her see how rattled you are.

'I receive hundreds of texts, any text in particular?'

Lee looks over at Mullins. He looks back at her, shrugs his shoulders then looks at me. The mood in the room has shifted. I'm now under attack.

Detective Lee is waiting for me to say something. She pulls her chair forward a bit as if getting closer to me is going to make me talk. Maybe she thinks she's putting me under pressure. She's wrong. I know pressure. This is not pressure.

'No, I don't remember getting any text from Avril Ryan,' I say.

'Well, I have the transcript here, the text was sent to your number.' She recites my phone number. 'That is your number, isn't it? And it was your number three years ago because I checked.'

I'm doing my best not to show how panicked I am beneath my confident demeanour. The truth is, I feel like throwing up on the spot. Is it possible Avril Ryan was planning to blackmail me? She's the one who sent that text. Did Tara get one too? Oh my God, did Tara kill her?

Clenching my hands into fists, trying to stop them from shaking, I watch as Lee opens up the file Mullins hands her. She glances at me, then reads the text message out loud.

'*I need to speak to you urgently, yourself and your friend are in danger, please ring me back at this number as soon as you can and don't speak to anyone until I see you.*'

Lee closes the file marked 'Avril Ryan'. She hands the file to Mullins and turns her attention back to me.

My mind is somersaulting. Should I say something now? Should I say I never received that message? That the text I received simply said, '*I can destroy you*'.

Once again I drag strength from the air around me. Breathing deeply, I calm my mind and tell myself not to say anything until I speak to Tara.

'Honestly… I did not see that text.'

'But you texted her back.' The detective's eyes are open wide like two spotlights shining on me.

'No, I didn't.'

'Yes, you did. I have the transcript here, right in front of me.' She takes the file from Mullins again and opens it up, looking at the page before glancing back at me. She must see how shocked I am, the blood draining from my face. Surely she's questioning if I am in fact telling the truth.

'It's from your number, Faye. You arranged to meet Avril Ryan at Huntley Lodge.'

My mouth is gaping open. This can't be true. What is going on? My vision blurs. I rub my eyes.

'No,' I say. 'I didn't! I never sent Avril Ryan a message.'

Did I? Lots of things in my past are vague but surely I'd remember that. I look at Mullins then back to Lee.

'I didn't arrange to meet Avril Ryan. I never saw that woman in my life. I never saw that text message either.'

Chapter Fifty-Seven

'Faye… Faye…' someone is pushing my shoulder. I open my eyes and see Aoife standing there. Her soft blue eyes are open wide and staring down at me.

'What happened? Are you alright?' she says, sitting on her bed opposite me. 'I saw her in there, but it was too late to do anything.'

'What?' I open my eyes fully and sit up in the bed. 'You saw who?' My head is still muzzy and my mouth dry. I lift a bottle of water from my bedside cabinet and empty it in one go. It's like a cold shower washing through my body, making me more alert. I'm in my room. Aoife is talking to me. Oh fuck, the cops were here. I close my eyes again and rest my head back down on the pillow.

'You should have told me, Faye. I could have said it was mine but it all happened so quickly, I…'

What is she talking about?

'Or I could have given a sample for you. I could have left it in the bag early Monday morning before you came back and then they wouldn't have discovered it was stale urine.'

Oh Christ, she's talking about the urine sample. Aoife isn't aware that my tragic story of trouble and strife has moved onto the next chapter. What I wouldn't give for a bag of pee to be my problem now.

'It's okay Aoife, it doesn't matter now.'

'But I would have,' she says.

It strikes me as funny how open to deception people in here are willing to be.

'Well, you would have been wrong, Aoife, believe you me. Take my advice. I'm learning the hard way. Toe the line in here, Aoife, get it over with as soon as you can. I'm back to the start now, no privileges, not even my phone.'

Aoife jumps off the bed and pulls her phone from under the mattress.

'Look,' she says, holding it close to her chest, grinning from ear to ear.

'Congratulations,' I say, wishing she'd go away and leave me alone. I'm so confused. I need time to think.

The detectives finally left after telling me they'd be back in touch soon. Detective Lee said I was to go nowhere and was only short of laughing when she looked around the room, highlighting where I was, as if to say I shouldn't find that request too hard to keep. I didn't care. I had too much to worry about for her bitchiness to be a problem.

I still can't get my head around what she said. Is she lying? Is she even allowed to lie? Was I supposed to jump up and contradict her, tell her what was really in the text and reveal that Avril Ryan was in touch with me? If that was her plan, it failed.

I kept my mouth shut. The only thing I uttered to her after that was to tell her that if she planned to keep harassing me while I was at such a delicate crossroads in my life, I would be getting a solicitor. I didn't like her response, which was to recommend I did so. Now I have to make a phone call to my father and tell him what's going on. Ask him to get me a solicitor. If this doesn't kill him off, I don't know what will.

Aoife has skipped out of the room, leaving me alone. Thankfully, I have a session with Fionn first thing in the morning. He'll tell me what to do. What to do about Tara. Should I call and tell her what happened with the detectives? She did say to contact her if they were back on to me but it's just a few days to the wedding. I don't want to ruin that too.

I'm looking at the ceiling, doubting everything in my head. What if I did have something to do with Avril Ryan's death and I blanked it out? That can happen with alcoholics. They have special erasers inside their head to help them rub out parts of their past that are too difficult to live with. Is that what happened to me?

No, it isn't. I know exactly what happened back then. It was the most painful time of my life and instead of erasing it like I should have, I relived it every day, allowing it to destroy me... and now I find out it wasn't the truth.

Turning my head around I put my face into the pillow to soak up the tears and the sound of pain seeping from my body. Did Tara get into trouble when I left her? I don't want to think about it. Am I going to be arrested for something I didn't do? I don't want to think about that. Are my mam and dad going to live the rest of their lives sad because of me? I definitely don't want to go there. There is only one thing I need to think about. How do I fix all this?

Chapter Fifty-Eight

Tara

In three days' time I'll be married. I'll be Mrs Tara Jones, and this makes me happy.

This morning I packed a lot of the clothes I'm taking to Australia with me. Summer dresses, bikinis. I put the winter stuff in bags for the charity shop. I thought I'd be sad pulling out all those memories from the wardrobe, but I wasn't. I was elated and it took my mind off the investigation. I imagined myself in my summer clothes lying on the beach or strolling around my house in shorts and a T-shirt and now I can't wait to get there. Lucas has decided to leave most of his stuff behind him. He says he'll have no need for it when he gets home.

My father rang earlier asking if there was anything I needed him to do. There wasn't. He said he had his speech ready and was really looking forward to the wedding. It was good to hear him so upbeat.

It's just a waiting game now. Everything is set to go, thanks to Amy and her hard work. She kept a lot of the stress and worry that goes with planning a wedding away from me. I'm not sure how I would have got to this stage without losing a few years off my life if it wasn't for her, especially with all that has happened.

Lucas is spending his last day at work today. He was sad leaving the apartment this morning. He'll miss his colleagues, though he hopes to still be dealing with them over the phone and Zoom when he gets to Australia because he has applied to be stationed in the European section of the Melbourne office. Which he's pretty sure he'll get. I really hope he enjoys his last drinks with his workmates tonight. They're giving him a send off and I'm sure for Lucas it will be pretty emotional because he loved working here. He said he hopes his colleagues in the Melbourne office are as great as the people he met in the Dublin office. I hope they are too. I want Lucas to be happy.

I'm disappointed Faye never rang back. I really thought she would. I left two messages because the phone kept going straight to voicemail without even ringing. I hope she hasn't changed her number or lost her phone. She's probably just busy but I want her to know I'm here if she needs to talk about anything. If she's worried about the investigation.

When Andriu rang late the other night I was surprised. He asked if we could meet up and I told him it was a hectic week for me. Then I felt guilty. Andriu came all the way from London for my wedding and I was brushing him off. So I arranged to see him tonight, here in the apartment at around eight. I hope he doesn't stay long because I plan on soaking in a bath, putting on my PJs and relaxing in front of the TV for the night. Tomorrow, things are kicking off with the rehearsal at the church, then dinner at my dad's favourite bistro. This is my last chance to have a quiet night in.

The frost that covered the balcony earlier this morning is beginning to freeze over again. I'm hoping the weather gets a bit warmer by Saturday otherwise we'll all freeze to death in the church. It's a big old church and no matter what they throw at it, it never seems to warm up. I was there last week with Amy and the florist and we were all shivering with the cold the whole time.

I step outside onto the balcony. The cold air wraps around my body. Crossing my arms over my chest, I listen to the siren in the distance. Somebody somewhere is in trouble. I think of the detectives. I haven't heard from them in a couple of days but that means nothing because they could be anywhere, finding out anything, getting ready to pounce. They did say they would leave me alone this week because of the wedding and I hope they keep their word.

When I told Lucas what Sean said about not mentioning the 'Cabhrui' website, he said I should follow Sean's advice. He's the professional. He knows what he's doing. But it doesn't sit well with me, all this deception. Maybe the detectives would lose interest in me if they knew the truth. But what is the truth? What happened to Avril Ryan at Huntley Lodge?

In the background, my phone rings so I hurry inside but I'm too late, I've missed a call from Sean. I redial but it goes straight to voicemail. Then my phone beeps. He has left me a voice message.

> *Tara, that friend of mine who works at the courts got back to me earlier today. Muriel was right. Avril Ryan did file a harassment complaint against a man. I'll forward on his identity. It was a few years before she went missing. The investigators will already be aware of this. But you asked so… enjoy the wedding.*

Damn it. I was hoping there might be something in that discovery to send the detectives down a different path but if it was years earlier and, as Sean says, the family will have told the cops about it anyway, it's of no use to me. Shaking my head, I promise to let go of my thoughts about Avril Ryan and concentrate on the wedding.

—

A few hours later the buzzer sounds. Andriu is here. He arrives at the door with a bottle of wine in his hand which I thank him for. He must be planning on having a drink. I wasn't but I feel obliged to join him.

'Is Lucas here?' he says, walking over towards the balcony and looking out. 'Great view, this place must cost a bomb.'

'No, he's gone for a drink with some of his colleagues. It's his last day in work so… how are you getting on? Have you met up with Faye at all?'

Andriu shakes his head, still looking out on to the city. 'That's what I wanted to talk to you about, Tara.' He turns around and nods at the bottle in my hand. 'Are you opening that?'

'Oh yes.' I hurry to the kitchen area and take two glasses from the shelf, putting them on the table before opening the bottle of wine. 'I'll just have a small glass,' I say. 'I've a few heavy days ahead.'

Andriu takes his glass and sits down on the chair opposite the sofa. I sit on the sofa.

'Here's to your future, Tara,' he says, leaning in to clink glasses.

'Cheers.' I feel a bit awkward in his company all of a sudden. A flashback of the last time we were on our own having a drink all those years ago comes to mind. I know we were both drunk but if I hadn't pushed him away anything could have happened. I couldn't believe that he tried to seduce me. He was Faye's boyfriend, for Christ's sake.

'You wanted to talk about Faye,' I say, hoping he doesn't suggest she had something to do with the murder again.

'I did meet Faye,' he says, leaning forward in the seat. 'I think she followed me. I can't be sure but...' Andriu takes a sip from his glass without taking his eyes off me. 'Tara, what do you know about Faye since you last saw her?'

'Nothing really. She's a doctor, I'm not sure what hospital. I think it's somewhere on the south side.' Then I remember her mentioning a clinic. 'Or she could be working in a private clinic.'

'Faye is not working as a doctor.'

'What?' I can't believe what I'm hearing. Why is Faye not a doctor? Andriu must have it wrong. I spoke to her secretary.

'She is, Andriu, I rang her at the clinic and her secretary answered. She said Faye was doing her rounds. She is a doctor, Andriu. What makes you think otherwise?'

'I don't want you getting upset, Tara, especially before the wedding, but I think you need to know this in case something happens.'

I can feel the blood rushing to my head. The glass in my hand feels heavy all of a sudden. What is he going to say?

'Faye is in a clinic getting treatment. The thing is, Tara, I think she's gone a bit mad. She's dangerous, Tara. She followed me the other night. She pretended to bump into me. I think she might have been in the pub, sitting at the bar, watching us.'

Chapter Fifty-Nine

Faye

It's after ten. The usual silence bounces off the walls of the building like it does every night. It's eerily creepy, knowing everyone is now lying in their beds, doing their very best to think of a reason to wake up tomorrow. All you need is one.

Sometimes the muffle of tears can be heard hiding behind walls. Or laughter. When that happens it's like someone is being bold and it's exciting. It's also a reminder that this too shall pass. Better days lie ahead. I want to believe that. I need to believe that.

With my mind unable to rest, I kneel up on the bed and pull the curtain to look outside. The darkness steals the picture of the walled garden that this window frames. The tall trees by the back wall are now only a suggestion, a blurred shadow, drawn by the half moon.

With nothing to see, I move away and return to the comfort of my duvet.

Dad surprised me earlier. I explained what had happened with the detectives and he told me I wasn't to worry. He would get me the best solicitor he could find. No one was going to accuse his daughter of anything. He told me not to utter another word about it to anyone until I spoke to my solicitor. Dad made me feel safe.

I didn't directly mention the 'Cabhrui' website, or how I had helped Tara, but I did tell him he would find out something about me. I told him I didn't think it was a bad thing and I hoped he wouldn't too. I might be pushing my luck with that wish. But it doesn't matter, he doesn't have to agree with what I did. I just hope he understands.

Mam was frantic on the phone when she first heard. After calming down, she asked me was I okay to stay here or did I want to come home? I told her I had to stay here. I had to get better.

Her tears were muffled but I knew she was crying and when she said she was proud of me the word rang like an angel's song in my ear. *Proud*. I'd almost forgotten that word existed.

I'm nervous. I've never faced so much uncertainty and yet I feel stronger than I have in a long time. Do I owe my recovery to Avril Ryan? The knowledge I have gained over the past few weeks has helped me get to this point. It would never have happened if Huntley Lodge hadn't appeared on the TV that night. I would never have opened those doors. I would never have received a call from Tara which fueled my journey into the past. Stalking was probably not one of my finer hours and realising how much I hated Tara Moore was scary. But I'm ready to let it all go now. The past. Andriu... Emily...

'Fuck.' Clarity crashes into my head. The text from Avril Ryan. I'm supposed to have received it the week Tara's mam died. But what if it was the same night she died? That would explain why I didn't see it. I wasn't in possession of the phone. I wasn't the one who replied to that text and arranged to meet her at Huntley Lodge.

I jump up in the bed... No... Sweet Jesus, it can't be. But it makes sense.

'Aoife, Aoife.' Tossing the duvet aside I rush to her bedside and shake her, not caring if I frighten her. 'Aoife, wake up!'

'What?' she says lifting her head from the pillow. 'I wasn't asleep.'

'Aoife, I need your phone.'

'But...'

I rush to the wall and switch on the light. Then I hurry to the pile of unread leaflets and cards that I've collected in my drawer. It's hurting me to breathe. My eyes are stinging.

'Where the fuck is it?' I'm tossing paper after paper onto the ground when I finally see it. The card is caught in the edge of the drawer. I pull it loose and put my other hand out to Aoife.

'The phone, Aoife.'

She hesitates at first. She will lose her privileges, but something about the terror I'm showing convinces her. She jumps up, reaches under the bed and takes out her phone. She switches it on and hands it to me. Standing in a long blue nightdress, Aoife crosses her hands over her shivering body and stares at me.

I bless myself, then dial the number that's printed under Detective Siobhan Lee's name. If I'm right, Tara Moore is in a lot of danger.

Chapter Sixty

The call goes straight to voicemail. My hand is shaking. I leave a message asking the detective to ring me back, saying that I need to ask her something. But I can't wait around for her to reply. I have to do something. I have to talk to Tara. Her number is on my phone which is now locked up somewhere in this building so I can't call her. Catherine took great pleasure taking it out of my hand after the disciplinary meeting. I had made her look like a fool in front of her boss and she was not happy about it.

'What will I do?' I say out loud. Aoife is looking at me, chewing her nails.

'What's happening?' she says, nerves apparent in her startled eyes. 'What's going on, Faye?'

'I need to contact my friend,' I say. 'She could be in danger.' I'm already pulling on a pair of jeans.

'You can't leave, Faye.' Aoife is trembling now, feeling a responsibility to stop me.

'Don't worry Aoife, this is absolutely necessary.' I lift my sweatshirt from the chair in the corner. 'Have you any cash?' I say, pulling the top over my head.

'You're going to get into a lot of trouble,' Aoife says. 'Don't do it, Faye.'

'I have no choice. My friend is in danger.'

I pull open the drawer where I keep my money. We're only allowed five euros per day for the shop that comes around on a trolley. Stocked with sweets, fruits, magazines, it's like the meal on an airplane. Things I wouldn't normally care for but have now become the highlight of the day. I've only ten euros left. That won't get me into town in a taxi.

'Can't you ring someone? Ring the police, or your mam – someone's number you have in your head.' Aoife is right. I should ring someone, but I know what will happen. No one is going to believe me. They'll think I'm just freaking out, looking for attention again and then they'll contact the clinic and I'll be watched all night.

'I did ring the detective. They didn't answer… Can I have your money? I'll give it back to you,' I say.

Aoife opens the drawer on her bedside locker and takes out her remaining ten euros. She hands it to me, watching me calculate out loud how much I think a taxi will cost. Then she does something I wasn't expecting. She takes one of her shoes out of the wardrobe and puts her hand into it, pulling the insole out. Aoife removes two fifty-euro notes and hands them to me. I say nothing, looking at her with both disbelief and admiration. A part of me is surprised Aoife is breaking rules, she seems so quiet and obedient, but she is in here so…

I smile at her then grab her and hug her. 'Wish me luck,' I say.

'Be careful.' She hands me her phone, watching as I gently open the door and leave the room.

–

The corridor is empty, with just one main overhead light on. There are still people in the TV room; I can see the shadows from the TV dancing on the walls through the glass window. When I reach the lobby, there's nobody there. The shutter is pulled down over the reception area. I move towards the big blue door. I could have attempted to make my way out through the emergency exit but that would be a lot riskier because the alarm might go off. The smokers are allowed out into a smoking area at the side of the building so this door is usually left open until twelve at night.

I am turning the lock when I hear footsteps behind me. Without turning to see who's there, I slip out through the gap and close the door behind me. Then I run, down the driveway, out through the big black iron gates and onto the street. My heart is pumping. I look behind but the door is still closed.

The road is busy; normal life is still in full swing. Across from the clinic, a row of cafes and pubs light up the street. The buzz is terrific… on that side of the street.

I'm cold. I couldn't take my jacket in case Catherine spotted me walking towards the exit. She knows I don't smoke. I would have had to pretend I was going to the kitchen for some water.

I walk down to the corner of the street to wave down a taxi. Clinging to Aoife's phone, I check the detective hasn't called back before getting into the car. I ask the smiling taxi driver to take me to Reilly's Bar on the quays near the Financial Centre. I have no intention of going to the bar but it's the only landmark I can remember near Tara's apartment block. Sitting in the back seat of the taxi, I take a few deep breaths. I know I'm crossing a line here. I do not know where this will end but I have to talk to Tara. I need to warn her. Suddenly, I wonder what I'll do if she's not there. She could be anywhere the Wednesday before her wedding. Probably running all over the town finalising things. God, I hope she's there, that I don't have to wait out in the cold again for hours for her to return home.

The taxi cannot go quick enough. Every traffic light is running against us. My fears are mounting as I consider what I'm about to do. What if Tara doesn't believe me? She has to believe me. I have to be right; there is no other explanation for it. Tara is going to freak so close to the wedding, but she has to know what's going on.

When the taxi eventually pulls up outside the pub, I get out and pay the guy. My heart is racing, my body trembling from both nerves and the ice-cold wind that's racing down the quays.

The smell of beer slaps me in the face when I walk past the open door of the pub. A young man exits, crashing into me. I move on, telling him it's okay but he repeats his apology over and over after me. 'Sorry miss, sorry, Jaysus, sorry.'

When I get to the door of the apartment, I search through the numbers on the intercom until I get to 431.

Chapter Sixty-One

Tara

What? My head begins to spin. Really, could Faye be that mad? Poor Faye, is this my fault? Did I push her too far? A million thoughts rush through my head. Why didn't she tell me? Did this breakdown have something to do with Avril Ryan? Faye seemed pretty normal to me the last time we spoke but I didn't know at the time she was in therapy. I thought she was a doctor at the clinic. She let me believe she was.

'When did you find this out?'

'I got a bit suspicious when I spoke to her so I contacted her sister.'

'You spoke to Deirdre?'

'Yes, it was sad listening to her sister tell me how she had spiralled out of control. The girl I lived with and loved for so long was like a complete stranger. A mad woman.'

'But…' I have no words.

'I know I shouldn't have cheated on her back then the way I did, and I regret that. But she was freaking me out. Something definitely happened to her, Tara. She changed overnight into a paranoid nervous wreck who I didn't know anymore. And now…'

'What?' I lean forward, eager to hear what he has to say and dreading it at the same time.

'Tara, if Faye was being blackmailed by that woman who was found dead in the pit at Huntley… it would make sense that she's the one who killed her. That could be what made her mad.'

I stand up and walk into the kitchen, refilling my wine glass. What is he talking about? Why does he think Faye was being blackmailed? Does Andriu know what we did? Did Faye tell him about my mam's passing. She promised not to, so how did he come up with that theory about blackmail? Faye would not have broken her promise to me. Andriu must have found out some other way?

'I'm not saying she killed her on purpose, she might have got into a row…'

'Stop it, Andriu.'

I don't want to hear this. What if he's right? If it's true that Faye has, as Andriu puts it, gone mad, and if she is no longer a doctor and is in care, then I have to consider that his theory could be right. Something must have pushed her over the edge. My stomach is churning and the wine is making me a bit dizzy even though I haven't had much. I was the one who brought that woman into Faye's life. If I hadn't given her Faye's name as the clinical assistant none of this would have happened. I don't know what to think. Who to believe. Where to turn.

'I told the detective.' Andriu's voice is like a blade cutting through my thoughts. I turn to look at him sitting on the chair, his eyes searching for my reaction.

'You told the detective what?'

'That I think there might have been an accident at Huntley Lodge, that Faye might have been the subject of Avril Ryan's blackmailing scheme.'

'But… when did you talk to them?'

'Yesterday, they rang me.'

'I'm sorry Andriu but I can't believe this. Could that really have gone on and us not know something was up? Poor Faye.' I think about how she left Huntley Lodge. The way she cut me out of her life so easily and things slowly begin to add up. Something did shake her. But murder? Faye? No.

Andriu stands and walks to the bottle of wine, filling his glass. I can smell his aftershave but it's like poison to my senses. What is this man doing in my apartment? Why is he here telling me this, three days before my wedding? I need to talk to Lucas. I want Lucas.

'Andriu, I need you to go. I'm sorry but…'

'I understand,' he says, putting the glass down on the counter. 'Just be careful.'

'What?'

'Well, if she was able to get out of the clinic last weekend and she's blaming you for what happened… just be careful, Tara. Faye is unhinged, she's dangerous. She might want to confront you like she did me.'

There's a weight pressing down on me now, I might collapse any minute. My heart is breaking all over again. Poor Faye. Suddenly her words echo in my head, her drunken words. *You ruined me Tara; this is all your fault.*

My fear is growing. I take my phone to ring Lucas. I hate asking him to come home when he's having his leaving drinks with his workmates, but I need him here with me. I need to feel safe. If what Andriu says is true, maybe Faye has followed me too. Maybe she knows where I live. I'm about to dial Lucas's number when the intercom buzzes. I put the phone down and go the intercom to see who it is. Andriu is putting his jacket on when the voice comes over the speaker.

'Tara, it's Faye, I need to talk to you.'

Chapter Sixty-Two

Faye

I'm freezing standing here. Tara is taking her time coming down to me. I can't see why she didn't just buzz me in. After a few minutes, a girl opens the door and I slip into the foyer. I walk to the elevator and press the button. When the door of the elevator opens my heart sinks. Shit. It's him. I was not expecting to see him here.

'Andriu,' I say, faking a smile. I don't quite know how to play this. This was not part of my plan.

'Tara doesn't want to see you, Faye,' he says.

I look around at my empty surroundings. What will I do? 'I just want to wish her well for the wedding, I won't be long.'

'She knows what you did.'

'What?'

'She knows you killed Avril Ryan.'

My body shudders. My biggest fear is being realised. Andriu has convinced Tara that it was me. I need to get to her somehow. She needs to know the truth.

'Let me go up to her,' I say.

Andriu steps closer to me. Then, out of nowhere, he pushes me against the wall. 'Go home, Faye, or back to the asylum you came from.'

I've never felt this threatened before. Every part of me is trembling, standing here staring down at a murderer.

'No, I need to talk to her.' I step away from the wall. My body is trembling but I have to be strong. I have to get to Tara.

'It's over, Andriu. I know it was you. You had our phones the night of Electric Picnic, the night Avril Ryan sent me a message telling me I was in trouble. You read the message. You deleted the message. But not before arranging to meet her. You killed her. She was warning us about you.'

Andriu says nothing. Grabbing me, he puts his hand on my neck, pushing me further down the hallway behind the stairwell. I struggle under the pressure, trying to keep my feet on the ground. No one can see us here. I can barely breathe in his grip. I'm panting, dragging in air. My throat gurgles. I can't speak.

'No one is going to believe you, Faye, you're fucking mad. Certified. Everything points at you. Even Tara believes me.' His words burn like flames of fire. His eyes, blazing with hate. Andriu is framing me and Tara is backing him up. I want to say that Tara will believe me when I tell her how he contrived to turn me against her. But the words are stuck in my throat, choking me.

The front door opens and I can hear someone walking into the building. Andriu lets go of his grip on me and I drag as much air into my lungs as possible. One more minute and I would have collapsed. Andriu would have left me there. Maybe I'd have died. Maybe I'd have lived… I wanted to live.

I realise I'm in a lot of danger here. But so is Tara. What if he hurts her and disappears again? My fingerprints are on the elevator. The buzzer. I broke out of the clinic. I'll be blamed. Rubbing my neck, I step away.

'Go away, Faye. Leave us. There's a great big river out there if you're looking to escape.'

Bastard. I drop my head as if defeated and I cry. 'I'm sorry Andriu… I just thought we could get back together. I won't say anything. I know no one is going to believe me.' I sound as pathetic as he wants me to. Then I walk towards the exit like I'm giving up but my head is in overdrive planning what to do next. I push open the door and walk outside.

The detective hasn't returned my call, so I try her number again and this time I leave an urgent message. I tell her to get over to Tara Moore's apartment quickly, that she's in danger. At this stage, I don't care what trouble I get into; I just want to make sure Tara is safe.

After hiding around the corner for a few minutes, I go back to see Andriu has left the hallway. He didn't leave the building, so he's gone back up to Tara. I've never seen him like this. Crazy with anger. I'm scared now. Scared for Tara. What will I do?

I need to get to her to warn her but how? I could knock on her neighbour's door and tell them she's in trouble – maybe they'll have her fiancé's number or a key. Time is ticking. I look to my right to the bright lights of Reilly's Bar in the hope that Lucas or someone who knows her might be in there.

Chapter Sixty-Three

Tara

I walk around the apartment with tears flowing down my face. My teeth are gnashing with fear. Faye has come to my apartment just like Andriu warned me she might. I'm finding it hard to believe Faye would hurt me, though. She might just have wanted to confront me. To tell me how I destroyed her life just like she did that night on the phone when she was drunk and she blurted out her hate for me.

Of course if Andriu is right and she did kill Avril Ryan, accidentally or not, it means she is capable of some level of violence which, accompanied by rage, could result in disaster. I could have been in real danger if I was here on my own. I'm so lucky Andriu called tonight.

I hope he's talking her down. Trying to get her to leave me alone. He has been gone a long time. Opening the door of the balcony, I see that the night sky twinkles like a scene from a Disney movie. It feels more like a Stephen King movie down here.

I look over the side of the balcony to see if I can spot Andriu and Faye out on the street. There's no sign of them. The street is empty. A stray black cat crosses the road, bringing me luck, I hope. Its tail sways from side to side as if conducting its body. I consider how free that cat is. How lovely it must be to be the conductor of your own symphony, your own life. I take a deep breath in an attempt to calm myself. That will be me soon, I hope, when I get to Australia.

I take one last look down the street but I can't see either of them. They must be in the lobby. Maybe Andriu has brought Faye inside to calm her down. Maybe he called her a taxi and is waiting with her for it to arrive. But what is she doing here in the first place if she's supposed to be in hospital? Did she just leave? Is she really that unhinged?

My phone rings. I rush to answer it, hoping it's Lucas but it's not. It's the detective. What the hell does she want? Maybe they know about Faye. Maybe they're ringing to warn me too. For a split second I consider not answering it because I don't want to hear any more bad news but then my finger swipes the screen. I have to know what's going on.

'Hello.'

'Tara, this is Detective Lee. I'm calling because I received a message saying you were in danger. Are you okay?'

'Yes.' I struggle to sound confident. What will I do? Will I tell her what's going on? That I think Faye could be the person they're looking for and she's downstairs now trying to get to me? I feel so bad, hanging her like this, especially when Faye is right – this is all my fault. If I hadn't asked for her help for my mam, none of this would have happened. But if she has lost control… I am paralysed with indecision, not knowing the right thing to do. But then it hits me – how did Lee know I might be in danger?

'Who called to say that I was in trouble?'

'Faye Connolly.'

'What?'

'Yes, she left a message on my voicemail. She seemed pretty anxious. I know she's not well but I have to follow through.'

'She's downstairs trying to come up to me,' I say, realising none of this makes sense. If Faye is dangerous she wouldn't be reporting herself, would she?

'Tara, I'm going to send someone over. Keep the door closed. Stay calm, Tara.'

Jesus, my head wants to burst. I can't believe what's unfolding. My breath is catching but I manage to utter the words 'I'm okay here, Andriu is with me.'

'Andriu?'

'Andriu Fitzpatrick.'

'Oh we've been trying to contact him, he's there now?'

'Yes, he's downstairs talking to Faye.'

'Okay, Tara, there is someone on their way over now.'

With a trembling hand, I take the phone from my ear. I'm confused by what Lee said. Andriu told me he had talked to the detective yesterday – or the day before, I'm not sure. But why did Lee say they've been trying to contact him? Does she need to see him again or has she not spoken to him at all yet? My head is spinning; it's impossible to make sense of what's going on. I decide to ring Lucas and ask him to come home as quickly as he can.

A knock on the door makes me jump.

'It's only me.'

I rush to the door to let Andriu back inside before turning my attention back to the phone in my hand. I notice I missed a WhatsApp message that Sean sent earlier. A screenshot of the man who Avril Ryan had charges out against. Sean's friend in the courts must have sent it to him. I click on it while asking Andriu if Faye has left and telling him the cops are on their way.

'She won't be back tonight, Tara,' he says. 'Who are you calling?'

'Lucas... I—' The face on the screen causes me to freeze. Andriu is looking over my shoulder at an image of himself on my phone.

Chapter Sixty-Four

Faye

'Is there a Lucas Jones here?' I call out over the music at the small crowd in Reilly's Bar. But no one seems to know or else they're just ignoring me. I notice a blond man with his back to me at the far side of the bar so I rush over and step in front of him to see his face. It's not him though. The barman reads my anxiety. He comes out from behind the bar and asks me what's up.

'I'm looking for Lucas Jones. I need to find him. He might be in here.' My head darts from table to table, searching for the tall, blond Australian man. But I can't see him.

'Do you know Tara? She was in here last week? Tara is in trouble and I need to find her fiancé.'

'Sorry but you're going to have to leave, you can't come in here shouting all over the place.'

'But Tara's in danger.'

'Of course she is,' he says, putting his hand on my shoulder. I shrug it off.

'Don't fucking touch me,' I say. 'Listen, there's a woman in trouble in the apartment block beside you. She could get killed. I have to get in there.'

'Ring the police then,' the barman says, standing in front of me, making sure I don't go any further. Everyone

294

is looking at me now. They all think I'm mad. I look mad standing here in a light tracksuit top with no jacket in the freezing cold, shouting at customers. My head is a mess, my eyes red from crying. My face is probably flushed due to the lack of oxygen getting to it when Andriu was crushing my neck. These people probably think I'm high on drugs. That's what it looks like.

I turn to leave. The barman is walking behind me as I make my way to the door.

'I'm not a junkie, Tara is in trouble, we were here last Friday night. Do you not remember me?' The young man is ignoring me. He might not even be the same guy who was working on Friday because they all look the same to me. Even the women. In my head they're all blended into the one person. The person in black who serves alcohol.

'I didn't look like this. I was in disguise,' I say, realising the more I speak, the madder I sound. I walk through the door out onto the street.

The barman shouts after me: 'And don't come back.'

I look up at the apartment block and think, what can I do now? My stomach is swirling and I feel like throwing up. I'll have to knock up one of the neighbours but first I have to get into the building. My head is aching from worry when I notice a police car coming around the corner. Is it here for me? Shit. Will they believe me? The clinic must have discovered my escape. But how would they know I was here? Unless there's a find-my-phone app on Aoife's mobile. Whatever it is, I don't care anymore. My mouth tastes like acid. I'm dragging air into my lungs with no rhythm whatsoever. Just dragging and holding and breathing out and in and… I have never been this scared but I have to do this.

I jump out onto the street in front of the police car, waving my hands to force it to stop. The car pulls up an inch from my body.

'What the hell?' the policeman says, opening the door and jumping out.

I rush over and beg him to help me. 'My friend is in danger. She lives up there.' And then, as I glance up to where I'm pointing, I see two bodies on a balcony. The man is pushing up against the woman, forcing her to the edge. It's them. It's Tara. I recognise her hair, the bob hanging over the glass balcony wall. He's squeezing her neck, pushing her backwards over the balcony.

'There, there,' I shout. 'Look!' I'm pointing up to where Tara is fighting for her life.

The second policeman is out of the car now and both of them race towards the building. They push on every button and immediately the door is released. I run after them.

'It's the fourth floor, number 431,' I tell them, then return to where I can see the balcony.

'Tara,' I scream 'Tara!' I want her to hear my voice. I want her to know help is coming. But she's slipping, I can see it. 'Fight, Tara, fight.' A few people have gathered now; they must have seen the police car from the pub window. What's keeping those policemen getting to her? 'Tara!'

Then I see the dark shape of the two policemen rushing onto the balcony. Tara is grabbed by one of the men while the other one struggles with Andriu before pulling him to the floor. They have him. They have her. I collapse to the ground with relief and put my head into my hands. Someone sits down beside me and puts their arm around me. The stench of body odour assaults my senses. But I welcome it; someone is holding on to me. I cling to the stranger's arm, tears soaking the sleeve of their hairy jacket. My body is shaking. Out of somewhere a coat is put over me. I can't look up anymore. It's over. There is nothing left in me to give.

The barman has joined the commotion, bending down to apologise to me for not taking me seriously, but I shake my tortured head and smile at him. It's not his fault. He didn't know, how could he know? He can only judge from his experience and to him I look like one of the druggies that he has to throw out of his bar on a regular basis.

'It's okay,' I manage to mutter.

'Can I get you something? A brandy maybe,' he says. I think about the strong alcohol hit at the back of my throat, dissolving into a bitter fruit flavour in my mouth. Then the burning heat travelling through my veins, doping every cell in my body. It would be easy, very easy. No one would blame me after what I've just been through. But I would.

'No thanks, I don't drink.'

Chapter Sixty-Five

The ground is the first thing I feel. The cold, damp stone freezing my bottom as I sit here and wait. I don't know what I'm waiting for. What to expect now. But I don't care. Tara is safe.

A car pulls up behind the crowd that has gathered, and I look up, hoping it's my dad. It's not. It's Detective Siobhan Lee. She steps out of the vehicle like John Wayne getting off a horse. Lee stands with her hands tucked into the pockets of her jacket, surveying the crowd and looking up at the balcony. I'm really not up to answering her questions now. But I know I have to. She needs to know this has nothing to do with Tara. It was Andriu who received the message the night of Electric Picnic when he had our phones because of our bid to create the perfect alibi. Andriu who deleted the message from Avril telling us we were in danger, then texted Avril back and arranged to meet her at Huntley Lodge. It was Andriu who sent me the message from Avril Ryan's phone the day he killed her. 'I can destroy you.' He was trying to freak me out, setting in motion his plan for a cover-up.

When I think of Avril Ryan arriving at Huntley Lodge expecting to meet me and Tara, a shiver travels deep through my body. The poor woman must have got the fright of her life when Andriu opened the door. The man had robbed her of everything she had, including her confidence, then disappeared into thin air when she found the courage to take him to court. Avril would not have stood a chance against him. Andriu would have been well prepared, knowing that if Avril Ryan did ever get to speak to us, his true character would be revealed. His depraved past, out in the open.

I thought it was the end of my life when he left. How wrong I was. Avril Ryan tried to save me from him and it turns out she did. Her death forced him to abandon his plans to manipulate me, to control my money and my life. He had to run away in case the body was discovered. But he couldn't just leave us like that. He had to destroy my friendship with Tara. He wanted us to be enemies so he could easily manipulate an alternative reality of what happened the day Avril Ryan was killed.

Andriu knew that if he let me think it was Tara he had slept with he would drive a wedge between us. End our friendship. If Avril's body was discovered, his plan to frame Tara would be easier if she and I were not in touch and hated one another. But then, when the body was eventually discovered and he found out that I wasn't the respectable Dr Faye Connolly he was expecting to find, he switched plans. I became his perfect candidate – unhinged, alcoholic Faye, driven mad with guilt about what I had done. A credible murderer. Andriu decided to frame me for Avril Ryan's murder and it almost worked. But there's one thing he didn't allow for. Tara and I had been friends since we were kids. She knew me.

–

Tara is hugging me, the warmth of her body a welcome, familiar comfort. We stand, locked in our embrace, afraid to let go of one another. I see my father a few feet away. His tall strong frame stands like a warrior against the dark night. Mam is with him. Crying, of course. Crying like me. I let go of Tara and rush over to them. They both embrace me, wrapping me up between them, making me feel safe.

In the distance I see a man running towards us. It's Lucas. He rushes over to Tara and holds her tightly.

'I'll be back in a minute,' I say, unlocking myself from the comfort of my parents and walking over to Tara and Lucas. Tara can barely speak she's crying so heavily in his arms. I place my hand on her back and offer my other hand to Lucas.

'Hi, I'm Faye, Tara's best friend. I'm pleased to meet you.'

Lucas smiles at me. God, he really is handsome. Lucky bitch.

Chapter Sixty-Six

Tara

I am now Mrs Jones. Wife of Lucas Jones. I'm about to walk onto the dance floor for the first dance of the evening. The wedding was as perfect as I could have hoped for. The church was wonderful. When I pulled up outside, I could see the bridesmaids waiting in the foyer and I began to shake. My father noticed.

'Everything is going to be great,' he said, urging me to relax. 'Remember, Tara, your mam is by your side.'

I looked up at the sky, at the bright winter sun beaming down on us and I closed my eyes for a minute. I pictured Mam sitting there, her eyes gleaming above her smile and I felt a warmth pass over me. Then the car door opened and I was thankful it wasn't the coldest day of the year. Amy rushed to help me out of the big fancy Rolls Royce. We took our positions in the church doorway and waited for the music to start. The arch of white roses in the centre of the aisle made way for an abundance of coloured flowers on the altar and it was stunning.

Amy and Emily were first to walk up the aisle ahead of me and I could feel a lump in my throat when my father took my hand. I wanted to cry but I remembered Amy's words from earlier on when I got a bit emotional in the house.

'Whatever you do Tara, don't cry. It will ruin your make-up.'

I swallowed hard and squeezed my father's hand. We walked up the aisle to the sound of the organ playing 'Here Comes the Bride.' Everyone turned to look, smiling, their good wishes following me up the aisle to where Lucas was standing.

When I saw him, I could see no one else. Just Lucas. His eyes opened wide when he looked at me. His smile was electric, charging me. I inhaled the moment and let go of my father's hand.

The priest was young and light-hearted, cracking jokes and making the whole event less formal than I thought it would be. He had been told about the incident that had unfolded on Wednesday with Andriu and when he took my hand he squeezed it, then looked at Lucas and said, 'You have a very brave woman here.' I wouldn't have described myself as brave. Faye was brave. But I did put up a good fight.

Lucas took every opportunity to squeeze my hand or smile at me throughout the ceremony, relaxing me and helping me enjoy myself. After the register was signed and the photographs taken, I walked down the aisle to the cheers and congratulations of all the beautiful guests. It was when I got to the bottom of the aisle that I saw her in the corner standing with her mam. Faye smiled at me. Then she lifted her foot up behind her and rested it against the wall. I laughed.

'Just a minute,' I said to Lucas, taking his hand from my arm. Faye was pale and thinner than I ever remembered her being. I walked over to her.

'You look as beautiful as I expected,' she said and suddenly I didn't care about my make-up. Tears could fall wherever they liked. I pulled her tightly to me and hugged her.

'You have to take care of yourself, Faye,' I whispered.

'I will Tara, I promise.'

I walked away from Faye, knowing it might be the last time I'd see her. Maybe we'll get close again, maybe we won't. Maybe she'll come visit me in Australia or maybe she won't. None of it matters. Faye was always there when I needed her. I will never forget that. But I'm starting a new life now without the crutches of my past holding me up. And so is Faye. There is nothing I don't wish for her. But mostly, I wish her peace.

Chapter Sixty-Seven

One Year Later

A golden-brown cocker spaniel comes over to where I'm sitting on the bench. His fluffy head pushes up against my leg as he shakes his tail. I bend down to rub his head and he licks my hand. His tongue feels warm against my cold fingers. A moment later, his owner calls out to him and the dog runs away.

The trees are all bare this time of year, their leaves a soggy carpet below the feet of the joggers running on the track that meanders through the forest behind me.

The park is full of people walking, some by themselves, others in couples or with dogs. Across the way, a team of footballers are training and beside them, a group of cricketers are practising throwing the ball.

I'm sitting here reading a book, embracing the peace that I find every time I come to this park. The big oak tree standing for years in the one spot reminds me to be happy. To accept what I have, to stay still and enjoy it.

I haven't returned to my job as a doctor. Not yet, anyway. At the moment I'm getting great pleasure in helping out at the old folks' home near my parents' house. I don't live with Mam and Dad anymore. I have my own apartment, living my own life, learning responsibility again. I see them every weekend, though. Mam is still making my favourite dinners and Dad checks with me that my bills are paid. It's not their fault. They know me as one thing: Faye, the one who needs all the help she can get.

I managed to salvage a friendship with my sister, though it doesn't really satisfy me. Being friends with Tara has spoiled me and keeps my standards high. I'm beginning to think every relationship I ever have will be measured by that one. I get the odd message from Tara which is nice. She's loving her life in Australia and is expecting her first baby next year. I called in to see her dad once, just to say hello. He wasn't there, though.

There will be no investigation into our connection to the 'Cabhrui' site. Sean the solicitor assured us the evidence was too weak. Tara's mam had done enough to make it look like she ended her pain without anyone else's help.

It took a lot of time, but I've learned to forgive myself for being so stupid. For not seeing the signs that are so obvious now. How Andriu manipulated me from the start. How he tried to tear me and Tara apart.

Talking to Fionn has helped me see that I hadn't the tools to deal with such a nasty person. Sometimes experience is the only tool that works, he says.

Andriu is in jail now. I don't have the finer details because I don't care about him or what becomes of him. I do think of Avril Ryan, though. How she saved me from him. A woman that I have never even met. If Tara and I hadn't given Andriu our phones on the night of Electric Picnic, Avril Ryan would still be alive. If Andriu hadn't given Tara a lift to pick up the Nembutal for her mother, Avril Ryan would never have seen him. She would still be alive.

I often think of her arriving at Huntley Lodge thinking she was coming to meet me. How brave she was being, helping someone she didn't even know. I shudder to think what went through her head when Andriu Fitzpatrick opened the door.

The sky is darkening by the minute. I can no longer see the writing on the pages in front of me, so I close the book. She'll be here shortly.

The smell of coffee is tempting but I'll wait, we'll have one together. After a few minutes, another dog arrives at my side. This one is big and fluffy with a black coat and white paws that make him look like he's wearing socks. I rub his head and cuddle him as he nuzzles into me.

'Hi Ben, who's a good doggie?' I say, lifting my head to greet his owner. 'Hi Aoife… fancy a coffee?'

A letter from Jackie

Dear Reader,

Sincere thanks for reading my fourth novel, *Her White Lie*. I'm grateful to you for sharing your precious time with Tara and Faye.

If you enjoyed the story, I would love to hear your thoughts via a review. Knowing what you think of the novel is important to me.

This story is not true and all the characters are fictional.

To those of you who have already read my first three books, *Familiar Strangers*, *The Secrets He Kept* and *Five Little Words*, I thank you for your support and reviews.

You are welcome to contact me anytime with any questions or comments. I'm available on Facebook and Twitter.

Best Wishes

Jackie Walsh

https://twitter.com/JackieWalsh_ie
https://www.facebook.com/jackiewalsh.ie/